THE MEMORY TOURIST

BY

GLENN HAIGH

The events and characters contained within this novel are purely a product of the author's imagination and are therefore completely fictional. Any resemblance or similarity to real people or real events is simply a coincidence.

For you my beautiful friend, Deborah, with your skin like snow not a pimple or blemish on show-with all my love. I miss you every day xxx.

Acknowledgements

I would like to thank love and all those who love me and whom I love, without that this would not be possible; love is the ink with which I have written this novel.

One

After it happened

I am sitting on the very back pew of the church that Priya got married in. It is the church that all her children and Freya will be christened in. It is the church that eventually all our funerals will be held in. Two minders dressed in coats of dazzling white flank me. They have no emotional attachment to the event-taking place; they are here to do a job. They have been assigned to me. They do not pity the grieving who stand on frail legs and wail into another's trench coat around us. They are not here to sympathise or indulge in the sorrow. They simply stare ahead towards the front in complete confidence that I will stay bound to my seat between them. I am glad to have them; I would not want to witness the trauma and grief I have caused so many people without the impartial presence of my minders.

The song begins. It's Nights in White Satin. The wailing subdues, overridden by the music, to a secondary but consistent sobbing. Instantly I am taken aback, I know the other girls are too, to the relentless playing of it in our shared house and the day that they fell about laughing when I described to them why I had always liked it so much. It made me feel safe, I told them. It made me feel that somehow and somewhere out there was a knight in white satin and that one day he would ride up to me on a white stallion encased in an ethereal golden light; he'd fight my demons and ride off with me sitting behind him, my arms clinging to his waist, rescuing me from the darkness and despair. When the raucous of their amusement had subsided

Priya sensitively pointed out that the song's name is a metaphor, more of a euphemism Garth felt, and not literally about Knights in White Satin. I was crushed.

"It's not even knights as in men who fight for your honour. It is nights, as in the darkness that follows daytime. How could you get that wrong?" Rita said.

I look over at her and remember her words. It looks as if her neck has sunken into her body, her head resting directly on her shoulders. In the middle, Priya and Polly sit either side of her. They are all holding hands without being aware that they are. Priya's face is ashen and she isn't wearing any make up. Her hair is pulled back into a tight ponytail. Prim and proper Priya has gone, grief has stolen her and is trying to pass off the alien sat three pews down from me as her but I'm not fooled, it's not her. Grief hasn't stolen Polly, pretty little Polly. Instead grief has poured cement down her throat hardening her internal organs disabling them. Looking at her it's hard to tell if she's even breathing. She definitely doesn't blink. The concrete solid in every limb means she is unable to lift her hands up to her face to interrupt the unbroken flow of mascara-contaminated tears.

The church doors begin to open and sunlight spears through the gap creating circular pockets of light on the harsh stone floor. Then they are fully opened and the full stare of the sun strikes the entire congregation and lights the way to their destination for the pole bearers. I can see the nose of the white coffin and just a snippet of the white peace lilies sitting on top of it. Garth dressed in white satin, and to the right of my minders and me is the front pole bearer. His eyelids droop so much it's almost as if he carries the full weight of the coffin inside of them. He is robotic and methodical. His will fights off the threat of emotion, his bottom lip numb to the pain of his top teeth piercing into it, a warning to the tears waiting on the substitutes' bench that they are not welcome on the pitch.

We used to be so close, so co-dependant. Like a meadow, all connected and each one relying on the other in order to exist: Garth the lush green grass like a carpet connecting all other things in the meadow; Priya the crystal clear water in maternal duty providing the nourishment we all needed to grow and flourish; Polly the flowers decorating us all in colour, vibrancy and a sweet scent; Rita the tall, strong trees with wide reaching arms offering shade and shelter in all weather conditions; me the dandelions gone to seed, whimsical, easily swept away and flighty. Like a meadow our friendship could command the attention of people. Just as people in a car driving past a beautiful meadow would be attracted to its charm onlookers would react in the same way to our friendship. Shopping in the supermarket together the conversation between us would draw in an audience, entering the entrance of the hospital to start a shift our banter would turn heads and then in the pub, after our shift had ended, our laughter would fascinate those around us. That was then, this is now. Now our meadow is desolate and destroyed. It's as if one day the pound signs in the eyes of a passing property developer flashed a particularly brighter neon than usual and taking advantage of the farmers adverse financial situation bought it. Now only patches of it exist here and there, small patches of lush green grass sitting behind the glum and unfriendly faces of the red brick squatters, which are all clones of one another. A circle of broken-hearted trees pining for those they have witnessed slain enclosing the estate within, employed in a strategy of fraudulent promise by the sale ravenous developer. The river still flows behind it all and still bursting with nourishment but now hankering after something to nurture. The worst thing for my friends, who still remain inside the friendship, which I stand outside of looking in, is that they know the property developer who has ripped them apart very well. It's someone they trusted and loved right up until the point the property developer commissioned the bulldozer to flatten them all without mercy. Me, I'm the property developer and more than anything they struggle to cope with this, struggle to cope with the fact I have brought them all here to this day.

As the coffin slowly travels down the aisle I whisper to my minders. *She really was very short. I never really realised just how short she was.* They do not acknowledge me.

When the coffin is rested at the front of the church the wailing stops altogether. It is still happening but everyone contains it within themselves. The vicar, a heavy set woman, who always used to wave and smile at me as she passed me on her bicycle when I was a child or whenever I visited my parents after I left home, starts talking. Her words float out into the congregation like bubbles, when people try to catch them they burst leaving behind nothing, no imprint on anyone's memory. Once she has welcomed everyone and given a glowing account of the girl whose body is in the coffin waiting to go into the insect riddled earth, an account I am unable to relate to, she invites Garth to read the poem he has written. Shaky legs try their best to carry him forth, although their struggle is obvious and they pause twice to alleviate the burden of the weight they eventually succeed.

He takes out a folded piece of paper from his top pocket, unfolds it and after drawing in breathes deeply into his lungs he starts to read. "When I look up at the stars, through your sky light at night, of your eyes I think." Empathy swirls in the congregation; I can feel it, read it even as if it were written on the pages of a book. He pauses to look at everyone. My mum gives him a weak smile; forcing the corners of her mouth to curl up, in spite of the heavy weights hanging from them. He presses on. "Of how your eyes danced so bright and full of life, the stars remind me." He inhales breath and forces his back straight, lifting his head. "When I'm in the snow of your skin I think, of how soft and pure your skin was, not a blemish or pimple on show, the snow reminds me." He closes his eyes and bites his bottom lip; a single tear squeezes itself free escaping his defences. "When I wade through the fallen leaves in the park, on an autumn afternoon, of your hair I think." His shoulders begin to rise and fall and he dips his head. I should feel guilt and shame, I have done this to him, but I don't feel either. The vicar takes a step forward, and catches him as he sinks to his knees. She sinks with him and on their knees she supports him, offering her shoulder, which he rests his head onto and sobs. She curls one arm around him.

She prises the poem from his grip and whilst she reads the last line of the poem, he sobs onto her shoulder. "Of how thick and vibrant, flecked with colour, your hair was, the leaves remind me."

Suddenly the internal turmoil everyone has been managing to contain collectively bursts outwards and the wailing and sobbing is deafening. The vicar folds up the paper the poem is written on and places it into Garth's pocket where he had taken it. Then she takes Garth's head and cradles it to her, kissing the top of it, whilst he dissolves like the rest of the congregation.

I do not stay to watch the coffin lowered into the ground. This does not mean that I do not see those who fall to their knees and sob into the earth, some beating it with their fists. My minders return me to the place I call home now.

Two

After it happened

I'm in a room padded with white walls, bathing in the clouds. I'm aware of life churning on without me, mechanically and obsolete. The people I once knew all churning like exhausted cogs in a factory I once belonged to. The monotony of life churning on in one direction, to a destination I know and they don't. The world they live in, the people I once knew, is different to my world. We are at reverse ends of the universe where at their end they are unable to acknowledge my higher intelligence and my powerful imagination. I feel no superiority over them because of this, though. I know I was once like them, dwelling in their spectrum of the universe and that I was, like them, ignorant and blind. They are different to me now but over the rainbow all worlds are the same and all creations are equal. One day they will be my equals again, here or there, balance will be restored once again. I try to guide them now, the people I once knew. My endeavours to enlighten them are futile. My words are weightless now, they have no strength or substance and they are as weak as whispers in the wind.

I am lost in my own world, deeply rooted in my own imagination; I am almost irretrievable to myself. To the people I once knew I am absolutely irretrievable and this laments them terribly. I'm lying back on a cloud above them, untouchable, unreachable, my absence of logical mind and the presence of my freed limitless mind and creative imagination through which my very being exists is inconceivable to them. They could not even begin to comprehend the parallels of our existences. My arms are fully outstretched behind my head, pointing north like the wings of an angel. I'm making a cloud angel furiously flapping my arms in the white mist. Small pieces of the cloud detach and slowly float up and above me like bubbles, wispy and hazy like floating gauzes over my eyes. I watch them dance like creatures conscious of mind, with living energy and logic. They whirl and whir, twisting upwards. They hover in mid-air briefly. Then the speed of the whirling and whirring increases until they amalgamate and they take the form of mini suspended tornados. I see faces in them. The sad and hapless faces of the people I once knew. They are inert and delicate like light pencil sketches but the frustration is hardwearing. It is frustration of helplessness, as they cannot access me now; I am beyond their reach even more so than I always have been. One of the faces is Garth's. His face is etched with worry and longing, I haunt his thoughts; I am lodged painfully in his memory, like a sore splinter on the sole of his foot it is disabling. He wants to help me but his faculties fail him with any conceivable approaches to reaching me. Poor, poor Garth, so kind and generous, so undeserving of the aching void I have inflicted on him and so weighted down by it that he can hardly lift himself out of bed in a morning. His beauty has been wiped away by my betrayal and abandonment, beautiful sun filled eyes muted to wintery dullness now, dark and deep like tunnels only palatable to rats and all things hideous, damp and dripping. Poor, poor Garth his bitterness eats away at him like worms eating rotten flesh in a grave and although the blame is mine I'm isolated from repairing any of the damage I have done, for as inaccessible am I to him he in turn is inaccessible to me and my words now alien to his ears and with no weight. I cannot reassure him that despite the decay and the desolateness, all is well. I am well.

I look to another of the mini tornados whirling and whirring and just as delicate and just as still, as if like Garth's the face is a faint pencil portrait, I see Priya's face. Resourceful and determined Priya, the mother hen with all the answers and remedies immobilised with the same isolation that Garth feels. It is me who is on the outside, living beyond what is considered normality and she and Garth whom are safely inside the box. However despite this they are alone in their frustration and grief. Standing in different shoes with different views, neither experiencing this very same tormenting event in equivalence; this is the cruel law of interpretation. It's the twist of any given scenario or situation that means one single event, is not felt in the same way by the people experiencing that very same situation. I never understood this before, it is only now that my mind is freed from its previous restrictive confinement that I see this: Garth and Priya are both subjects of the same situation. I am that situation, but they receive the transmission of this differently. Priya bakes scones and bread and then deep-cleans her house, blinding her senses with the fumes of cleaning products. Garth on the other hand chooses to torture himself with memories of the times when I was able, however loosely, to live inside the box with them. He lay on his bed; as I lay on my cloud, staring into space fast-forwarding, pausing and rewinding information, processing it over and over until he is numb.

There are two more mini tornados whirring and whirling with two more faces, of people I once knew, delicately and motionlessly etched within them but I don't want to play this game any more. It is no longer fun. I will visit the emotions of Rita and Polly soon but not in this moment, not now.

I roll onto my stomach and slowly hoist up my lower legs behind me like tower blocks over shadowing my body. The gleaming white laces that match the brightness of the white soles of my gold glittery pumps dangle down like ribbons as I gently wave my dainty feet in the air whilst light-heartedly humming. I penetrate my cloud with one of my fingers and seamlessly doodle with uninterrupted sweeps of my finger, carving out pictures like I used to do when I visited the seaside with my parents, in the sand. Mum and Dad would sit beside me, smiling down on me, their only child, with such adoration and pride. I used to make their lives full and bright. Not now. Now I make their lives empty and dark. Kneeling in front of a finger-deep outline of a crab, seahorse, mermaid or similar nautical creature my dad would indulge my childish creativity by lavishing praise on me, in exaggerated tones.

"We have a future artist here, Ciara! One day her work will hang in a gallery and people will flock from far and wide to see it." It was the same line for anything I created, whether it was from recycled rubbish, using water paints on canvas, textiles, clay, flowers, photography or idle doodles on paper, in snow or in sand. Sadly he does not know that he was right. I do have creations hanging in galleries and my work is viewed and adored. If my words were not whispers in the wind I would be able to educate him and Mum of this, which would bring them much needed comfort.

In those days long gone, the days of the visits to the seaside the three of us would take, my mum would sit on her legs trying hard not to giggle and expose my dad's, undetected by me, excess exaggeration. Stroking my hair in constant up and down motions dispelling sand from the crevices of my curls like fairy dust, she would be largely mute. Mum didn't have much of a voice whilst I was growing up; she left the conversation and the humour to my dad but she was a dutiful and devoted mother and wife and so the nurturing and caring my dad left up to her; they complemented each other like a lock needs a key, one could not function without the other. We were together then, three elements of the same existence, a happy family.

They're not with me now, my parents; they're not over the rainbow like me. Their minds are not free from the binds of their world like mine, they don't see what I see and they don't live in a bubble like I do. They are all alone in a world I once belonged to. Hollowed now like a rotten tree eaten from the inside out, nothing but insect riddled bark. To them they seem empty for all but a heavy heart that beats with no purpose or promise, compared to when I was with them when the beating of their hearts and circulation of blood around their bodies had meaning, had the reward of being parents. Parents to a daughter they saw as beautiful and who they adored despite her flaw of being unable to recognise this, despite her being the elephant in the room.

Into my cloud I doodle a love heart and then I quickly scribble it out. It's too silly, like a schoolgirl would doodle. I doodle a map instead, an intricate masterpiece weaving, curving, curling and sprawling all over the cloud. It's a complex map etching out my former life, the life I once lived, in the world I once lived it in. I draw the events and the people I encountered in that life, the things that happened in that life. My finger whizzes around as if battery-operated sketching and sketching, until the past of my life has been engraved into the cloud. Swiftly I inhale then exhale one long stream of blustering wind from my mouth like a dragon breaths fire until the mind map has disappeared into the air. Then my doodles move from past events to future events. I doodle Garth's union to Al and the birth of their daughter Freya. My doddles take the three of them all over the world. I doodle pictures of Garth and Al on dusty roads in far off lands, lined with primitive housing, Freya in a harness carried alternately by each of them, a wake of children chanting excitedly after them and waving their hands in the air. I move onto Priya and my doodles sprawl out like the branches of a tree prophesied the future events of her life and at least for some of her future, her life with her husband, Mr Green. The speed of my finger increases as her future life begins to get more demanding and somewhat overcrowded. I smile to myself; overcrowded will make her exceedingly happy, she will be overjoyed to fulfil the quota of children she always said she wanted. Eventually, after Priya's mind map has developed more branches, twigs and sprigs than a huge ancient oak tree I move onto Polly and Rita's. They're a pair just like Garth and Al. Sparse is the eventuality of their mind map in comparison to the other two mind maps, like a tree in a harsh relentless winter, brittle and bare. It does not take me long to complete theirs. Unhappiness is not an inevitable consequence; a bloom-less and withered tree does not indicate a fruitless future, and their future will be everlasting brightness beyond all comprehension, just in a different dimension to their initial intention.

Resting my chin in the palm of my hands, my elbows sinking slightly into the cloud, I gaze upon my doodles and smile. I'm happy that my friends' futures will be bright despite the fact that none of them can now accept me as part of those futures.

Three

After it happened

The trees in the graveyard are like old women waiting to die, groaning and creaking with age. Wind chimes adorn them like elaborate costume jewellery hanging from their nimble and frail limbs; they chime sinisterly in the wind, like props in a horror movie. An orchestra of porcelain, wood, stainless steel, tin and glass, a mixture of conventional tubes and novelty shapes; the teddy bear wind chime with a faded face is the most sorrowful; its misery chiming out through the wind like a small child separated from its parents by a thick fog, cries out in distress.

Garth and I are sitting on opposite sides of the mottled mound of moist and freshly turned earth, which is yet to sink. We are not communicating, he cannot acknowledge me. I may as well not be here at all. At this present time he is unable to forgive me for what he holds me responsible for, a heinous crime in his eyes. I feel no guilt despite knowing that the deep purple stains under his eyes are my responsibility; the tears spilling down his cheeks are my doing; his sunken shoulders and hung head are inflictions I have caused.

It is just a body, a vehicle that is no longer needed. The best friend you knew, her essence, it still lives on elsewhere and in every fibre of everything. I promise you this you will meet again when your soul is also free.

My words cannot penetrate the horror that has infected his thoughts. Worms have wriggled and beetles have scuttled their way through his ears and gorged on his thoughts. They devour his logic like, his thoughts tell him, and they devour the body of his best friend lying in the grave between us.

"I'll never forgive you," he says sobbing into his hands.

You will, I reply, reaching out to him placing a hand on his that cannot penetrate his numbness to me. *You think you won't but you will.*

"Never. I won't be able to if I tried to." He shakes his head firmly. "You are a murderer, as far as I'm concerned, even if other people do think differently."

You will think differently one day.

"Never as long as I live will I ever think differently, it's just not possible."

You're unable to see now, you will when grief becomes bored of bullying you and moves on to another rookie. You will see clearly then.

He closes his eyes and then with a wince his eyelids fly open again, impulsively reacting to the pain of the propaganda being stapled to the back of them; flesh decaying and melting from her bones. Finger nails and toe nails growing long and curly, turning yellow and brittle. Eyeballs sinking into her skull and her smile becoming nothing but teeth on bone; this is what greets his eyes every time he shuts his eyelids. Abruptly he doubles over, retching loudly he lurches at the side of the grave, vomiting uncontrollably like he does on the day it happens, the day he finds the body.

"It's your fault my best friend is rotting underground," he says when there is simply nothing left to vomit.

Drawing himself up, clutching his stomach with one hand, he wipes away remnants of vomit with the back of the other. In this moment, in contradiction to the circumstances of this memory, I want to let out a high-pitched cackle and if it were in the times of the days before this I would let out a belly-rumbling screech at the sight of him. His sadness, his lifeless eyes or his regurgitating stomach bile beside a grave, these are not the things that are making me want to cackle. The pillar box red bobble hat pulled down over his brow so that its rim sits on top of his silver framed oval spectacles, which in my opinion always gives him the slight likeness of a mole, is making me want to laugh. Cackles would have risen from my belly infectiously, which, like a common cold, would have polluted the air and incubated within him and our friends, in the good old days, the days before this, causing them to exhume identical guffaws of their own.

It happened, this infection of cackles that no-one's immune system could ward off, and on the day Garth was introduced to his rather ridiculous and rather extra-woolly woolly hat. It is a Christmas present, a Secret Santa gift. We have all been told to bring one for our Christmas meal and drinks. As always we meet in Ye Old Victoria, the quaint little pub, opposite the hospital where we all worked, on the corner where

Victoria Close and Harold Place meet at a point. The old-school semi-circular pub, with its six-inch glass-panelled windows was a frequent haunt of ours. For a period of time, the exact length I cannot confirm it's a haunt my friends abandoned after it happened. As usual our very own Christmas Elf, Garth's self-imposed title, which is a customary grace of all e-mails and post-it notes we receive pertaining to the event, coordinates everything. As is tradition a specific Christmas theme is in play. On this occasion we must all dress up as reindeer. In my opinion this is a vast improvement on the previous year when he forced us to appear as Santa Clauses stuck up the chimney. It is frightfully nightmarish trying to jam six pillow-stuffed Santa-suited revellers encased in cardboard chimneys in one of the wooden and stained-glass-encased-booths of the Ye Old Victoria. Not to mention the almost physical impossibility of balancing a bum the size of a rubber dingy on bar stools.

I try to conceal my elation as my Secret Santa gift succumbs to Garth's heavy-handed interrogation turning docile like a puppy playing dead as he squashes and squeezes its squidgy and pliable form. I have to sit on my hands and bite down on my bottom lip to prevent myself from getting the jibber-jiggers, which would seal my fate in alerting him to the fact that I am the red bobble hat knitter. Eventually Garth rips at the paper and reveals the gift inside. He gasps in utter horror.

"It's always me who gets the homemade hand-me-down," he says folding his arms crossly over his chest and furrowing his brow. The cackles spread amongst the four people who are not offended by his comment.

"It's the thought that counts," I say, trying desperately to sound casual and not too desperate to convince him. "Really," I say lifting it off the table and stuffing my hands inside it to give it body and soul, "I think it's really rather sweet. Priya, did you knit it? I'm sure I saw some red wool in your dresser drawer when I was looking for a pen last week."

"As if," Priya sniffs, "I do not knit. How sad is that? I have much better things to do with my time."

"Well, really," I begin.

"Oh give it up, doll. We all know little miss make it, bake, it take it, paint it, arrange it, did it," declares Polly.

"I didn't," I mumble unconvincingly at five hands on hips reindeers with accusingly raised eyebrows and jingle-jangling antlers.

"Oh I give up. Next year I'll buy something tacky and unimaginative like a candle and incense set," I say resentfully.

"Oi," Rita snaps, "I don't have oodles of time like you. Maybe I should get a sick note from my doctor three times a year and then I can…" she trails off and horror fills her eyes, the elephant is in the room.

For a moment five fiery reindeers become five frightened reindeers all darting eyes and skittish legs as if they have accidentally strayed from the safety of their country estate onto a busy dual carriageway and into the path of a speeding freight lorry.

"Oh great, trust Rita to bring the elephant into the room." Then with good grace Garth pulls off his antlers and snatches up the red bobble hat, thrusting it down on his head.

"You look like the mole from them children's comics."

The elephant has gone; our amusement forcing it out of the room. For Garth and the others, around the time of this graveyard memory, it seems that nothing, not even a construction forklift used to build the skyscrapers of Dubai, could shift it from the room now. In this memory it stands stock still behind the grey love heart shaped head stone.

Four

After it happened

I am a terrible friend and I cannot blame the four people I have become disconnected from for the conflicting emotions they feel. Exile is a fate I have brought on myself; it's my decision that has blanketed me from their ability to accept me as their friend now. The truth is I never belonged with them. My place was always somewhere else; I was like a pink flamingo in a concrete compound, my existence in their world was extraordinary, I was too exotic for the concrete jungle that is their world.

I always knew I was extraordinary from a very early age and it didn't come as a shock to me like it did for the people close to me. On my seventh birthday I decided that I was too old for the beautiful vanilla sponge cakes iced in pink with marzipan princesses and butterflies on top of them that my mum usually baked for me. Instead, at my request having seen its picture in one of her home baking books, she baked me a chocolate sponge cake coated in thick white chocolate frosting that reminded me of the moon because of its small craters and tiny peaks. On the top, to decorate it, the marzipan princesses and butterflies had been replaced with vibrant coloured and plump-looking raspberries arranged into a love heart shape. A few of them had somehow gotten squished; perhaps my mum had handled them a little too harshly as she manipulated them into shape. The juice from the squished raspberries had bled into the frosting and I remember thinking that the raspberry heart on top of the cake was exactly like my own heart, delicate and easily bled. I looked around the room at all the other seven-year-olds at my party, including Garth, and I couldn't identify one of them whose heart I could compare to the bleeding raspberry heart on top of my cake like I could mine; I was different to them all.

Just like the body in the grave that Garth and I visit so often, he and the other three of my friends are being slowly eaten away. Grief, not parasites of the earth, is eating away at them. I wish I could get through to them and make them understand why this had to happen but they do not have the knowledge and understanding of the world that I have; they cannot see that all events are intrinsically linked. Life is like a row of dominoes, events ripple out to cause other events and these are all pre-determined before we are even born. Her body is meant to be lying in the grave, it's an event that is meant to have happened and everybody is and was powerless to prevent it. My decisions, my existence, my being the way I was then, are all necessary and pivotal in setting off the chain of events that eventually led to her body being in the grave.

The time for her is right. Some people are meant to die young, others old. She is one of the people meant to die young. It's written in all our blueprints, which are like road maps of our lives that we write before we are reborn. It's all there, the things that will happen to us, from the day we are born. Like a ladder, the rungs, are laid out for us. Twenty-four rungs is what her ladder had, and she climbed all of them before her ascent was complete. Garth's has ninety-eight rungs. Polly's and Rita's have more rungs than the girl they grieve for but significantly fewer than Garth's. Unfortunately it's just the way it is. I don't regret the decisions I made nor do I regret the place those decisions have brought me to.

My friends wonder if I am paying too harshly for my decisions, they may avoid talking to me or to each other about it but parts of them tick with terror that the regime I am now under may be too unforgiving and forcefully castigating. A life sentence; never will I drive a car or take a bath again. They find this hard to comprehend sometimes. In reality where I am, the place my decisions and actions have brought me to is not entirely different to where they are. The obstructing slabs that separate us are not as absolute as they think they are and I'm not as restrained as they fear. I still experience beautiful parks and gardens, like the ones the five of us used to go to on our days off. We would pack the wicker basket that would be full of sandwiches and treats into the boot of the car along with blankets and head off into the countryside. We'd lay on the blankets in the grass, arranged in a kind of human linking puzzle, a head touching a head, an arm over an arm or a leg over a leg. We would love gazing up at the slug-like clouds, fleshy and leisurely in their edgeless garden of blue. We would chat idly for hours, laughing often when someone said something random like the time Polly asked if it was possible that clouds are pockets of air and we thought she was being ironic but in fact she was being serious and had not realised that they actually are pockets of air. Alone and apart from them, I am still able to visit these parks and gardens with sweet smelling flowerbeds like oriental buffets, a collection of mouth-watering colours and appetising smells. For hours on end, like we used to do together, I still watch busy bumble bees buzzing in and out of the buffets greedily gathering what they need, just like they do in the place that my friends exist in, though I am never in danger of being stung. The difference is that now my imagination is the regulator of such places, my mind is the only vehicle I have, the only vehicle I need. It's why I'm never in danger of being stung, because it's all in my imagination.

Sometimes the word 'incarceration' crosses the minds of my friends and this is their view, from the position they stand, of my fate for the decisions I have made and because there is a body lying in a grave at my hand. Huge amounts of time are spent pondering this possibility. Garth sits on the doorstep looking out into the distance, turning the word over and flattening it down as if the word 'incarceration' is a duvet and he is making the bed. He tries to imagine the types of people I am confined with and can only imagine unsavoury characters, phantoms that he wouldn't want to meet on a dark night down a dark alley. Cohabiting with me now there are people who have made similar decisions to myself that have led them to be here. Like me, it's their fate and over time they learn to accept this. There are girls here like me who have left people grieving beside the graveside of someone they love, loathing the person responsible; the girl who drank too much wine and then decided to get into her car and drive to the supermarket to get more ploughing into a bus stop when her vision blurred. She is here with me and because of her decision there is more than one body rotting in a grave with a best friend hunched over each, weeping into the soil just like Garth weeps for his best friend now.

When he thinks of how my existence might be now, gruesome images blot Garth's concentration. He wonders often how the place I now dwell might have altered my physical appearance and my personality from what it was. If he would allow himself to see me he would discover that my appearance here is just the same as it always was. I still answer to the name Dee Winters. I'm still five foot and one inch tall and very slight in build. I'm still petite featured and large in the chest department. My hair is still thick, curly and the colour of autumn leaves: browns, oranges and reds. My eyes still dance like stars. My skin is still as soft and glistening as snow, not a pimple or blemish on show.

I'm still very much me. They are very much not themselves. This is my fault. I murdered a part of them when I sent the body to the grave, decomposing and melting into the earth because I no longer needed it.

Five

After it happened

I am sitting in the back of his silver Peugeot. I haven't planned it this way; I just think about him and then I find myself here with him, part of what he is doing at precisely the point I have thought about him.

I only know it is a Sunday because of guesswork based on the clues I can extract from what is happening. It has got to be a Sunday because he always drives to our parents for Sunday lunch and I recognise the route he is taking as being the one we would often do together to go home and visit our parents. I sit in the back behind his seat. My feet are up on the edge of the back seat and I'm hugging my legs to me. I watch his static eyes and I register their lost jazz. I wonder when they will dance once more. Everything is different about this journey to how it would be if he could accept my presence. Usually he would have the camp disco tunes blaring out and all the windows wound down to annoy the other drivers on the road. Usually his head would be swinging from left to right as he belted out the chorus to our favourite holiday tune, which reminded us of sun-soaked Spanish holidays as teenagers. "To the beat of the rhythm of the night, dancing to the morning light, forget about the worries on your mind, you can leave them all behind." It doesn't happen on this trip. His sobbing is the only sound in the car. His worries could not be more pressing on his mind today; there is no leaving them behind.

Music had always lifted us. Music got us through every bad patch in our lives. My break up with Casey Briggs, Garth's break up with Casey Briggs, failing our first driving test, our first patient death and when Garth's first car, an original thirty year old battered mini that he bought for fifty pounds headed to scrap yard heaven three weeks after he bought it, music lifted us. Recently music fails where it always succeeded; it is as if the music has died and been buried along with the body Garth and I visit in the grave.

Garth regards the CD player in his car with a look of resentment; he wants to rip it out and hurl it through his windscreen into the road along with all the CDs in his glove compartment.

When we arrive Garth and I walk side by side down our respective back garden paths. There is a two-tone painted wooden fence separating us. It is yellow on my side and red on his. I'm still close enough to be touched by him if he reached over the waist-height divider, if he had the inclination to do so. We both stand on the first of the two back steps leading to our childhood houses. His stare is fixed ahead at the yellow front door of his house and mine is turned away from the red front door of my house and is instead fixed on him. He doesn't notice the twitching of the kitchen blinds and his mum's concerned eyes peering out. I register the relief instantly swim into them on discovering he has arrived safely. Seconds later the front door flies open and his mum appears, taking in his tearstained cheeks and blood shot eyes she takes both his hands in hers and draws him inside, folding herself around him when the door is closed.

Once inside my own house I stand with my back to the door staring up at the staircase, which my dad has just begun to descend.

"Is that you?" my mum calls from the kitchen. "Dinner is almost ready. Will you set the table, please?"

Neither of us knows exactly which one of us she is speaking to. My dad pauses mid-way down the staircase and stares in my direction, an expression of disdain painted on every inch of his face. I hang my head without feeling ashamed, I just think it would be better for him if the eye contact was broken. He shakes his head and continues down the stairs, shuddering as his shoulder brushes past me. I follow behind him into the dining room and sit at the dining table whilst my dad sets it for two people, leaving the space that I am sat at empty. He sits down and nervously waits for my mum, who arrives carrying two plates of steaming Sunday lunches, one for him and one for me. She is wearing oven gloves so that the heated plates do not burn her hands. She stops abruptly and the smile she nailed onto her mouth this morning, as she does every morning now, slips from her face into one of the dinners she is carrying causing a surge of gravy to slosh over the edge of the plate and splash onto the carpet.

"Why didn't you set a place for Dee?" Anger shoots through her gritted teeth like nails from a nail gun.

He looks towards me. "You know exactly why," he replies, slamming his hands onto the table. "God damn it, do we have to go through this every Sunday, Ciara? Has she not ripped us apart enough, love?"

My mum bends slightly and hovers both plates an inch or so above the table. My dad glares at her, his eyes forbidding her intention. She ignores them and releases her grip on the plates. They free fall the inch and land clumsily, flinging food from them on impact.

"She is still our daughter and always will be. Nothing can ever change that. Nothing she could ever do could stop me loving her."

"She has ripped our hearts out!" My dad bangs his fists on the table again, causing the plates to jolt and fling more food onto the table. "And still you defend her! People cross the street to avoid us; they all know what she did, what she was, Ciara; they all know."

"What do you mean by 'What she was'? You make her sound like a psycho. That isn't the case. It wasn't like that."

"You know what I meant, ill, she was ill," he taps one side of his head. "They all know she had problems."

"Why do you hate her so much for it? It wasn't her fault. She didn't invite it. No-one does, it finds the person and the person doesn't find it."

I want to intervene but I know I can't.

"I'm not discussing this any further, I refuse to waste any more time on her. She didn't consider us, did she, when she did what she did?" He looks in my direction again. "She is no longer part of our family and that is final. Do you hear me? I mean it, if you ever take her side over mine again, I swear on the grave I'll-."

"You'll what exactly?" My mum's face is twisted like a wrung-out wet tea towel. I have never seen her facial features so distorted and fury-filled. "Go on, you'll do what? Leave me? Well go on then because if you are asking me to turn my back on her, if you are asking me to forget she ever existed I won't. Do you hear me? Am I making myself clear?"

My dad slams his hands down on the table one last time and heaves himself out of his chair with so much force that it rears its front legs like a startled horse before slamming them back down on the floor. Standing in front of her now they stare down their noses at each other like angry bulls readying to lock horns. Before it happened they never raised their voices to anyone let alone each other and they never said a bad word between them. They were always such a placid and united couple.

"Well, what are you waiting for?"

"Is that what you really want, Ciara?"

"You know what I want. I want you to accept our daughter back into your heart. That's all I want."

There is silence and then with the look of someone utterly defeated my dad backs away, dropping his head so that his chin rests on the top of his pigeon-breasted chest and he sobs. My mum's facial features instantly untwist and she lurches at him, wrapping her arms around him.

"I really wish I could forgive her. What you want, I want too. I just don't find it as easy as you do. I resent that, I really do. Maternal instinct, I wish I had it too."

"It's not easy, it's really not. You just have to give it time."

Later, when my dad is in his shed painting shelves to put up in my old bedroom, I stand behind my mum as she unloads the dishwasher.

"He will forgive you, Dee. He's out there now painting the shelves for your bedroom to put all your art trophies and awards on. Sometimes he just bottles things up too long, it's harder for him." She places a plate down on the antique pine worktop above the dishwasher and gazes wistfully at our reflections in the window in front of us, seeing only her own face looking back at her. "He blames himself for what you did. He thinks it means he failed you as a father. He thinks it means he failed me as a husband." She places one hand flat on the worktop and then presses the underneath of both of her eyes with her other hand hoping to suppress the tears. "I don't want you to worry about what you saw tonight, we will get through it. We will be strong for you. We won't let you down this time."

Six

After it happened

I am standing three quarters of the way down Harold Place, just by the red pillar-box outside number twenty-one. I have no idea how long it has been or where this event fits in the timeline of the on-going existence that I have left behind.

Everywhere is covered in snow. The areas untouched by human activity, such as the top of the pillar box, the tops of walls, window ledges, un-walked-on pavements and roof tops glint with a thick layer of crisp white covering as if they are iced Christmas cakes. Cars trudge slowly through the thick grey sludge on the roads. Their wipers labour hard in back and forth motions struggling to prevent the falling snow from covering the windscreens that they are duty bound to protect. Their lights on full beam shine out like the eyes of prowling monsters, searching far and wide for any signs of life. Angrily, their back tyres spin mercilessly, causing an up-spray of grey sludge. It looks cold. I struggle to remember what cold feels like.

I turn away from the road to face number twenty-one. Something inside the house is drawing my focus to it. A soft glow from the hallway light floods through the stained-glass panels in the top half of the front door. I can see the mahogany wooden staircase and its sumptuous toffee-coloured carpet. The heavy aubergine curtains of the front bay window are closed against the darkness outside in which I stand but a small snippet of light sneaks through a slim gap in them. The laughter of children wafts out into the street like a sickly sweet scent. Strangely I feel myself pulling forward like metal to a magnet. I am standing inside the bay window. The front room décor greets me with a warm and friendly welcome, painted in two colours. The bottom of the walls, from the top of the thick cream painted skirting board right up to the matching dado rail, is a rich dark purple colour. From the dado rail right up the cream ceiling cornice the walls become the colour of light purple. There is cosiness and intimacy in the photographs of precious moments hung around the room. There is one in each alcove of the chimneybreast. Two hang on the back wall of the room facing where I am stood in the bay window. There is three more hanging along the sidewall, the wall separating the hallway from the front room. There is a family of four repeated in all of them, at various stages of their life together and in various settings. Some are photographs that have been taken indoors and some are photographs that have been taken outdoors. Each one is a different collage of events from their lives such as holidays, weddings and christenings, all frozen in time. As they are parallel and equally spaced around the room they remind me of a comic strip, a comic strip of the family's life together. There are other people in them but despite this the family whom this house belongs to stands prominently out from them as if they were 3D images. There is a blonde woman with dark skin and bright green eyes. A man, her husband, is tall and strong with crowfeet in the corners of his eyes and he has a huge smile. Two little boys both look very much the products of their parents, each with bright green eyes and huge smiles; one has his mum's ears and his dad's chin whilst the other has his dad's ears and his mum's chin.

The boys from the photographs are in the room now, from the sound of a spatula grazing a baking tray and the smell of pizza wafting down the hallway into the room I detect that one or both of their parents are in the kitchen, which is down the hall past the staircase and the dining room. I watch the boys play with a train set, which dominates the entire circumference of the lounge carpet. Each boy sits either side of the model tracks, wearing a conductor's hat on their head and holding a remote in their lap. Both have focused looks of concentration as they wield their remote controls. Their tongues are clasped between and protruding from their lips in the left corner of their mouths. Neither boy is aware of my presence, of me watching them. Two trains whizz by each other on parallel tracks and every so often one of the boys shouts out, 'choo-choo,' and makes motions with an arm as if pulling a cord on a steam train.

I look over into the corner of the room, sensing that we are not alone. An old woman wearing a black cape and bonnet, with grey hair pulled back into a bun is sat in the corner of the far chimney breast alcove in a high backed rocking chair. She is watching, with a steadfast stare, over a third little boy in the room who is sat in the middle of the circular model train track wide eyed, excited and throwing his head back in laughter at his two friends who are unable to see him. He has a plump face, with a porcelain complexion and curly blonde hair, sitting beneath a straw hat with a blue ribbon. He lived in this house a long time ago, a time when sickness conquered medicine and many little boys perished of fevers.

He notices me and unexpectedly as if the room is made of chocolate and is being subjected to intense heat its features melt away. The light purple colour above the dado rail begins to drip away gradually revealing a royal blue colour, bathed in the soft glow of oil lamplight. The cream paintwork flakes away revealing dark wood. The framed colour photographs on the walls evaporate like steam and in their place hang pencil sketches and black and white photographs in oval dark wood frames and large paintings in heavy ornate frames. They are positioned randomly and the walls look overburdened by them; not a bit like the walls of the present day who prefer the organised minimalism of the photographs and frames that they wear now. There is a pencil sketch of the boy, the only child in the room now, hanging on one of the walls. Just his head and shoulders have been sketched. His eyes are the shape of almonds and heavily lidded. His wide smile is slightly lopsided and he has three dimples one in each cheek and one in the centre of his chin. He looks blithe and like a child should, innocent and untroubled. He is five and it is the year he departed this world. There is a blazing coal fire in a tall dark wood frame with an inset mantel mirror. On the mantel, in a heavy silver ornate frame, is a full-body black and white photograph of his mum. She is tall and slender, bony around the neck and shoulders with a flat chest. She appears to be of grand status, wearing an extravagant off-the-shoulder gown and a choker at her neck with a jewel at the throat. She sits by a plant in a velvet chair with a rounded back and she is looking to one side.

It's Mother before she became sad and before her voice went away.

On the other side of the mantel there is a framed picture of Queen Victoria wearing her small diamond crown. It is in a matching frame to the one that his mother is in.

Mother liked Queen Victoria. She said that with a woman in charge the world might be a more organised place.

They are not words I am hearing. They are thoughts entering mine; I am gaining the information telepathically. The boy is sharing his memories with me and I hear them as if they are spoken by the soft, humble voice of a confused and worried child. I am glad that I am unable to feel sadness, like I am unable to feel snow.

He shows himself playing with his wooden Noah's Ark and all the brightly painted animals that went with it; he is playing with a man. *Father always played with my Noah's Ark and me after church on a Sunday.* His father is a tall bony man with a thick handlebar moustache and wearing his Sunday best. He is laughing softly and ruffling his son's hair. *They were both so happy before I got sick.*

The memory as delicate as the snow outside begins to thaw and the room slowly reverts to how it was when I first entered it. The features in the room flake back just as they flaked away and eventually it is exactly how it is in the present day. The two boys of this world return to the room blissful in their game of trains and completely unaware of and unaffected by the memory the boy not of this world has just shared with me. The soft glow of light intensifies as electricity re-enters the equation. I smile at the harmony of this household, two families of different worlds and times, one living and one not cohabiting together in blissful happiness.

Seven

After it happened

Mysterious and loud footsteps echo into the room and as suddenly as I found myself inside number twenty-one I find myself outside it again by the pillar-box.

The desolate street I left is now disturbed by footsteps and voices. They are men's voices. Garth's voice is one of them and he is walking straight towards me. He is ten feet ahead of me. I look into his eyes. His eyes are dancing again, full of life and of love. He is wearing his silly red bobble hat, a red Puffa jacket and red wellington boots. He is positively animated and chatting to his companion merrily.

"Guess what the little madam said to me this morning?"

He looks up at the person walking with him whose arm he is linking. He, Garth's companion, is taller than him by a few inches, leaner and he holds himself differently with his shoulders back and his head high, as if he doesn't have a care in the world. Not like Garth, who has a slight sag in his composure as if he is a man full of woe, which is not the case at all. His clothes also bear a striking disparity to what Garth is wearing. He is wearing a long black trench-coat with the collar turned up and a dark grey scarf knotted at the neck. His trench-coat comes to just below the knee, from which point I can just make out dark blue jeans, which are almost camouflaged against the navy blue sky. On his feet he wears brown leather boots.

To an uneducated onlooker they appear to be as mismatched as vegetarian sausages and beef stock gravy. I know, with the benefit of the learning the library can offer me that they are, despite appearances as well suited as pork and applesauce. His hair and eye colour are too dark to recognise against the shadowy background of the night. As I contemplate what colour they could be I am reminded of how Garth likened my hair to autumn leaves in his poem of me and I decide that this man's hair and eye colour is the same as mine and that in fact this is one of the attractions for Garth: reminders of me.

"Garth, I have no idea what Freya said to you this morning but I'm sure you are going to enlighten me."

The man's voice is deeper than Garth's and there seems to be a hint of sarcasm in his tone as if he is mocking Garth. I smile realising that Garth has drawn the same conclusion as me and responds by nudging him in the arm.

"You're no fun, Al. You're supposed to guess and keep guessing until you get it right." Then he adds, "And I don't much care for your tone of voice. It smells a funny colour."

Al, shaking his head and laughing, replies, "You are so random, Garth. Everything has to be a game. Can't you just tell me and we can have a normal conversation about it like civilised adults?"

"No."

Garth gives Al's arm a squeeze and then they both stop right in front of me, inches from where I am. If it were possible I would be able to feel his breath on my face and the icy cold nib of his nose on mine. We would probably rub noses like we used to if he was aware that we are nose to nose.

Garth withdraws his arm from Al's and turns to face him. Garth pushes himself up against him and wraps his arms around his waist. Al drapes his arms around Garth's neck and they embrace. Garth clings to Al. They are so utterly content and enamoured; I'm witnessing a very tender and intimate moment. Their chins rest on each other's shoulders. The sides of their heads are connected at the ear. Their eyes are closed. I watch the love and mutual adoration whirl around them in their auras like a protective casing. It is good to see the old Garth back again. Al strokes his hands in up and down motions on Garth's back. Eventually Garth gently prises himself away and the two of them stand slightly apart holding hands. For a moment I think of Garth and me at primary school and suddenly I'm imagining him and Al, like we used to, whirling around in a game of ring-a-ring-a-roses.

"So Garth, what did Freya say this morning?"

"Guess," Garth laughs. "You have to guess."

Al rolls his eyes, shakes his head and smirks. "Okay, I'll guess," he says closing his eyes in concentration. "Nope, I can't guess. You'll have to tell me."

"No. You have to guess." Garth stamps his foot, causing the bobble on his red bobble hat, which incidentally really is looking very tired and warn out, to wobble furiously.

"I'll read your mind instead."

Al places the tip of his finger on the ridge of Garth's nose right between his eyes. Al closes his eyes and so does Garth. Then Al begins to hum like a bumblebee, only louder.

After prolonged humming Al finally says, "I'm picking up on something. Yes it's coming through nice and clear now," then he stops and makes a wincing movement accompanied by a sound effect as if his vision is painful to receive. "I've got you in the kitchen. You are pouring milk from the jug into Freya's glass. She is eagerly spooning Honey Nut Loops into her mouth. She has swallowed them down. Now she is saying something. Hang on a minute. Yes it's coming. She says, 'Daddy I think we need a bigger chimney next year so that Santa will be able to get the pony down it that I am going to ask him for, again. That's probably why he didn't bring it this year like I asked him to because a pony is too fat for our little chimney, don't you think so?"

Garth's eyes spring open and he gasps. "How did you..." His eyes change and narrow with accusation. He snatches Al's finger away from the ridge of his nose. "Hang on a minute, you already knew didn't you?"

Al laughs and Garth pulls his hands away.

"You are so gullible, Garth! I could hear her from the lounge, besides which she said the same thing to me at bath-time last night and I told her to put it to you at breakfast this morning. You know, good cop bad cop."

"Charming, I get to be the bad cop who says, 'No' do I?"

"That's the idea." Al grins flashing a set of pearly white teeth.

"You're a bugger, you really are. I have no idea why on earth I married you."

"My devilishly good looks, quick wit, immense intelligence and fat surgeon's pay cheque and pension."

"Actually it is just the fat surgeon's pay cheque and pension that's the deal clincher, the rest is mere fabrication on your behalf."

"Whereas I just took pity on you and thought if I didn't take you off the shelf no-one else would and you would be there until you croaked it from some dust related illness."

Garth darts quickly forward passing straight through me without warning. Lunging at the garden wall of number twenty-one he scoops up a handful of snow in both hands and quickly swivels round to face Al.

"Don't even think about it, Garth."

"Oh I'll do more than think about it," he replies as he compounds the snow in his hands into a ball.

Garth hurls the snowball at Al. It whirls and whooshes through the air towards him. Al knows it is coming and he throws his arms up to protect his face but he is too late and a snow bomb explodes on his sport-inflicted crooked nose, spraying his face with fragments of the snow.

"You little devil," he calls out, lunging forward. "Come here. You have asked for it now."

Garth turns quickly and heads off in a sprint, squawking and flapping, and looking behind him squawking louder in alarm at Al's speed in chasing him. Al is too quick for him and when he is close enough to feel secure that he will be successful in doing so he begins to dive for Garth's waist. Like a lion on the African plain he pounces on the balls of his feet, stretching out his front and back limbs to full capacity. He closes in on his target and clamps down on the prey. Al wraps his arms around Garth at the naval and Garth strains like a wildebeest under the lion's strength. The wildebeest thrashes about with great effort, desperately trying to give the ferocious lion the shake off. The lion lets out a marauding snarl as they both crash down towards the ground. The wildebeest calls out with fright.

I'm finding it fun to watch and I stand beside them, the unfelt presence, laughing.

The ferocious lion forces all of his body weight onto the wildebeest and lifts his feet off the ground so that all his weight is concentrated top heavy. Garth buckles completely and his legs give way beneath him. Their bodies plunge towards the ground. I find myself laughing again. This is the Garth I remember. A young man with a zest for life, he looks a little older in the face now and for him to have a child and a husband some time must have passed, but however long it has been I am pleased with the end product time has restored; a care free, exuberant character that made my days in the physical world so much more pleasurable. I am glad he is moving on. I am glad he is finding a better place and is forgetting. Not me. He is not forgetting me but what happened and how it happened.

The two men fall to the floor, one on top of the other. Garth squirms under Al's body weight, his face is pushed into the snow and his four limbs flare out paddling as if trying to swim. He wriggles furiously and turns his body position so that they are facing. They lay like this for a while. They gaze into each other's eyes, smiling at each other. Garth reaches up and touches Al's hair, tangling his fingers in its thickness.

"I love you."

"I love you too."

Garth moves his face upwards and Al moves his downwards until their lips meet and fuse. After a lingering connection, Al stands up and forms a human bridge over Garth, one foot either side of Garth's torso. He stoops down and offers Garth one of his hands as a crane to help him to his feet.

"Come on babe," he says. "Let's get you up. Polly and Rita will think we have gone to the Netherlands to milk a cow and not gone to the supermarket for a pint of one. Freya will be running rings around Rita by now, she'll be demented."

Garth and I laugh and both nod in agreement. He's not wrong. Rita is, I can see in my psychic eye, crouched down in the cupboard under her and Polly's staircase in a game of hide and seek, with Freya and is praying, to me ironically, that she isn't found. They do this a lot, my friends, pray to me for things they want to happen as if I'm their own personal guardian angel. 'Please Dee, help me get the promotion coming up at work,' 'Please Dee don't let there be a delay on our flight for our summer holiday,' 'Please Dee let it be sunny tomorrow because I'm having a barbecue,' 'Please Dee don't let the supermarket be busy today because I have a hair appointment at 3pm and I need to dash in and dash out.' More often than not I will oblige. They never seem to realise though, that I am pulling strings on their behalf. Instead they are over generous to coincidence.

"No," Garth giggles cheekily and childishly, "I'm not getting up. Not until I have made a snow angel, like me and Dee used to."

Al slaps a hand to his forehead, "Blimey Garth, you are irritatingly youthful all of the time. You and Dee were in your early twenties, that's two decades ago."

Eight

After it happened

Two decades, I don't know how much time this is.

I am as pleased as someone without emotional processes could possibly be that Garth told Al he won't get to his feet until he has made a snow angel like me and he used to. When we are in spirit and not too long after we arrive in the spirit world, our emotions become detached from us. We have no use for them anymore; they simply evaporate when we leave our bodies like steam leaves hot food. This happens at the same time we are given our spiritual and psychic powers back, the powers that we lose shortly after our births; they linger slightly. When Allison becomes Freya and I visit in those first few days after her birth her eyes engage with mine and I read her thoughts, there is recognition but as she develops as a physical person her spiritual faculties dwindle until nothing lingers at all. As a toddler she tells everyone about the beautiful angels, a girl angel and a boy angel, who sit at the bottom of her bed and read her stories about fairies and princesses. As a teenager when Garth and Al remind her of this she has no recollection of it. It's the same for everybody.

Although I cannot feel pleasure I know that I would if I could, and it's the same for all spirit people who are remembered by those they left behind. I know that if I had physical faculties I would be pleased that Garth is keeping my memory alive even after, according to Al, two decades. Not a day goes by since it happened without him mentioning me to someone and there is something in every day he lives that prompts his memory of me and spreads my memory in other people, like drawing Al's attention to the fact that making snow angels was something I loved to do.

Eating scones once lashed with jam and cream in the window of a beach café he tells his companion that I love cream teas and would be so jealous of them. He was right too. If I was able to feel jealousy I'd have done so in that moment- watching him take delicate bites of his scone and then sweeping his tongue over his lips to mop up the cream and jam that coated them. This must have been before Al's time because Garth's date, a young fresh-faced man with mousey hair, a brown cord jacket, a long multi-coloured scarf and a copy of Doctor Who? in his frayed and worn canvas satchel is definitely not Al. Although there is something of a theme forming as, like the man in this memory, it is the point when Garth manages to cover the end of his nose in cream that Al falls head over heels in love with him. Only in the train station café on the day I engineer the meeting between Al and Garth it is the cream from his hot chocolate and not the cream from his scone that covers Garth's nose. Although I have no sense of time now, I can sequence from clues, like my detection that the nerd, as I would have called him if I were still in the physical, must have been before Al's time. I also know, because I was present at the event, that it is the nerd who breaks Garth's heart. I'm sitting on the bed in Garth's room when the nerd tells him he has been offered a fellowship at a university in Brazil after his PhD in physics and would be leaving in a matter of days. Garth is enraged and calls him a torrent of names, hurling trainers at him as he dashes across Garth's bedroom floor and flees the house never to be heard from again. It's weeks according to the conversation Priya and Polly have one evening sharing a bottle of claret by candle light at the dining table, before he actively seeks out another lover. This, they remark, which I agree with, is so out of character for Garth.

Al smiles every time Garth mentions my name, casting Garth a look. Its mixed theme is always the same: love, understanding, compassion and regret. Al only knows what I look like from Garth's description of me, because there are no photographs of me, he tries desperately to imagine what I was like, the way I laughed, what my sense of humour was like, whether or not I would have approved of him. Sometimes because Garth mentions me so often he finds himself asking me advice about Garth, particularly asking me for inspiration when it's time to shop for his birthday and Christmas presents. Often in the mornings when it is raining outside and there is nothing to get up for in a hurry they lay together, Al's arms wrapped around Garth and Garth's head resting against Al's chest. Intently and keenly Al listens to our stories, gorging greedily on them. He empathises with Garth by chipping in with supportive comments. Telling Garth how beautiful I sound and how special our friendship was, reassuring him of how lucky he was to have experienced that kinship even if it was only for twenty-four years. Al tells him that he wishes he'd had the opportunity to meet me too, he regrets that he and Garth did not meet earlier so that he could have.

When Garth tells him that he won't get up until he has made a snow angel Al steps back, holding his hands up as if surrendering and then he lets them fall to his side. Garth moves his legs in and out in rapid motion; simultaneously waving his arms away from his body and back again. The night is full of laughter. Garth's and Al's laughter punctures the otherwise silent evening air. I'm laughing too, but mine is silent laughter, unable to puncture the silence like theirs. Seeing Garth rapidly moving his legs and arms in and out provokes my memory of one of the winters we shared together. It plays out in front of me just like the memory belonging to the little boy residing in number twenty-one Harold Place that he chose to share with me. We are running through the park one dark night, hand in hand. Garth and I, we are belting out a rather dubious rendition of 'The hills are alive with the sound of music'. Rather, Garth is panting it out because we are negotiating a pretty steep hill at the time. We want to reach the top to look out over our town, which is blanketed in white. It is something we decided to do on impulse whilst wrapped up under a blanket on the leather settee in our front room drinking hot orange juices and staring out of the window at the shimmery snow, the dark blanket sky and the twinkling stars.

"You're going too fast. Slow down," Garth says, pulling on my arm as he trails just behind me.

We break apart because I shake him off my arm and carry on the last few feet to the top without him. When I reach the top I start star jumps like the woman from my exercise video, the one I do in front of Garth whilst he sits watching me, eating popcorn. Scissoring my legs in and out, in and out and flapping my arms like wings. I let one arm deviate into a fist pump as my legs swing out and back in, and my other arm drops back into my side and out again. Looking back on it now I had quite impressive co-ordination, even if I do say so myself. I spin around to get visual clarity on Garth's progress and find him how I left him, hunched over, kneeling in the snow and clutching a stitch.

"For a nurse you are very unhealthy."

"For a nurse you are very unhinged."

We both laugh and I outstretch a hand just like Al did, during the memory I just left before visiting this one, to crane him up to his feet. He throws out his own hand and firmly grasps mine, allowing me to bear the full burden of hoisting him up. His body weight causes us to topple over and crash to the ground. We roll around in the snow laughing, loud laughter, carefree laughter the mantra of our friendship.

I return to what is happening in the present to the memory Al and Garth are currently forming. Al is pulling Garth to his feet now and draws him close to him. He kisses him deeply and then hand in hand they both walk away passing through me and down the street. I turn to watch them go and I blow a kiss into the air after them. I watch it hang in the air travelling through it slowly like particles of dust until they reach Garth and Al bursting over them like fairy dust. Soon they become little black dots swallowed up by the falling snow and then, until another time, I leave them and return home to my beach hut.

Nine

After it happened

I am not imprisoned; where I am now is supreme freedom. I can visit those I love and have left behind any time I want, and although they cannot accept me anymore I have the security of knowing that one day they will. It is not necessary for me to journey the wall that separates me from those I love just to observe their progress and intervene, if necessary, in the events they experience to safeguard their welfare. I can do this from here without crossing the divide. The Sanctuary of Comprehension and Development, or the library as I also call it, provides all of the resources I need to monitor and support the continuing existence, in my temporary absence, of those I love and have left behind.

Different people here know the Sanctuary of Comprehension and Development differently. For Allison, a friend of mine that I met here, it is known as the Residence of Awareness and Advancement. For all of us it's a source of knowledge and a place from which we can send out healing and power to those who require it. It's a place of reflection and contemplation. Ultimately this magnificent and sacred place is a combination between a library, a museum and a records bureau. For all of us who visit it there are columns and columns and columns of bookshelves that never end in length or height, housing blueprints. There is one blueprint for every person we left behind and they document all the experiences they will go through and all of the things they will achieve according to how they wrote them. Each experience written within the blueprint is called a lesson, 'the school of life,' exactly like someone studying for a PhD designs their own research path the blueprint documents all of the research to be undertaken. The tragic and the joyous experiences they will go through are of their own deciding exactly like choosing aspects of a PhD. I chose to be the elephant in the room, to learn from it, to experience it and to bring those experiences back home with me and Garth chose to be gay and to be the friend of the elephant in the room, to research these aspects of life for the same reason just as Allison chose alcoholism and domestic violence as her research topics for when she was Allison and beauty, intelligence and the experience of same sex parents as her research topics for when she is reborn as Freya.

It appears differently to each of us when our imaginations conjure it. For me it is a series of huge linked pyramids in a row, three times the size of those in Egypt and made entirely of solid gold. The entrance is at the top of the middle pyramid. Sometimes I will levitate up to it, other times I will climb the tall vertical gold staircase, which is guarded by flying Siamese sphinxes, in solid gold. They stand tall on six legs and in one of their four arms, two on each side of their bodies directly below their wings they hold a jewel encrusted joust twice their height. For Allison it appears as a huge circular castle standing in a sort of rockery and made of sand so glittery it must be brushed with diamond dust. Each of the four turrets has diamond-shaped windows that weave around them in a pattern from the bottom to the top, like ivy. Around the circumference of the castle there is a moat and the guardians of the castle, beautiful mermen with white hair and silver tails swim in synchronised configurations often using the silver fins on their arms to become airborne.

Although we are able to access the blueprints of our friends that tells us how their lives will unfold without us and allows us if necessary to be in the right places at the right times to help them, time is not something we have any concept of here. Morning, afternoon or night, minutes, hours, days or weeks and past, present or future it is all blended like a fruit smoothie. Compartmentalising stages of our existence is not a functional necessity here. Based on this the information that I have access to of Garth, and all of my other friends' lives are not chronological. When I read Garth's blueprint for the first time I know that he will from the point I left him fall in love deeply with three men. He'll be deeply hurt by one of them, he'll hurt one of them and he'll marry another. I have no comprehension of in what order this will happen when I first read it. That there will be three great loves in his life is all I'm sure of. Ages, duration of the relationships, dates, times and chronology are all inconsequential details.

I know the facts about the wedding, all except when it will happen in time sequence. It's a no-expense-spared event. Glorious sunshine is a prominent feature of the day, which is my wedding gift to them; shafts of gold pierce the clear blue sky. A marquee eclipses the grounds of a stately home positioned in front of an immense lake, which has a wooden boat deck covered in ribbons and flowers, lanterns and candles. Prestigiously dressed and porcelain-looking residents, unseen to those in the physical, stand in the protruding leaded windows looking out at the intruders of their grounds. I see them and wave, but they don't wave back. Garth's groom is tall and handsome. He has a crooked nose, which is an old sporting injury. They meet on a rainy day waiting in an open-air station for a train that is delayed, a birthday gift from me to Garth. Garth suggests they have a hot chocolate in the station café whilst they wait. Al finds himself uncharacteristically agreeing, not realising the little voice in his head egging him on is me.

On their wedding day they wear tailored morning suits in blue velvet with matching top hats, quirky bow ties and brilliant white roses in the lapels. Three-tired cake stands containing mouth-watering afternoon tea delights stand on trestle tables covered in vintage tablecloths. Between the polished silver stands of dainty finger sandwiches, scrumptious glazed cakes and yummy plump scones the tables are decorated in rose petals, wooden antique mantle clocks with sprouting springs, cracked faces and missing hands and elaborate ornate candelabras are draped with pearls. They drink tea from delicate white and blue china teacups, poured from peculiar teapots and champagne from crystal flutes with blackberry liqueur. They and their guests dance under Chinese lanterns on the wooden deck by the lake. Refined dancing to live music, musicians playing wind and string instruments. Guests float out on the lake on swan boats taking their champagne with them in the evening throwing back their heads in laughter. Priya and Polly are bridesmaids in blood-red evening gowns with ribbons in their hair. Rita is Garth's witness and best woman.

I also know that Garth and Al will have a child through surrogacy. She is called Freya because this is what I and Allison decide when I help Allison write Freya's blueprint in the east turret of the diamond dusted sand castle that Allison conjures. As well as her beauty and intelligence we write that Freya will have thick hair, which is prone to tangles and knots and will be difficult to tame. Garth hates it and there is many a tantrum, his being the loudest, when it comes to brushing it before school and putting it into a ponytail. Once, and this makes me laugh every time I think of it, she becomes old enough to do it herself, they save a fortune on hairbrushes because Garth stops hurling them at walls in frustration. On one occasion his brush throwing sees them visiting the hospital when it bounces back off the wall seeking revenge and whacks him above the left eye causing a rather nasty gash. Being a nurse, this sees him plagued with taunts from all his colleagues for a while afterwards. He sits in the waiting room with Freya sat cross-legged at his heel playing with her ragdoll. The surroundings that he is in provoke his emotions. He wishes that I were still with him. I am.

I also know that he travels the length and breadth of Europe, like we planned to do together. He buys a battered VW campervan, which reminds him of the battered Mini we once waved off to scrap yard heaven. He restores it to its former glory, painting it purple and white. He and Al with Freya on a sun-filled summer morning drive down to Dover and cross into the continent and then disappear into a road-trip extravaganza, the sun setting behind them. On this trip Garth meets a stunning white mare so pure looking that he would swear she was a unicorn if it wasn't for the absence of a horn. He confides secrets to her that not even Al knows and he never tells Al about her. The following day when he returns to her meadow he finds she is no longer there, and he strangely misses her.

Ten

Before it happened

As a child, my parents owned a caravan. It was an old thing turned green from white with age with a thick brown belt of colour around its middle. It was moored on a caravan park on the spell-casting Cornish coast swirling with charm and mystery. A huge stretch of sand dunes separated it and the hypnotising Atlantic Ocean with all her well-kept riddles and skeletons. The magnificent golden coastline curled around the caravan park and my dad used to say that it was like the sand was wrapping its massive arms around the caravan park, hugging it to keep it warm.

I loved going there for holidays. As soon as school broke up my dad would pile the car high with all our camping gear and we'd head off in the early hours of the morning when the sky was still pink. Sometimes Garth would come with us. Right beside our caravan there was a footpath made from logs sunken into the sand dunes. It wound and twisted and reminded me of the yellow brick road but it wasn't my favourite thing about this place. My very favourite thing was the procession of colourful beach huts standing on the fringe of the sand dunes facing out to the sea all day long, watching curly-haired blondes with blue eyes, pounding the surf. They had all the warmth and friendliness the Cornish people they are famous for, a glossy smile always painted on their faces.

Pointing at a particularly glossy white one with an equally glossy bright red roof, door and window frames, sitting on my dad's shoulders, I jiggle up and down. "When I get older I am going to live in a beach hut just like that one."

My mum chuckles affectionately rubbing my knee she stretches herself as far as possible, looking up into my excited eyes. "You silly girl, you can't live in a beach hut. You can't even sleep in them over night. It's illegal."

"Silly Mummy," I laugh, throwing myself backwards almost completely toppling off my dad's shoulders. "Sleeping in beach huts is not illegal."

My dad wobbles and jerks and makes the sound effects of someone on a unicycle with really bad balance. My mum flies her hand up to the small of my back to steady us.

"Yes it is, your mummy is telling the truth, Dee."

"No she's not, silly Daddy."

"I am, Dee; I'm telling you the truth."

I giggle. "Mummy, Daddy what does illegal mean anyway?"

Both my parents laugh loudly. "It means you would get arrested," my dad says.

"Would I get arrested by the police?"

"Yes, you would."

"Would I have to go to prison?"

"Yes, you would for a very long time."

"How long, exactly. Like one hundred years or something?"

My parents laugh unanimously again. "Oh, definitely, you would have to go to prison for at least one hundred years, maybe even more."

"Nooooo," I cry, burying my head in my hands. "But you two would be really old, much older than you are now when they let me go."

Now that I am here after what happened, I do live in a beach hut on a beach just like the one in the memories I visit. My beach hut, to anyone standing outside of it, looks just like any one of those from my childhood that spent all day staring out at the panorama ocean, small and box-like. This is an optical illusion because, once inside, my beach hut is a palace of grand proportions. I love sitting in my kitchen at the glass dining table in a wicker chair beside my distressed oak dresser. Sometimes James, Allison, both of the Murray sisters or all four at once sit with me. With unending views over the unending sky-layered ocean, my bedroom is sumptuous and luxurious. Its circular perimeter is lined with gold oval and ornate freestanding mirrors. James and I, when we stand in front of them, reflect differently in each one. Our favourite is the one that shows me as a Geisha Girl and him as an Arabian Knight. At the very top of the beach hut there is a roll-top bath, twice as long as a normal bath so that me and James can sit at each end staring up at the stars when the roof folds back like the soft top of a sports car.

There is an annexe, which is my art studio; full to bursting with all the creative works I created in the physical. They still exist in the physical, distributed now amongst various people. Replicas dreamt up from my imagination are here, though, displayed in my art studio. The oil painting of a fruit bowl that hangs in Garth's kitchen hangs here in my studio. The fabric canvas of a palm tree that hangs in Priya's bedroom hangs in my studio. Like she does, I often take it down from its hanging place and run my fingers over the fabrics. However, unlike her I have to imagine I can feel the fuzzy felt, smooth silks and coarse cotton. Three photographs of Aryl blown up to the size of large mantle mirrors hanging in glass frames in Rita and Polly's hallway, before their tragedy, hang also in my studio. In the middle of my studio on white podiums under glass cases are my sculptures that now dwell in my mum and dad's attic, gathering dust. The clay sculpture of a little girl sitting cross-legged on a tree stump hugging a teddy bear to her, the bronze wire sculpture of a naked tree in winter and the aluminium sculpture made from recycled Coca Cola cans of a woman's face with ringlets. My costumes too, the creations of my blue and cream sewing machine, which is here, for all the fancy dress parties and occasions my friends and me, attended. The originals again are distributed in various places, some in a dressing up box in Freya's play room, a keepsake one, the Fred Flintstone outfit that Garth wears to Rita's twenty-first and the Wilma one I wear are framed and hung in Al's study, others are gathering dust in my mum and dad's attic. Sometimes me Deidre, Morgan, Allison and James, my friends here at home, dress up in them and parade around pretending to be various characters.

Like an avatar in a virtual world, from one of Freya's games that I sit and watch her play sometimes in the back of the VW whilst Al and Garth sit up front taking it in turns to navigate foreign roads, I am the creator of my own world and my friends the creator of their own worlds.

They all live here with me. When my imagination built my beach hut, the higgle-piggle and topsy-turvy house belonging to Allison was already here. Instantly I thought of the precariously balanced towers made of inconsistently sized and shaped building blocks I would watch Allison build as Freya in her toddler years. James's house did not appear until I went to meet him and brought him home. Thousands of feet above my beach hut and Allison's topsy-turvy tower, James lives on the top floor of a skyscraper constructed entirely of glimmering ice; the walls, the floors, the ceilings and the doors; everything is ice, even the radiators. His furniture too is all made of ice, his table and chairs in an ice fitted kitchen. His ice bathroom sports an ice shower capsule and an expansive Subbuteo table. His lounge has a u-shaped ice sofa unit strewn with thick furry throws. Above the electric blue flames of his open flame fire, hangs his cosmic ice plasma screen continuously broadcasting Formula 1.

The collection of bubbles arranged like a rabbit warren that Deidre and Morgan Murray live in materialised after I had brought James home. When they arrive the girls explain that firemen can see through bubbles, unlike the wardrobe in their bedroom before they came here. In their 'chill out' bubble there are white floating beanbags and coloured plastic tables, a huge floating cinema screen and a popcorn machine. In a huge bubble at one end is their stables and horse gymkhana, where Eyelashes, Deidre's jet-black horse and Ginger-Ale, Morgan's palomino horse, reside and where the girls ride them when they are not riding them on the beach.

My dad hoists me off his shoulders and into his arms.

"How old do you think me and your dad are exactly Dee Winters?" My mum asks tapping my nose with her finger.

"Hmm, really old I think, maybe two-hundred-and-twenty-two, somewhere around there. Is that how old you are?"

My parents' bellies split with laughter, which infects me and without really knowing what I am laughing at I join in.

"No, young lady that is not how old we are."

"She has a vivid imagination doesn't she, mummy?" My mum nods at him and then he continues. "If only all you needed in life was an imagination, there would be no stopping this one."

If only you could see me now, Dad, you'd see that an imagination is exactly all I need in the life I have now, I say before turning my back and leaving the memory to return home.

Eleven

Before it happened

Deciding to be a nurse had more to do with the fact that Garth was always sure he'd be a nurse and his passion rubbed off on me; it wore me down over the years.

There was another reason. The fact that I was doing abysmally in my first year of A-level Maths, Physics and Chemistry diverted any pie in the sky intentions I'd had of becoming Dr Dee Winters. Instead I became Ward Nurse Dee Winters.

As small children we played doctors and nurses on a daily basis, Garth and I. Garth was always the nurse and wore the outfit he made me ask my parents for at Christmas without telling them the real intended recipient of the gift. I totally understood why Garth didn't want to ask his own parents for the outfit, consisting of a navy blue knee-length pinafore, white frill-edged apron with a big red cross on the front and full-blown Florence Nightingale headdress. I laugh raucously along with my physical child self at Garth, prancing about like a show pony in one of our bedrooms, wearing the ridiculous nurse outfit and the fishnet stockings from the chemist, whenever I visit the memory now, as a tourist.

I was always the patient and mostly a road accident victim. My being a cyclist knocked off my bicycle by a bus and killed was a morbid obsession for him. When

I visit those memories now I laugh at myself, my arms and legs smothered in tomato ketchup for special effect and bandaged in toilet paper. I can't, and I never did see the point of me being wrapped head to toe in toilet paper, it sticking to the ketchup smothered on my skin like a zombie Egyptian mummy from a low budget horror movie when I was meant to be dead. I did try to tell Garth this on many occasions but he didn't listen.

As I watch now, as the memory tourist, I grin at Garth as a little boy, so bossy.

"It's my game so you will do as you are told, Dee Winters," he says, stamping his foot hard and frowning.

"And, what if I don't want to play your game?" I say back, my hands on my hips and a mass of curls bouncing around my face as I wiggle my hips.

"You have no choice. You are my best friend and my best friend has to do what I say," he replies, this time stamping both of his feet one after the other.

There is no point arguing with him so it always stops here, I do as I am told and my spirit self leaves the memory and returns home.

In all honesty I think Garth's real motive for wanting to be a nurse largely comes down to the fact it gives him full licence to pander to the every need of dishy doctors like a doting puppy. 'Yes, doctor,' 'Certainly, doctor,' 'No problem, doctor' and 'Yes I'll hold it for you, doctor,' became his every day mantra when we did become nurses. Admittedly this had appeal for me, the idea of becoming a doctor's wife and falling in love with him over the passing of a syringe. Unjustly my dishy-doctor conquests didn't compete with his tally; it was a brand new doctor in weekly rotations for Garth during our early training days.

On Garth's part coercion exists but to be fair to him, as I said, there are other contributing factors existing swaying me towards a career as a nurse opposed to a doctor. Outstanding in Biology, I have a natural fascination for the human body. Regrettably, being a Biology boffin is only part of the package. To become a doctor you need full-on nerd and all-round science geek credentials. A science geek I was definitely not because I was so appalling at Chemistry, Physics and Maths. The only A-Levels I achieved was an A grade in Biology, a B in General Studies accompanied by a very dismal and substandard E in Chemistry. I'm leaving out Maths and Physics because they are off the scale of failure altogether. Nursing, all this in mind, seemed a sensible option therefore. Actually, I need to revise that statement: at the time it seemed like my only option. It was that or re-sits, but as my teacher pointed out with an air of I told you so sarcasm about him on results day, re-sits generally apply to those who fall at the last hurdle and are finger tips from success; not those, like me, who fall at the mid-way hurdle and are therefore whole legs and arms from success.

Very unfairly the reasons Garth's A-level four grade Cs were much more stable than my erratic achievements is entirely circumstantial. He didn't have a chemist for a dad, thus it wasn't expected of him to excel in the sciences. Quite simply he got better grades than me because he didn't do all the sciences.

Another of my favourite memories to visit is the day I tried to break it to my family that I didn't want to do all sciences. Now this very moment, my spirit self sits by the grandfather clock in the left alcove of my grandma and grandpa's, my dad's parents', dining room. My physical self announces it rather boldly and with no caution whatsoever to my family's feelings during a normal Saturday afternoon visit. "I'm not studying all the sciences, I have decided. I'm going to do Biology, Psychology, Sociology and History like Garth," I say nodding my head with my arms folded over my chest.

Scone and raspberry preserve almost chokes all four of them. So severe is my grandma's reaction that in ranting at me she neglects concentration on the Earl Grey tea she is pouring from her large china teapot. Instead of into my grandpa's china teacup, she pours a ribbon of steaming tea right into his lap. My spirit self is able to exhume the laugh, which my teenage physical self is suppressing, at the awkward scene of my dad looking bereft and comforting my mum who is tearfully rambling about the glee Mavis and Erin will squeeze out of this. "There is enough juice in this gossip to keep Mavis and Erin going for a whole year, they are going to love this," she snorts into a handful of tissues.

As if there isn't already enough guilt bubbling in the pot there is the matter of my grandpa yelping in pain and my grandma fussing over his groin with a bag of frozen peas. I pity my physical self, looking down at the table, picking raisins out of her scone and avoiding everyone's eye.

The deal is done. Minutes later I'm assuring everyone I'm joking and dutifully commit to study all sciences.

I want to be able to intervene and give myself advice; I want to tell myself that doing all the sciences and failing miserably is something I wrote for myself in my blueprint. I want to assure myself that being a nurse, albeit for a short while, is my destiny and that I wrote that in my blueprint also but that to get to it, to unlock that event that I have written, I must take all sciences and fail them. I want to tell myself it's scripted chronology, a snowball event set in motion even before I was born. I cannot intervene, though; I cannot advise myself. It's impossible. Although I am able to intervene in memories in construction to help blueprinted events happen I am unable to change past events, I cannot intervene by whispering into the ear of those involved in historical memories to alter those memories, they have already been and gone and are set in stone, they are already accomplished to the letter of the blueprint in which they were written.

Although I do not intervene in this memory there are others that follow it that I do try to intervene in, memories which I'm allowed to intervene in. Like the times my mum, after it happens, sits on her own in a quiet place somewhere in the house blaming herself for how she behaved in the memory of my declaring I didn't want to do all sciences. "Did we expect too much?" she asks herself out loud. "Should we have been more understanding? Is it as simple as that? If we'd let her take Biology, Psychology, Sociology and History would she still be alive? Did we lead her to failure? Did we lead her to her death?"

I try to intervene, my unfelt hand on top of hers trying to calm its shakiness, my words of reassurance that the two things are not connected trailing through one ear and out of the other, nothing but wind whistling in them.

Twelve

After it happened

During my journey home my grandmother told me the story of her own passing from the physical world that happened just after my mum's seventeenth birthday. My grandmother told me of how proud she is of my mum because of what she did for her. The evening before the funeral my grandmother was brought to the family home. She described how my mum prepared her. It isn't something I knew, my mum had never spoken about the events surrounding my grandmother's death. Given that my grandfather had died years earlier after his tractor overturned when my grandmother died this left my mum and her five brothers' orphans. My grandmother explained that like with all Irish funerals there was an open casket service before the funeral. It is such a touching memory that my grandmother described to me that I decided, once I had settled in at home, to witness it for myself and so I do as a rookie memory visitor.

I've just had a glass of ice-cold homemade lemonade with Allison and I am sat on the terrace of my beach hut, my bare feet are buried in the soft warm sand beneath the terrace. I begin to imagine the memory my grandmother shared with me when she escorted me home before introducing me to my induction minders. My beach hut and its surroundings begin to drip away. New surroundings begin to build around me. First a hill and then a huge oak tree with sprawling roots and branches, a red squirrel clutching an acorn twists up and around the tree in cork screw motion and disappears into its home, a hole at the top of the tree. Fields materialise from nowhere. Fields of corn their ears swaying in the gentle breeze searching for the sounds of the three young men and their secret lovers, which they are used to concealing; fields that look like assault courses with arrangements of hay bales strategically placed, I can just about hear the ghostly echo of the laughter from the two little boys that would normally be climbing and tumbling the bales; lush green meadows dotted with buttercups being greedily enjoyed by livestock, strangely I expect to see a young woman of seventeen sitting in the grass writing down her thoughts in poems.

At the bottom of the hill a river begins to flow and swans begin to hiss at my presence. Over the river springs a humpback wooden bridge, I walk over it unperturbed by the hissing swans that know that any form of physical attack will be futile. On the other side of the bridge materialises a cottage. It's a quaint squatted cottage. It is knobbly from the large uneven stones it is made from which are painted white. In places the paint is cracked and flaked revealing some of the grey crumbling stones beneath it. Ducks waddle around in the front garden and chickens peck at the grain between the cracks of the flagstones in the garden path avoiding the splatters of dried blood that the rain is yet to wash away.

On the brow of a gradual sloping hill behind the cottage I can see three strapping young men, my mum's older brothers. They are sitting in silence. Each one has the sleeves of their crisp white shirts rolled up to their elbows. They all have their black jackets laid out on the ground in front of them and they all chew on a piece of straw. They stare ahead of them in silence. They are unable to see the figure walking up their garden path looking up at them, their future niece. As a child I loved hearing all of my mum's memories of her childhood in Ireland. It always seems so idyllic, enchanting and lovely like a mystical kingdom full of fairies and leprechauns. Today is such a contrast to any story my mum ever told me. The image of her descriptions has somehow been cheated of its vibrancy and lustre like a bright painting that has been painted over with black paint. There is nothing unwelcoming and unpromising in the stories she described like I am witnessing in this memory.

I walk up to the front door, which is made from wooden planks and painted pale blue and then I pass straight through it into the cottage. On the other side two young boys run straight through me one chasing the other with a tie, my mum's younger brothers, young enough that their resilience is strong enough to hold off understanding, for a little while longer at least, which grief will challenge soon enough. I stand long enough to notice two large rooms either side of a stone staircase.

Without using the staircase I find myself in the back bedroom facing the window. I can see my uncles through it and they are still sat on the brow of the hill silently waiting. I turn into the room. She is at the coffin brushing my grandmother's hair and she is singing. Her back is to the window, and me. I have never heard my mum sing before; she must stop after this day. My uncles on my visits to Ireland as a child shared stories of her singing and they said she had the voice of an angel. Hearing it for myself now I understand that they were right. Her sound is enchanting, words sung in Gaelic, words I don't understand but the motion of them; the purpose of them I understand clearly. She is singing about beauty and loss. Her words are like the wind, wistful and temperamental. She gazes down at my grandmother as if she is merely asleep with love tinged with only the tiniest amount of sadness in her eyes. Placing the silver handled brush down on the dressing table between the coffin and the bed she picks up the silver framed matching mirror and holds it into the coffin hovering it over my grandmother's face.

"Look, Marmmie," she whispers softly, smiling. "Look how pretty you are."

She isn't wrong; my grandmother's face is wrinkle free with a complexion that is as soft and smooth as my own and my mum's. The blusher that my mum dusted onto her face before my intrusion into the memory gives her a pink girlish glow.

As spirit people we are able to remember our age when we leave the physical although it has no meaning once we are home and there is no hierarchical system according to our age. My grandmother told me that the day she slipped on a loose paving stone bringing in the washing and hit her head hard on a jagged rock in the garden she was thirty-nine. Sometimes when we cross over and come home, some spirit people can feel cheated and they don't instantly respect that they have chosen it to be this way in their own blueprint. A spirit person can become distressed, before emotion is detached, because they feel it is not their time and because they have concerns about leaving vulnerable things behind, such as a seventeen-year-old daughter in charge of five male siblings. My grandmother was one of these spirit people. As a spirit person it was the opposite for me the day my soul left an empty body in the bath, I had instant acceptance.

My mum replaces the mirror beside the brush on the dressing table and reaches for a string of pearls. "Here you go, Marmmie. Your wedding pearls." She leans into the coffin and strings them around my grandmother's neck. "I know you wanted me to wear them on my wedding day but I think they should go with you."

I watch as she moves around the coffin sweeping her hand around it making her way to the other side. When she reaches the other side using both hands she picks up a jewellery box from the top of a dark wood chest of drawers standing on tall thin legs with brass handles on the drawers. Her down cast eyes look up briefly, just for a second. They fix in my direction and burn directly into me. I know she can see me but nothing falters in her expression. She turns her back on me and sits on the bed. She places the jewellery box on her knee and opens it fingering inside it for a moment or two. Then she pulls out a mother of pearl brooch, which belonged to my great grandmother.

"I don't know who you are or why you have come. I know you are here and I am not scared."

I disappear from beside the window and I reappear sitting on the bed beside her. My mum does not flicker but I know she can feel me beside her. She stands up and leans into my grandmother's coffin, pinning the brooch onto the blue dress she has dressed her in. "I saw you in the garden the day she died, stood beside the washing line. I know you came for her. Please keep her safe."

I did visit the memory of my grandmother's last day in the physical and I watched what happened but I am not the one who takes her. She went with my grandfather before I was even born.

Thirteen

Before it happened

Garth and I are born on the eighteenth of December of the same year because we choose it this way in our blueprints, which we write together before we are born.

Winding tinsel around our Christmas tree, my mum goes into labour at precisely the same moment Garth's mum, next door, goes into labour hanging her Christmas cards on string across the mantle. Side by side the ambulances arrive at the hospital and our mums, still at this point not introduced, are wheeled in one after the other, like car and caravan.

Polished with empathy, our mums give each other an intense look as they are speedily wheeled through the hospital. Their minds are simultaneously recalling the previous occasions they have seen each other in their gardens hanging out the washing, exchanging brief glances and chance smiles, watering the flowers in the front garden and painting the window frames in the summer. Huffing and puffing, clutching their bellies as they are wheeled quickly by hospital porters, an identical regret: *it's a pity I never said hello*, travels through their minds as they round the corner and disappear into separate delivery suites.

I love the fact that he is older than me. Garth is born at 3pm and I am born at 3.10pm. As a pig is from a giraffe, as babies Garth and I couldn't be more different. I am large and round, like a pig. Garth is stretched out and scrawny, like a giraffe. I have no hair at all except for three wiry sprigs on top of my head and Garth has a fluffy strip of hair down the centre of his head. My eyes are docile and round and Garth's are oval and have hidden depths.

Utilising my limitless imagination I am standing at the far end of the ward now on the day we were born, in front of the window. I am listening, with sympathy for those who endured it at the time, to the one-day-old Garth and me, relentlessly screaming one piercing stream of constant ear-splitting sound, which is like the whistle of a kettle boiling. Two nurses jump to attention, spring from behind the desk of their station positioned at the opposite end of the ward and hurry forwards. One is short and plump and has a fresh face, the eagerness and nervousness of a trainee tango together in her aura. The second is the same body mass as the first, only stretched out to be long and thin. She has grey hair, the irritation and fatigue of experience tango in her aura. The tall, thin nurse dashes towards my cot, her stringy legs threatening to snap off at her apple-like knees as they take gigantic steps as if she is jumping from one stepping stone to another across a river. Lifting me from my cradle she latches me to her ribs. The short plump nurse waddles like a duck, her backside toing and froing and her flat feet making slapping noises on the floor. Plucking Garth out of his cradle she casts a fleeting glance at her superior in age and service and attempts to mirror the cradle she has on me on Garth. Singing a rather atrocious duet of 'Rock-a-bye-Baby,' they rock us from side to side. My nurse is as shrill as a high-pitched drill and Garth's nurse is as throaty as a frog.

Both are completely out of tune and out of time to one another. In spite of the well camouflaged soothing, which is far from tender, our screaming does not get worse, but it does not ease off either.

Flummoxed, my nurse turns to my bewildered mum and says, "I have never heard babies cry like it. It's as if they are sickening for something but all their needs have been attended to. They have been fed, bathed and changed." She removes one of her arms from the cradle around me and covers my forehead with her hand. "The little mite doesn't have a temperature." She looks across at Garth's nurse and asks, "What about your little mite, Beryl? Does he have a temperature? Bless his little cotton socks."

With caution worrying, I syphon from her thoughts, that removing an arm from the cradle may cause her to drop him, Beryl covers Garth's forehead with her podgy hand. She lingers it there for a little longer than my nurse did, needing more clarity, with inexperience. Then she replies, "No, Doreen God love him, he doesn't."

"There is something not quite right. Something sets me on edge, Beryl. I think Dr Mulligan should take a look, just to be on the safe side."

Our mums look on hopelessly, feeling redundant and unable to offer any wisdom.

"They are certainly trying to tell us something."

"Don't be daft, Beryl," Doreen scoffs. "They are not trying to tell us something. They are barely a day old, silly girl. Snuggle him to you more, just like I am with this little one." Self-importantly she instructs Beryl walking towards her, "Look like this." She jiggles me to emphasise her point.

Following behind Doreen, knowing what will happen next, I wait for the silence, which comes the moment, the crown of my head is a fraction away from Garth's.

"Well I never," Doreen says. "That seems to me to be a lot of fuss about nothing." She looks at Beryl and says, "Yes that's right dear, snuggle him into you. I'll just pop this little mite back in her cot with her mum and then I'll be back to show you how to lay him down properly."

Only I know that Doreen is about to feel the sharp blade of humiliation puncture her gut at Beryl's natural intuition. Turning, she begins to walk towards my mum. Creating a distance between us, our relentless ear splitting screaming instantly resumes.

"This is silly," Doreen says snuggling me into her for warmth.

"Do you know, Doreen? I think I know what is wrong with the little mites," Beryl says. "I think they want to be together. I think they want to make friends. That's what they are trying to tell us, I told you they were."

"Make friends? Be together? Don't be impudent girl. They know nothing of friendship in the same way that you know nothing about nursing."

Doreen couldn't be more wrong on both counts; we knew of friendship a long time before we were born and Beryl has been a nurse many times before, once on the front line in World War I.

"I honestly think I am right," Beryl replies excitedly, nodding her head with an expression of someone who has just made a world-changing discovery, like a cure for cancer.

"Dear girl, I have been nursing on maternity wards for thirty-odd years. You are barely out of nappies in nursing terms. Babies do not cry like this because they want to be together."

"Let me show you." Beryl closes the gap between us, turning Garth in her arms so that our little crinkled faces meet. "There you go, little ones," she whispers softly, stooping down and planting a kiss on Garth's forehead. "There you go, little friends."

The moment we are reunited, the crying stops.

"Well I never. In all of my years I have never known anything like it. We'd better move the little mites next to each other. It seems the only way to keep them quiet," she says, her usual know-it-all smugness battered and bruised from the bashing it has just received from Beryl.

"I think this is what you call being inseparable from birth." Beryl laughs smugness taking a second swipe at Doreen's pride inflicting more bruising. "I hope you don't live too far away from each other. I think these two may become very good friends. We might even have a future Mr and Mrs here."

Now, Beryl couldn't be more wrong. In the next life, perhaps if we chose it to be so when we write our blueprints, presuming we will want to experience another life, of course, which we might not.

Doreen laughs. "I'd better get hat shopping, then."

Both our mum's laugh and mine replies, "We actually live next door to each other so they will be growing up together. You could be right about that Mr and Mrs prediction."

No she isn't, mum. No one hears me, of course.

Fourteen

Before it happened

I shun the camera in the physical world because I am terrified of it. I love to take photographs of other people and of other things, often very random things like street name signs, gate posts, litter and broken things. Once I take a whole series of shots of an arrangement of broken garden furniture I find in a skip, which I set up in the garden. The table is cracked, the parasol is shredded and the chairs have legs and arms missing. Garth helps me carry it back, making three trips in total, to my garden and assists me in my endeavour to take the perfect shots. We arrange them at the bottom of my garden on a stone circle that my dad laid one August for my mum's fortieth birthday, granting her wish of having a sun trap so she could enjoy al fresco dining. We lay the table with my mum's best china without her knowledge. We eagle-eye our watches every ten minutes for the entire afternoon to make sure we are finished and packed away before she finishes work. In an oriental, expensive-looking vase from Garth's mum's sideboard, we place vibrant red roses and position it in the centre of the table. All afternoon I snap away with my camera. I take shots lying on my belly with Garth holding mirrors in key positions to reflect the sunlight. I take birds'-eye shots sitting on Garth's shoulders. 'Al fresco decay,' I call it and it wins first prize in a national photography competition.

I absolutely love to take photographs; I just hate being in them. It's a fact that, after it happens, feeds Garth's and the girls' grief so that it swells all the more painfully and they hate me even more for being so selfish. There is nothing of me frozen in time for them to remind themselves of our friendship or me in general.

My granddad, my dad's dad, is the trigger of my mistrust of the camera. I am a very little girl of about six or seven with red ribbons in my hair. I am sitting on my granddad's knee in his big leather armchair by the fire whilst he reads me a bedtime story. I listen spellbound by his story telling voice breathing life into the characters who I watch spring from the pages and act out, the events he reads, on the rug in front of us. Locked in the moment nothing else exists. I do not even hear the click. Suddenly there is a flash of light. It's too late. The photograph has been taken. I look up from the story and see my grandma standing in the doorway facing the armchair smiling, with pride at us and holding the camera with both hands close to her chest.

"That is going to be a lovely picture," she says, nodding. "A very special moment captured forever and ever."

"The camera never lies," my granddad says, looking at me intently. "The camera freezes the truth in time, immortalising it. People can identify the mood of someone just by looking at a photograph of them. They can tell if they're sad or happy just from a photograph."

I find this deeply upsetting. I really do. Can the camera really look through my eyes into my soul and find the truth, telling it like a storybook? I sense, despite not understanding why because I am only very young, that mine is a very unsavoury story and one I definitely do not want to share. Fear weaves itself around my insides like a strong vine of ivy, choking me at the throat and constricting my windpipe. In that moment, as that little girl, I want to leap off my granddad's knee race over to my grandma, snatch the camera from her, throw it on the floor and stamp on it until it bursts all over her yellow and green swirly patterned carpet.

That choking fear stays with me and I am forever unable to shake it off. From that moment on I develop a terror of the camera. No-one is ever allowed from this point to snap me. Even seeing a camera I don't have control of will inspire the kind of panic whereby I will lose all sense and rational thought and I will begin gasping for air and shrinking away, trying to invert myself like a tortoise.

Professional therapists, before it happens, try through thorough investigation into my conscious to get to the root of a darkness that can sometimes sweep over me. None of them for all their wisdom manage to bring it back to something as simple as a photograph and an unfortunate wisdom of my granddad. Strangely, the simplest of events, the little things can have the most dangerous catastrophic consequences. Somehow, and I could never articulate it in the physical, I believe the camera has the power to expose me as something unsavoury. I can't really describe the feeling but it is a form of panic and a sense of paralysis that washes over me. I know that I can't allow myself to be exposed; I can't give the camera the opportunity to turn people against me by showcasing the ugly truth.

Developing an interest in taking photographs is my conscious way of masking my fear from the realisation of others. By being behind the camera I don't have to be in front of it and because I am good at taking photographs people prefer me to take them than be in them, like a personal photographer. Aside from this I feel, with my granddad's philosophy in mind, like I am some kind of truth investigator taking photographs of anything and everything in a truth crusade to unearth their secrets and show case them for the world to see; like my 'Al Fresco Decay,' exhibition, I was exposing the garden furniture's decay and abandonment, telling the story of this to the world, or at least a small part of it.

One of the first lessons I learned after it happened is that nothing, even the things we throw away, is insignificant and somehow although I cannot articulate it before it happens I realise this in the objects I chose to photograph, like the decaying furniture and the abandoned lip stick I once come across on the back seat of a bus. The lipstick, like the furniture, and everything else that may appear discarded and inconsequential is connected to something bigger and is a small piece of a big jigsaw. The discarded lipstick had a story, a truth to tell. It's the same for the decaying furniture.

The lipstick holds the story of a young girl experiencing heartbreak for the first time. The final and brutal last words of her long-term boyfriend like an out of control chainsaw inside her head severing slices of her brain causing other faculties to shut down, her speech to slur, her vision to blur. She had expected to marry him -everyone did- and they were the high-school couple with 'forever' written all over them. When the chainsaw has turned her brain to mush it slides down her throat in search of her heart. She blames her lipstick. Her lipstick is responsible for her pain. Her lipstick is the villain of the story; it is the wicked stepmother that has plotted against her to achieve her demise.

In a cowardly act unable to admit there is another girl, her boyfriend has told her, "I don't like your lipstick, it's too pink and it makes you look trashy."

Sobbing relentlessly and loudly for the entire bus journey back to her parents' house, loathsome bile, for the pink lipstick she is holding in her hands, boils in every blood vessel, yet untouched by the chainsaw, of her body, believing that it is the cause of her broken heart. She hates herself more for wearing it. Because she is too eccentric she has lost the love of her life. I follow her now sometimes, although she never knows I am there, and I am saddened by the lack of colour in her life as a result of what he told her. Her clothes are drab and her lips muted, she has never since that day purchased a lipstick and upon returning home that day threw every single one she had out of her bedroom window, firing them at the road like bullets, which exploded on impact. The penthouse apartment, overlooking the city centre, she lives in now is very sterile and colourless. She is resentful because colour is culpable for the broken heart that refuses to heal and the rejection that won't release her, colour has been completely dissolved from her life. Relationships, like colour, are devoid from her existence now and always have been since that day, the day I found the lipstick and photographed it knowing that it was much more than an abandoned lipstick, knowing that it was pivotal to some epic storyline of someone's life.

The events we would normally consider insignificant can have the most catastrophic consequences for some people. People like the girl I have described. People like me.

Fifteen

Before it happened

At eighteen-years-old we have outgrown the nurse's outfits that Garth makes me ask for at Christmas when we're in primary school. I decide when we are invited to the eighteenth birthday party of a girl in our biology class that we will make our own costumes.

Spreading tracing paper out on my desk we skilfully drew out the pattern of two very shamelessly provocative nurses' uniforms, in white with thin pink pinstripes. Extremely low-cut, almost showing our navels; high in length, barely covering our thighs and bum cheeks and as tight as a glove, our aim is for the eyebrows of all the other guests to raise so high that the ceiling of the village hall function room the party is to be held in becomes a huge hairy carpet. By the time the first bottle of cider was finished we had sketched the patterns, cut them out and pinned them to the material. By the time the second bottle of cider had gone we had cut the material to the pattern. Mirroring the start of the third bottle we were ready to stitch them using my beloved retro cream and blue sewing machine, one of my charity shop trawl treasures. I always tried to imagine who it belonged to before me. Going by the My Little Pony and Care Bear stickers I always assumed it belonged to a little girl. Now that I have met her, I know that my assumption was correct. She told me that after her treatment stopped working it was packed into black bin liners with the rest of her belongings and given away to charity. Her parents had felt it would be what she wanted, other people benefitting from her things, because when she was eight, three years before they had to pack her things up, she had declared that she wanted to carry a donor card, she told me that they were right and watching me use the sewing machine before we met had pleased her.

"You must spend half your life in charity shops," Garth slurred as I was attempting to retrieve my sewing machine from the bottom of my wardrobe.

I glanced back at him over my shoulder. Laid out on my bed, his purple t-shirt blended with my purple bedspread, he put his hands behind his head, angling his knobbly elbows out towards the ceiling. Then he crossed his legs at his skinny ankles, showing a lot of red sock as his bleached jeans rode up.

"I like old things. They have-."

He cut me off as easily as scissors cut paper before I could finish my sentence.

"I know. They have a history, a story to tell. You are so deep, Dee."

I fixed him with a stare. "I like to shop in charity shops so I'm deep? Shut up, loser."

"I'm the loser? I'm not the one who goes around wearing other peoples cast-offs," he smirked, lifting his mug of cider from my white, covered-in-boy-band-stickers, melamine bedside cabinet with his free hand.

He knocked it back in one gulp. "Take that hideous all in one vintage thing you're wearing. How many people do you think have worn it before you found it, where it should be, in the bottom of a second-hand shop's reject bin? One, maybe two, three perhaps, four or five even. No. Not five. There really can't be that many people who were deluded enough to think that offensive orange floral print is attractive. You look like my granny's curtains. My point is these people whose clothes you recycle could have had anything; some terrible skin disease, for example." He shuddered. "Christ, some poor cow in the sixties might have died in it after over-indulging at some flower power festival. Yuk, imagine that."

At the time I didn't realise how perceptively accurate, completely by accident, he was being with his last back handed-comment. Neither did either of us realise that the woman he described was in the room with us sitting at my desk.

I abruptly, annoyed at him, stopped pulling at my sewing machine, leaving it half hanging out of the wardrobe. Stopping it from tumbling out onto the floor was the fact that it was caught up in a tangle of shoes, handbags, belts and other garments longing for freedom at the bottom of my wardrobe. This is very pertinent to how I lived my life when I was in Garth's world: one big jumble sale.

"Garth, you make me out to be some kind of hand-me-down Sally. I buy second-hand clothes because I want to breathe new life into them," I snapped back at him stamping a foot and wagging a finger. I added, whilst wrenching a coat out of the wardrobe, "This is my favourite coat." I thrust it forward, "Look how beautiful it is."

"Yes, very beautiful," he ridiculed, not lifting his eyes from the task in hand, which was to refill the Smarties mug I got one Easter with cider.

"You 're not even looking." I snapped and stamped my foot again, triggering vibrations that caused my suspended sewing machine to jolt forward alarmingly fast, like a car precariously hanging over a cliff, any sudden movement capable of sending it crashing into the rocks below.

He replied, "I don't need to look at you, Dee. I know exactly the coat you are holding up. You bloody live in it."

"Okay," I replied, stuffing the coat back into the wardrobe. "Describe it to me, smart arse."

With his mug refilled he looked up at me, rolled his eyes and clicked his tongue. "Okay, Dee, I'll humour you. Come here and kneel in front of me."

I do as he asked without questioning his reason and kneel in front of him. Like Al will do to him years after I do what I do, Garth placed a finger on the ridge of my nose and began to make humming noises.

I giggled and broke away. "You are such a piss taker, Garth."

"Dee," he said in a serious tone, "you cannot interrupt a master at work. Now shut up and let me tune into your thoughts. Honestly, how am I supposed to read your mind with you giggling like a school girl?"

"I'm sorry. Okay, you can do your thing."

Placing my hands on my knees trying desperately hard to keep a straight face I closed my eyes. He placed a finger back on the bridge of my nose.

"Okay, I'm getting it now. It's coming through. I can see it as clear as day. You were holding up the lime green waist-length jacket, the one which is tight across those big bazookas of yours and then fans out to the waist, the one with the petal collar."

Huffily I pushed his finger away.

"Well I'm right, aren't I?"

"You think you are so clever but you missed out the little purse strung pockets and daisy button detail," I said scornfully.

"Oh yes. I forgot those," he replied in a tone suggesting that it was of little significance.

"The point you are missing," I said, getting to my feet and making my way back to the wardrobe to free my sewing machine, "is that, for one thing, buying the jacket means I have done my bit for charity and donated to a good cause and second of all, the jacket did not have the petal collar, the daisy button detail or the little purse strung pockets when I bought it. I brought an old and forgotten thing back to life, gave it a new lease of life. It had probably spent years in that shop being neglected and probably, for that matter, years abandoned at the bottom of someone's wardrobe before that." I cast a fleeting glance at the mass of garments jumbled in the bottom of my own wardrobe pleading with me to grant their freedom and I bit my lip guiltily. "I brought it back to life, introduced it to the world again."

Garth tugged at the pillow behind him and said, "Arc, the patron saint of clothes. I salute you, Dee Winters." Then he hurled the pillow across the room at me, adding, "Shut up, you daft cow. It's just a jacket. You make it sound like a bin bag full of kittens you rescued from a river bank."

"Shhh Garth," I hissed with a finger on my lips, "you will hurt my jacket's feelings."

"Weirdo."

I didn't reply. I simply stuck my tongue out at him and then turned to my sewing machine, which I freed from its tangle and placed on my desk under my bedroom window.

"You can sew first," I said. "I've done most of the sketching."

"I'm on cider duty," Garth replied. "That's a very important job, you know." He laughed.

"I know," I replied, making my way to him and snatching up the bottle by its neck. "And one you are crap at considering my mug has been empty for the last twenty minutes."

Sixteen

After it happened

I am stood in a meadow surrounded by buttercups, my hands fanning out like wings, my fingertips tickle with the sensation of the coarse grass they brush against. I close my eyes and instantly, at my command, the Sanctuary of Comprehension and Development pushes its way through the earth, gradually growing taller and spreading wider until it is fully erected. Instantly, this time using neither levitation nor the six-legged Siamese sphinx's guarded staircase, I find myself inside. I am staring up at a bookcase of infinite height, its top shelves disappearing into the black sky and silver stars. Slowly and gently like the first delicate leaf of autumn, one of the huge blue prints, bound in bark and tied with twine, which my mind has commanded to come to me, floats down and rests on a huge hexagonal gold plinth that has a pool of healing water in the centre of it.

Once more I close my eyes and raise my hands to my head and with my request the twine unties itself and evaporates into thin air. The heavy bark front cover lifts itself with ease, unburdened by its own weight. The thin translucent pages, like tracing paper, covered with gold leaf scrawl begin to turn in haste as if responding to a sudden and strong gust of wind. Within seconds the blueprint rests at the correct page, a page in the middle, half filled with gold leaf scrawl. The scrawl stops here despite there being a wedge of pages on the opposite side of the half-filled page; they are all empty. The author of this blueprint chose to stop halfway. I step forward with no emotion despite knowing what this means and knowing what event is looming. Underscoring each line of gold scrawl with my index finger I drink in the script the author has written for themselves and then lingering my finger on the last word I close my eyes and command my next move.

For many centuries in many lives we have had a connection; we are eternal soul mates and this bond is indestructible. The connection we share, which was written in our blueprints for past existences in the physical world and will be written in our blueprints for future existences in the physical world, is not always co-dependant. The bond is not always a strong one like the bond between Dee and Garth in my most recent life. We have written, and will write again, passive connections to allow us to learn from other people in the physical. Sometimes, like in our most recent life, the one where I am Dee, I choose to learn independently of him and instead share a close bond with another, Garth. In the background of my life, subtly watching over me he is there like an unwitting guardian. In Dee's physical life, my most recent life, he has a supporting role as the milkman. It's a role that when we wrote it in our blueprints together we took amusement from. Despite never knowing his name or anything about him there is always a mutual intense look of recognition, which I could never understand as Dee in the physical world, as I stand at my bedroom window brushing my hair. He jovially bounces down the back garden path carrying our milk and whistling and it's as if, when he pauses half way down and holds my gaze, he knows me as much as I feel deep inside of me that I know him; it's as if we can see each other's souls. He salutes with his free hand and winks. I smile and wave. We each feel comforted, safe in the world knowing that the other is in it with us.

The memory of him switches on like a light in my spirit psyche the instant I step out of my physical body onto the wet bathroom floor. The knowledge that he is still living a physical life arrives immediately after his name and the confirmation of his existence processes. If he had already crossed it would be him and not my grandmother bringing me home.

My eyes open. My command has been adhered. I am standing back from the edge of the quarry with sheep idly grazing behind me. Aware of my presence but unconcerned by it, they continue eating. Standing right on the quarry edge, the tips of their toes overhanging are three men of varying sizes. The tallest is stood in the middle and the smallest and plumpest is on the left of him.

"After three, right lads," his words fall over the edge of the quarry and plummet into the water below, lost forever.

The two men either side of him shoot sideways glances, doubt jumping up and down and waving frantically in their eyes. The smallest replies, "James, I'm not sure on this one, man. It must be twenty feet."

"It's twenty-five feet, I looked it up," the third man replies. "James, I'm with Danny, man. I'm not sure this is a good idea."

"Ben, mate, since when have you ever been on team big-girls-blouse with Danny? Don't be pussies, both of you. This is the reason we came camping."

"Big-girls-blouse, who are you calling a big-girls-blouse? You toss-." the rush of wind as Danny wobbles forward, his rant at James causing him to overbalance forwards, catches the end of his sentence and swallows it whole.

"Stand back, stand back!" James shouts. "Danny, stand back!"

James folds at his middle, making a grab with an extended hand for the neck of Danny's t-shirt. Danny's arms flare wildly at his side, desperate to lift rather than fall. It's too late, he's too overbalanced, his feet lift and forward he falls.

"Mate, dive! Dive!"

James looks at Ben and both men flop to their bellies and look over the edge of the quarry. They watch as Danny falls horizontally like a skydiver towards the surface of the water, which is so dense and stagnant it looks like a concrete slab and not water. "He'll never make it, the impact will wind him, and he'll drown!" James says jumping to his feet. "Get help." Then he gracefully springs on his feet. With his arms stretched above his head and his hands meeting at a point like a sharpened blade he dives towards the water set to slice through it, years of training and competition victories teeming in his poise and confidence.

Ben sprints through my apparition towards a family picnic behind me in a bid to use their mobiles to alert the emergency services. When he enters me, my form gently and temporarily fragments like tiny molecules. They hover in the air like soap bubbles and then they restructure, with no permanent damage, once his intrusion has ended.

At the water's edge bank holiday revellers staying at the quarry-side campsite begin to congregate. Some people are open mouthed, some shout out in terror, some hide their faces in their hands and some cover their mouths with their hands. They all watch transfixed as Danny rushes towards the greedy water set to become just another of the many cavernous meals it has enjoyed over the centuries of its existence. Their eyes flick from Danny to James. Instantly they recognise that the second man knows what he is doing and has expertise on his side. They are all rooting for his bid to save his novice friend to be successful, some people even cross their fingers. Others are muttering prayers. People are surging forward now and setting dinghies into the water that they clamber into and begin paddling towards the point they estimate the two men will enter the water, ready to offer any help they can.

Danny takes the water off guard, whilst it is resting after a hard day entertaining tourists, slamming into its stomach hard, causing it to baulk and then spew out of it a vertical fountain of water, which conceals both Danny and James from view. By the time the water has settled, those paddling out on dinghies have reached the point of impact, some lean over the side of their dinghies searching the water with their eyes like the lights of rescue boats searching for survivors after a shipwreck. Their search seems fruitless. Some have dived out of their dinghies and are in the water, bobbing their heads under the water's surface like ducks worthlessly attempting to see through the murky depths of the water.

I am standing on the edge now; it is almost his time. I sense it; he will be with me soon. In the middle distance the whirring of sirens punctures the stagnant air; they will be too late to save him. Suddenly someone emerges from beneath the water. Breaking through its surface rapidly, water cascades over their face like a liquid veil. It is one of the holidaymakers from one of the dinghies; he is swimming backwards towing another man against him. The man is spluttering. He looks as if he has swallowed a lot of water but he is conscious. Two men in one of the dinghies close by him reach out; they each hook an arm under each of the spluttering man's armpits and pull him into the dinghy. The man who towed him to safety clambers into the dinghy.

"Any sign of the other one?"

"No, he's a goner I'd say. This one's lucky not to have been snared by something. On the way back up I'm sure I sprang off a shopping trolley, it's how I reached the surface so quickly."

As the three men paddle Danny to the water's edge where Ben is waiting with paramedics, James appears beside me and as I had instant recognition of him when I left my physical body, he has instant recognition of me. He takes my hand, and we turn and walk away. Then, just like when Ben disturbed my form, James and I disperse into tiny bubble-like atoms that quietly and gently pop, disappearing into thin air. We are returned home.

Seventeen

Before it happened

With trees I have a kinship both in the physical and at home. I hear them and I feel them.

A deep forest sits at the back of my house swirling with a mysterious thick energy. Centuries upon centuries it has been the home of a very special tree. He stands tall and proud in the middle of the forest calling out to the other souls in his realm, guiding them spiritually. I spend a lot of time with him. Pressing my ear to his chest leaning against him I'm aware of unexplainable entities, aware of blood pumping through his veins, a heart beating in his chest and the formation of thoughts joining together, making perfect sense.

Garth will accompany me, humouring me. Treading carefully on the forest bed, crisp leaves rustling and brittle twigs snapping underneath us we would visit Aryl together. Aryl is the wisest and oldest tree of all the forest. His bark is thick and brittle and full of splits, lumps, bumps and pointing fingers. In a cranny of his magnificent, gnarled and knotted trunk we crouch and contemplate the meaning of life for hours. Sometimes we shield from the rain, wind or snow in the cave-like depth of it. The thick trunk, his torso, is almost as thick as a house. Splitting into four smaller trunks his necks twist out and spiral back on themselves. A thick carpet of moss lay between them. On summer days Garth and I would lay outstretched on it looking up at the blue sky and the fluffy white clouds.

Apart from the trees themselves I used to believe that we were alone. On the occasions I visit now, I realise this was never the case. There are many spirit people who dwell in the forest. The medieval temptress, burnt in the forest as a witch for seducing many village men and their wives. She is responsible for the mysterious scorched handprints, which appear on the trees. There is the caped and masked highwayman thrown from his horse during a heist. He can be heard firing his pistol on dark nights. Another spirit person in the forest is the little girl who fell from her tree house in more recent times. She is responsible for the ring of blue bells around the tree adjacent to Aryl. Protecting my friend Aryl and the other trees of the forest is the beautiful spirit of a native Indian who wears a buffalo skin dress and has her thick ebony hair in plaits. She passed in childbirth and decided never again to experience rebirth. Communication between us never takes place. Guardians don't communicate; they simply watch, protect and heal. One day I hope to be a guardian myself. I have much learning and many levels to aspire to before I am bestowed this honour.

As I think of it now I am drawn to the times long gone. Garth with his long curly bleached blonde hair is sitting on a bed of leaves his lanky long legs stretched apart. His skinny jeans show the ankle between the bottom of them and his black pumps, which have pink laces. His white Walkman with red Styrofoam headphones is cast to one side. My physical self is snapping away holding the camera at different positions, close-up shots, long distance shots, shots on my tiptoes and shots on my knees.

"I feel like we are the only two people in the world when we are here, Dee."

"I don't. Can't you feel them?"

"Feel who? There is no-one here. No-one but us ever comes here, not since that little girl died here."

At the mention of her name she appears, but only me in spirit form sees her.

"The trees, silly," I laugh. "They have souls just like us."

Garth laughs loudly; his laughing overpowers him, causing his heels to dig into the pliable mud. "You really are a nutcase."

"I'm being serious."

I am right behind them. The little girl is stood beside me holding my hand. Neither Garth nor the historical and physical me is aware of us. In the physical there is so much you are not aware of.

"Come off it, Dee," he sniggers, getting to his feet and leaning against the tree putting a hand on one of its gnarled knuckles. He takes a cigarette from the pocket of the open shirt he is wearing over a black and red vertically striped vest top and puts it into his mouth. "Light me."

I move forward, take a match box from the back pocket of my purple cord flares and withdraw a match, which I strike and hold up to his cigarette. I watch as Garth cups his hands around the flame and I light his cigarette. "You are lit."

Taking a deep drag, he pushes his head backwards, resting it on Aryl, blowing billows of smoke into the air. He holds the cigarette out; I take it and then take a gentler drag on it.

"You don't really believe all that shit, do you?"

"All what shit?" I ask, exhaling smoke rings, which he pokes his fingers through, bursting them like bubbles.

"That plant forms feel pain, all that biology bollocks."

Catching a delicate leafy branch jutting out from Aryl, one of his many children, in one hand Garth grips it. I sense his intention; I know Aryl senses it too. I feel his concern trembling through him so I rush forward screaming. "Don't you dare, Garth. I'll smack you right on the nose if you hurt him."

Garth's face washes with fright and he lets go of Aryl's child. I sense Aryl's anxiety dissolve, taking my own with it. Garth throws his hands up in the air. "Okay, don't shoot me."

"It's not biology bollocks anyway, Garth," I say. "How can you say that when we study A-level Biology. What is the point if you don't believe it?"

"We are studying human biology, Dee. I want to be a nurse to humans not a tree surgeon."

Intuiting Aryl's discomfiture again, I place a soothing hand flat against his bumpy body. "Shhh, you are scaring him. Tree surgeons are not friends of the trees, they..." I let my words trail off tuning into the vibrations of Aryl who shudders with dread at the very mention of tree surgeons.

"I know. They take a big chain saw and-."

Clasping a hand over his mouth, I warn him. "Don't say it. He has seen so many of his kind slain this way. He hates to be reminded of it." I close my eyes. "Listen. Can't you hear them?"

Subdued muffles filter through my fingers. "Hear what?"

Springing my eyes open, I look at him with agitation. "Can't you hear their screams, the screams of the trees that have been slain? Close your eyes and listen."

Postponing closing my eyes until Garth's are closed, I take his hand. We stand connected. Against Aryl is my left hand, my right hand is holding Garth's left hand and his right hand is pressing flat against Aryl. We stand in total silence. High-pitched sounds pierce through my ears like a nail being scraped down metal. Garth is numb to them, just like he is numb to my spirit self now.

Snapping open his eyes he says, "I hear nothing but the wind. You are off your rocker, babe. God, you are so happy ever after at the end of the rainbows."

Wrenching me by the arm, he tows me away.

I watch Garth and I disappear into the trees and then I leave too, returning home to James.

Eighteen

After it happened

Garth hastily hunts through boxes and boxes of old photographs whilst I sit on the windowsill watching him. He sifts through photographs from childhood days before we began school, chocolate smeared on our faces. He inspects photographs from childhood days whilst we were at school, the knot of his tie pulled loose to his navel. He paws at photographs of teenage days in sixth form, when we both had ridiculous blonde perms. He searches through photographs of young adulthood at nursing college and he cries over photographs of our final stage of life together, young adulthood as working nurses.

Delving into each box he pulls apart the contents, ripping the corners of the shoeboxes with disregard. He desperately looks into each photograph. Panic rising higher and higher with each one of them he tosses away, not finding what he is looking for until finally all of the photographs we own have been inspected. Hundreds of them, piles upon piles litter the floor in disorganised abandon. With his head in his hands, photographs stuffed into the triangle space of his crossed legs, he sobs heavily. I crouch beside him. Not one. Not a single photograph of me exists. He is distraught. He has nothing to remember me by and he is petrified he will forget me. The utter horror at the thought of one day forgetting me, of one day not being able to distinguish my eye colour or my hair colour, sets panic in him. I would feel regret at not realising how important a photograph really is, if I could. I've been so blind. I've been so stupid. Photographs are time portals that allow us to remember things how they were. They are precious keepsakes, which allow us to recall things that have gone, people who have gone. Photographs allow us to resurface memories that are buried deep in our subconscious under a mound of more recent memories. I was wrong to fear the camera. Wrong.

Crowded with questions, his thoughts are wasting time with trying to understand why: *Why did she hate having her photograph taken so much?* Beating himself up with what if: *What if I'd taken more notice?* Blaming himself with if only: *If only I had asked her, if only I had tried to understand more.* Torturing himself with maybes: *She couldn't even bear to see herself in photographs and I didn't realise. Maybe if I had she would still be here.* There is no advantage to it. Our path is set and mine in the physical is done. The 'what if', the 'why', the 'if only' and the 'maybes' are all irrelevant. Thinking this way is a huge waste of energy.

Eventually my redundancy to his sobbing is reprieved when something catches my eye. The full moon in a pitch-black sky catches my eye. I'm back sitting on the windowsill looking out at it, looking at him, Aryl.

Striking me is a way to help Garth remember me. Memories of our days in the forest with Aryl animate around me cinematically as if I'm in some kind of visual capsule. Suddenly, the black sky and the bright moon disintegrate and autumn colours draw me in. The flame reds and burnt oranges, the flash of my camera and the smell of cigarette smoke enter the equation. Laughter begins to fill my ears. Piece by piece the present rushes away and the past rushes in. Present Garth melts into Past Garth. His conservative boot-cut jeans and charcoal sweater over a white shirt morph into waxy skinny jeans, tight black and red striped vest and an oversized shirt. His short brown hair transforms into peroxide curls. Time reversed, we stand beside Aryl.

Once I live the memory I am drawn back to the present, as it is now. Garth in the lounge of our shared house, wallowing and surrounded by hundreds of immortalised moments we shared, which I am absent from.

Suddenly one of the photographs from a pile of them close to Garth begins to twitch at the corners caused by my energy. It lifts high up off the carpet, hovers momentarily and then floats gently back down again resting in Garth's lap. It's as if it had been caught by a sudden gust of strong wind, and this is what he believes for all of his psychical life. Gazing into the photograph his sobbing abruptly ceases as his mind begins to construct an image of me. Falling backwards he lets his legs fly into the air so that his feet are high above his head. Rolling around on the floor like a baby, laughing uncontrollably he holds the photograph close to his face.

I am already beside him in the passenger seat when he arrives at the car and drops into the driver's seat. Stretching through me to his glove compartment he takes out a stick of chewing gum, which he chews, removes from his mouth and then uses to fix the photograph to the centre of the steering wheel, laughing at it wildly as he drives.

Arriving at our destination Garth leaves the car and goes to the boot where he takes out Polly's cycling headlight, strapping it to his head over his red bobble hat. Switching it on, a funnel of bright white light shines out of it, which he briskly follows, unperturbed by the anonymous sounds of the forests nocturnal inhabitants, until he is deep in to the forest. I am already stood beside Aryl watching Garth come closer, by the time he reaches his realm.

Inspecting the photograph under the light of his headlamp to make sure he has got the right tree, he smiles and places a hand against Aryl's knobbly chest. "Hello, old friend. Do you remember me? Dee has gone. It's just me now. I'm all alone."

I sense Aryl's recognition and knowledge as to why Garth has come to him and he is receptive to his needs. Aryl tells him he is not alone and that everything, even him and all the other trees, in the universe are connected to him; nothing and no one is ever alone. Garth of course is sublimely unaware of Aryl's comforting wisdom. Perching on one of Aryl's gnarled and knobby feet, the entire forest is in total pitch black except for the small area in front of him, which is illuminated by his headlamp. Fumbling in his pocket he takes out a notebook. Holding it under the light he begins to scribble furiously. Looking for photographs of me, something to cling onto to ensure he never forgets me, he found nothing. What he is looking for he finds here. Remembering the snow days here, he writes about my skin. Remembering the stargazing we did here, he writes about my eyes. Remembering the autumn days we had here and the thick bed of leaves they brought, he writes about my hair.

I am in the forest, he concludes.

Whenever, throughout his entire duration in the physical, he needs the inspiration to recall me, he finds it here bringing strangers, and in time Freya and Al, with him to meet me. I am always here to greet them.

Nineteen

Before it happened

I watch and wait standing in the doorway of the pokey box-room, holding a warm mug of tea, counting every second down in my head. Twisting itself around his body is the Superman quilt he's had since before we were teenagers. With his earthquake-inducing snores the lampshade, matching his quilt, above his head vibrates. Sounding at 8am, Garth rolls over and whacks the alarm clock with his fist, shutting it up and spilling springs all over the top of the bedside cabinet. Pulling the pillow from behind his head he forces it over his face with a groan, not even noticing me.

"Come on. It's time to get up," I chirp. Turning over he groans again. His freakishly large feet and long toes hang out of the end of his single bed. Waving a hand at me over his shoulder he beckons me to leave. I begin to sing, "We're going to the chapel and we're gonna get marrrr-ar-ied. We're going to the chapel and we're gonna get marrrr-ar-ied. We're going to the chapel and we're gonna get marrrr-ar-ied."

"No we are not," he says flatly. "Priya is going to the chapel and she is going to get married, the stupid cow."

"You can't say that. It's a wonderful thing getting married. I hope I get married one day."

"Not at our age. Jesus we are twenty-one. It should be a different bloke every night, not his-and-hers slippers."

"Twenty-one and found the one," I counter in a sing-song voice. "I wish I could be twenty-one and have found the one. Instead I'll be thirty-five and never a bride." I make my way to his Superman curtains, which I thrust open, flooding the room in dazzling sunlight. "Ouch. That really hurt, you pig."

"How could it, little miss poet of the year? It's just a pillow."

"You threw it hard," I scold, rubbing the back of my neck. "My head thrust forward. I think you have given me whiplash."

"Wicked," he grins meanly. "You will look great following Priya down the aisle in your baby blue dress and a neck collar." He laughs.

"Oh you would love that, wouldn't you?"

"I would."

"Well, I'm sorry to disappoint you but it doesn't seem that bad after all. Come on, you have ten minutes."

"Damn. I'd be more at home in Casualty than at a wedding."

"You are such a grumpy old git, Garth. Weddings are beautiful occasions where two people pledge their eternal love for each other in public and promise to love each other forever, it's so lovely."

"It will be over within ten years and then she will be thirty-one and in the bin."

When I see Priya in the middle of the churchyard gate steps under the archway I suddenly believe in happy endings. She stretches out a lace arm, which has tiny pearls stitched at the wrist to take her bouquet from her Dad, a tall lean man in a charcoal morning suit. As he hands her the bouquet of closed-bud white roses their fingers graze and linger. Priya's dad, like all our dads, is a man of little words but the look in his eye- love- is more powerful than any words could ever be. For the first time in her life the exchange between them brings a lump to her throat and a tear to her eye. They smile at each other. Her creamy skin tones and textures appear radiant in the drenching of sunlight. Her round face is turned slightly and her bright blue oval eyes sparkle. Her naturally honey-coloured silky-soft hair is pulled tight into a bun and shines in the sunlight like buttercups in a meadow, an ivory clasp just above it holds her veil.

We all chose her dress together and decided on a beautiful silk and lace Victorian style dress, in the first vintage bridal boutique we visited. The sheer white sheen of it set against the sunlight makes me wonder about angels. She fits my vision of how an angel should look: lustrous. The high neck is rimmed with tiny pearl beading; there is more pearl beading under her modest sized breasts from there the A-line lace skirt billows out and sweeps down to the floor. The gentle breeze presses the front of the dress against her slender and long legs. Below the three pearl buttons at the back falls a long train that trails down the remaining stairs behind her like a waterfall of lace. Rita and Polly are fussing around its hem straightening it out and untwisting her floor length veil.

"I should be there to help them do those things," I say clambering off my scooter in the market place across the road from the church, not noticing the oil smudge on the hem of my dress. "I told you we would be late. Another thirty seconds and she will be half way down the aisle minus a bloody bridesmaid. She is going to kill us."

"Chill out."

"Chill out?" I cry.

I pull my helmet from my cow pat flat hair, which had been a very impressive beehive dotted with tiny pearls and butterflies before I had been forced to squash it with my helmet. It would have stayed that way too if we had come in Garth's car as planned, which would have happened if he had any insight to forward planning.

"Yes, chill out."

"Garth, you are supposed to be the bloody usher."

"So?"

"Ushers are meant to be there before the guests sit down."

"Why?"

I whack him with my bouquet of white roses. Actually, this only makes me feel a lot worse than I already do as the heads of two roses snap off and drop to the ground along with half the petals of the remaining roses. I give out a wail and then regard him with a look of contempt. As the memory tourist visiting it now I watch silently.

"Because, my idiot friend, the bloody ushers are meant to seat the bloody guests."

"And you are a bridesmaid, right?"

"Yes, you know I am."

"And, bridesmaids walk down the aisle behind the bride with the other bridesmaids, right?"

"Well, ordinary bridesmaids do but I am chief bridesmaid, which means I go first."

"Oh fuck."

"Garth," I say with both hands on my hips, a very distraught-looking bouquet on my left hip, "What do you mean 'oh fuck'?"

"She's going in. Run."

He sets off running.

"Garth, what do you mean run? Who is going in, going in where?" I shout after him.

He yanks on my right wrist, pulling apart my pearl bracelet, which Priya bought for each bridesmaid to match her pearls, in the process of spinning me around to face the other way. I tear my gaze from the pearls rolling all over the cobbled market place to see Priya disappear into the church. Rita and Polly are teetering behind her each holding a corner of her train.

"Come on, we are going to miss it," he shouts.

"Oh fuck," I cry, hitching up my dress.

We race across the road narrowly missing a convoy of cyclists coming dangerously close to breaking my neck on my powder-blue high heeled-shoes, which manage to pick up half the rubbish laying in the gutter.

"Where on earth have you been? Look at the state of you." A pristine and perfectly put together Rita hisses at me like a snake.

I manage in bare feet to catch up with them half way down the aisle. My heels dangling, one with a broken strap and the other with a coke can pierced through the heel, from the opposite hand to my rather sorry looking bouquet, which gives the impression of being dug up after it has been snatched out of my hand by a dog who buried it. In fact everything about me gives off an air of 'attacked by a savage dog'.

"Car trouble," I hiss back.

"What kind of car trouble, would that be exactly?" Rita asks caustically, "A bloody car crash?"

"The kind where Garth forgot to put petrol in it yesterday."

The two girls chortle, which earns a number of shushes from the congregation and a chastising look from Priya's mum. Priya swivels her head round and rolls her eyes at me. "Where on earth... oh my goodness gracious me, look at the state of you."

In her shock she forgets to keep walking and stops. Unfortunately, both Polly and Rita's eyes are on me and mine are on them so the three of us walk into the back of her and her dad. Thankfully we do not topple over her and apart from the embarrassment factor no long-term damage is done, nor is there any great delay in the ceremony.

"I'll deal with you both later. Now if you don't mind one of your best friends would like to get married today."

"I don't mind," I mumble and then add a very sheepish, "Sorry," whilst scuffing my toe on the aisle's red carpet like a scolded schoolgirl. All the way through the ceremony I look down at the dirty feet of my stockings with primary-school-girl-in-the-corner shame.

"Oh come, on wipe that dismal look off your face," Garth says once the ceremony is done and we are all outside. Rita and Polly link his arms and they find me skulking behind a huge gravestone, grappling with the demon inside me who is lapping up the opportunity to torture me with jibes.

"Come on," Rita says, reaching up to my hair and pulling out the pins. "It looks much better down, anyway."

Polly fondles about in her bag and produces a small hairbrush. Then she proceeds to brush out the tangles, whilst I stand there with my arms crossed over my chest huffily. When Polly has brushed my hair back to its natural full-bodied curls, Rita begins repositioning the tiny white pearls and butterfly pins. Garth, whilst my hair rescue is in operation, whips a tiny sewing kit from my silk pouch- he knows I never go anywhere without one- and stitches the strap of my high heel back together with baby blue cotton. Then on one knee he re shoes me. At the same time Polly takes a mini packet of baby wipes from her bag and cleans the oil smudge from the back hem of my dress.

"These baby wipes are the shit in cleaning off, well, shit funnily enough."

"Any stain."

"Yeah I'd love to know what they put in them. I'm surprised your face isn't a big mass of scar tissue, Polly."

A few minutes later I'm transformed from yesterday's bridesmaid back into today's bridesmaid. Rita takes my bouquet of roses from me, and then she takes Polly's from her also. She lays them down on a flat tombstone beside her own bouquet and unties the ribbons around the stems of each bouquet, releasing the roses. She adds my good ones to theirs and then splits the difference, creating three smaller but unnoticeably problematic bouquets.

"Voila," Garth declares, kissing his fingers and throwing them out into the air theatrically. "You shall go to the ball, or at least look decent for the photographs."

At this moment Priya rounds the corner hitching up her own dress to the knee. "Do I actually have any bridesmaids?" She stops dead in her tracks surprised to see my ugly duckling to swan in less than three minutes transformation. "Nice to see somebody has de-zombified Dee." She inclines her head to the nearest grave. "Do you get it?" We all stare back at her blankly. "I said, zombies as in the un-dead. Well, they're dead and then un-dead but without a heartbeat and pulse." We blink at her. "We are in a grave yard."

"Yes, we get it you stupid fool," Garth says. "It's just a crap joke."

Priya stamps a silk stiletto on the stone path. "It's a bit like you lot in terms of friends then, isn't it?"

"Heh-hem," Rita and Polly protest in unison.

"We were on time. We didn't let you down. And, thanks to us your third bridesmaid, as you put it, has just been brought back from the dead and so won't at least ruin your photographs," Rita defends both herself and Polly.

"I'm sorry," I say softly, scuffing my toe on the footpath and looking down at it.

"Oh don't worry, I know you didn't do it on purpose. You made it at least. That's the main thing, after all," Priya says throwing out her arms. "Now come here and give Mrs Green a great big group hug."

We all fly at her and encase her in a group hug, squealing with excitement.

Twenty

Before it happened

Life here, where I am now, after it happened, has no danger or stress. There is nothing lurking around a corner waiting to pounce on me when I least expect it, throwing me into disarray. There are no demons plotting my downfall. Here there is a lot of never ever. Never ever will my washing machine break down, never ever will my drainage system clog, never ever will my bath accidentally overrun and flood the house, never ever will my boiler burn out, never ever will my plants need watering, never ever will I get burgled, never ever will I pay a bill or risk having utilities cut off because I can't afford to pay them, never ever will I have to mop a floor or dust a mantel piece and never ever will I have to clean out my fish tank again.

They were waiting for me when I got here, swimming inside floating water bubbles all around me, until I created their annex on the side of my beach hut with my imagination. There are five of them, five very colourful and very big tropical fish.

In the physical before I came here, and I do now, I watch them for hours flipping backwards and forwards across the tank, never getting bored, all at different depths in the water, sometimes going lower to pass under or over the bridge in the bottom of their tank or swirl around the small rowing boat beside the bridge. Sometimes when my mood, in the physical, is bleak and when I feel misunderstood and detached from those around me I talk to them and tell them my problems. By the way Gayle hovers in the water staring out at me I know she understands. I know she is listening, I know out of all of them she worries the most about me, she is the most like me, empathetic and to her own demise tuned into the world and all its ways.

Everybody has gone straight from our shift at the hospital to the Ye Old Victoria for Karaoke night, everyone except me. Whilst the house is quiet and empty I clean out my fish tank placing, as usual, my fish into buckets to let the fresh water, once the glass of their tank is gleaming, come up to room temperature. Flicking off the light in the front room I ascend the staircase almost at a crawl, exhausted. Sleep has taken me when Garth's key is the first to turn in the lock of our front door. In drunken stupidity Garth leans too heavily on the open door as he turns outwards to kiss Malcolm, the final year medical student he's managed to seduce with tequila shots and his rendition of It's Raining Men. Garth hurls through the air backwards. Grabbing Malcolm by his tie, Garth tugs him off his feet and he takes flight too. The pair of them crash land after a very shaking and brief flight through the air and skid along the varnished floorboards, Malcolm body-surfing on top of Garth until with a dull thud Garth's head impacts the bottom step of the staircase and their body-surfing extravaganza abruptly ends.

Anaesthetised by alcohol, laughing uncontrollably, Garth rolls Malcolm off of him and promptly jumps to his feet. Still holding onto his tie, Garth heads at a quick pace into the lounge, towing Malcolm behind him. Once inside the front room the tie and the shirt, in one fell swoop is pulled part way, by Garth, over Malcolm's head. Assuming Malcolm can wriggle his way out of the rest of it Garth drops to his knees and yanks Malcolm's trousers to his ankles. Wrestling ferociously to release his head and arms that are stuck in his shirt and with his leg movements restricted by his trousers round his ankles like shackles Malcolm stumbles forwards over the top of Garth who was crouching down but at that instant decides to start rising himself still hunched over, which acts as a spring-board for Malcolm's tumbling body. As if part of a human cannon-ball circus act Malcolm fires across the lounge. Having gulped my sleeping tablets down with a mouthful of whisky the almighty crashing sound his collision with whatever it is his body impacts fails to wake me up. The two of them in the pitch black, Malcolm still with his trousers around his ankles and his shirt restricting his arms and his head, grapple around trying to reach each other. Neither one of them processes the fact that they are paddling about in puddles nor is either of them alarmed by the sloshing and slapping sounds resonating around them.

The next morning Garth in a pair of Batman boxer shorts is standing at the foot of the stairs looking very sheepish. I pause midway down and look at him.

"Your fish have had a little accident."

"What kind of accident?"

"The kind of accident that involves two grown men overcome by animalistic hunger for each other and, well, making total twits of themselves." He closes his eyes. "We kind of destroyed the entire lounge in a kind of body slamming, human free-falling freak show." Garth shaking his head waves his hand as if acknowledging he is making very little sense.

"Garth," I say, descending two steps closer to him. "Stop blathering and tell me what all this has to do with the accident my fish have had."

"Well, the long and short of it is we kind of, without meaning to-."

"Garth, get to the point."

"We knocked their buckets over. Why didn't you text me to say you'd cleaned them out?"

"You are kidding me?"

"About the text, yes of course."

"No, not the text you idiot, you are kidding about my fish aren't you?"

"Oh, about the fish, no I'm not kidding about that. Malcolm got the shock of his life when one of them started slapping about between his legs."

"You're idiots. You managed to save them though, right? You put them back in their buckets and filled them with water, didn't you?"

"We tried."

"What do you mean, 'We tried?'"

"Malcolm was freaking out, babe. One of them got into his Y-fronts and used it as a hammock. He was very startled. By the time I had turned on the light, after falling over the back of the sofa on my way to the switch on the wall, and then calmed him down enough to delve into his Y-fronts and rescue poor Derrick it was too late. Babe, it was carnage."

"Are they dead?"

"Define dead." Registering the narrowing of my eyes and the throbbing veins in my neck he quickly added, "Okay, that wasn't funny. Yes babe, they are dead. We are dreadfully sorry about the whole thing; I think Malcolm will need counselling. It could be the end of his medical career before it has even started."

From the window ledge part way down the stairs, where she is prone to leaving it, I grasp Priya's hairbrush and walk towards him hunched over. "Are you seriously telling me you drunken floozy, that you and your latest shag-piece of the week have murdered my beautiful, innocent fish?"

"Murder is a bit strong, babe. They are just fish. We can get you some more."

"They can't be replaced," I shriek. "I'll just roll around on top of you the next time I'm feeling animalistic passion with a bloke and suffocate you to death, shall I? And then I'll tell your mum that we can get her a new one."

He begins to laugh.

"Don't you dare laugh, this is not funny."

I begin belting him with my hairbrush until he restrains me by my wrists. "Calm down, you're being a deranged cow. I understand you are upset and we are very sorry."

Overflowing with tears I crumple into his arms. "They were my friends. I loved them. They never expected anything of me, never asked anything. They were easy to be with. I've let them down. Poor Derrick spent his last few minutes of life in the Y-fronts of some horny bloke. It's a terrible fate."

Then we both laugh, overwhelmingly.

Aryl takes care of my fish, I knew he would, which is why I chose a spot beside him in his forest as their final resting place. He guides them home and tells them I will join them soon. The five of us bury them in shoe boxes that Polly glues red rose petals to so that, other than in shape and size, they are unrecognisable as shoe boxes. Priya and Polly console me in a group hug as I sob and whimper, and whilst Garth reads the poem I wrote for the occasion. Malcolm hangs, slightly in the background and is comforted awkwardly by Rita. Every few seconds he mumbles something inaudible and feels his groin area as if not quite accepting that Derrick isn't still in there.

Twenty-one

After it happened

The day Al and Garth come across the old forgotten cottage, in a little tucked-away hamlet, surrounded by hilly meadows and forest, Garth is reminded of me. He is reminded of the day in my bedroom creating our naughty nurses' outfits, all the things I said about my lime green jacket; that I'd taken something erstwhile, forgotten and bleak and transformed it into something present, acknowledged and cheerful. *Dee would breathe life back into this decrepit broken down cottage,* he thinks.

"Stop!" he cries out. "Al, stop the car!"

Al, in alarm, slams down hard on the brakes. "What's wrong? Did we hit something?"

"No, we didn't hit anything. Look."

Al follows the direction of Garth's gaze. "It's a derelict cottage."

"No," Garth says, releasing his seatbelt and opening his car door. "It's not just a derelict cottage. It's so much more than a derelict cottage, so much more." He hops out of the car onto the grass verge and heads towards it.

"Garth, it's a broken-down wreck. It's no good to anyone," Al calls after him. "Get back in the car."

"Dee would disagree with you. Nothing is 'no good to anyone'. Everything has a use and a place and everything can be given a new lease of life, she would say."

He is right. I tell Al's ignorant ears. *This cottage will be your home and a very beautiful home it will make.* I am stood by the insect-riddled gatepost at the end of a once white and very pretty picket fence just inside the very overgrown garden.

Al joins Garth in the empty arched gateway, which is covered in ivy, of the cottage. "I want to go inside."

Al looks at the double-fronted cottage, taking in the little square windows that are so thick with dirt it is impossible to see through them. A mass of cobwebs as thick as candyfloss gathers in the overhang of the arched oak front door, which is as wide as two normal sized front doors. Skilfully crafted bird's nests on the windowsills of the second floor catch his attention as his gaze travels upwards towards the roof, resting his gaze on the roof he registers the lack of it. Crumbling, the chimney has almost entirely broken apart. Half of the slates are missing and Al can see right through it, back to front. "I'm not sure it is entirely safe," he says doubtfully.

"Oh don't be a chicken." Garth springs ahead, towing Al behind him.

Leaping over gaps, due to them being swallowed up by the ground, they follow what remains of the flag stone garden path. Reaching the front door before them, I pass through it into the cottage, lingering in what was the hallway when walls existed. Between the rooms there is almost no distinction except for rotten wood frames and damp fragmenting plaster. Running through the entire house is the hallway, a part-remaining wooden staircase, folding back on itself, at the end of it. On the half landing is a large stained-glass window, the bottom half of which is boarded up.

"It's locked," Garth says, pushing against the heavy door. "I didn't think it would be locked."

Leaning his right hand against it Al replies, "Nope, can't think of any reason to secure it. I mean, apart from the birds, who is going to claim squatter's rights on this dump?"

Hearing them outside discussing what to do next I join them and influence Garth's consciousness. I place my hands on him. He begins looking around them.

"What on earth are you looking for?"

"I don't know."

I place my hands on him again. Getting down on his hands and knees he begins foraging around in the wild undergrowth and brambles growing under the thick stone ledges of the cottage's front windows. "Don't just stand there, Al, help me look."

"Look for what?"

"I told you. I don't know. I will, when we find it."

"Garth, come on, we need to get back for Freya. Let's just go."

"No, we need to go inside. We have to. We are meant to be here."

"Garth, we are only here because you are rubbish at navigation and told me to come off the motorway at the wrong exit. We would be home by now if you hadn't messed up on the directions."

"Exactly."

"What do you mean exactly by 'exactly'?"

"What I mean exactly by 'exactly' is exactly that. It is meant to be," he says, pausing from his search and looking up at Al. "Something directed us here. I think Dee wanted us to find this cottage, maybe she brought us here."

"No, you directed us here because you can't read a map."

"No Al, it is fate. I can read a map."

"No you can't. You hardly know your lefts from your rights."

"I'm not arguing with you, Al. Stand and watch if you like but I am not going anywhere until I have been inside and I will find..." He pauses from searching the undergrowth to search his mind instead. "Well, whatever it is I am looking for, it'll be a lot quicker if you help me."

Al shrugs. "I think you are crazy but I know better than to try and change your mind once it is made up. You keep foraging on that side and I'll take this one," he says, going to the opposite side of the front door.

I stand behind, Garth, whilst he searches. Sometimes his hand is just inches from it and I will shriek with excitement. Then something else will catch his eye, a plant pot, an old spoon or an old toy and he will be thrown off track. Eventually he lays his hand on it. He can't see it through the thickness of the brambles but he has a firm hold of it and he knows he has found what he is looking for. He pulls it out. "Got it."

"Thank god."

"I told you I would know when I found it."

"I'm very pleased Garth that you have found a metal capsule thing. I still don't understand why you needed to find it."

"I don't either. I just know we need to open it. Maybe there is a key inside it."

My spirit form is bouncing beside him with excitement. *Garth, you're so clever.*

"Oh, this is ridiculous," Al says, striding towards him. "You and Freya really need to stop watching those girly fantasy movies. They are distorting your view of reality. Our daughter is going to grow up as airy-fairy as you." He snatches the capsule and begins to twist the lid. "There is no key in here."

The lid comes away easily and a large key, about nine inches in length, falls at his feet.

"You were saying."

"This isn't possible. I'm dreaming."

Garth stoops down and snatches up the key. "Close your mouth, darling. I can see your tonsils," he says using a finger on the bottom of Al's jaw to close his mouth. Garth rises to his feet and turns towards the door feeling for the keyhole with his fingers. It is positioned in the middle of the door.

"Go on, then. What are you waiting for? Open the door to the enchanted cottage and let's see what treasures lay within."

"Piss taker," Garth says, holding up the key and pushing it into the keyhole. He makes to turn it clockwise and then stops. "I'm a bit scared, actually. What if a witch lives inside?"

"She'll eat us for tea. Priya will adopt Freya, she'll be the daughter she never had and always wanted."

"I'm being serious. Some mad old cow might live inside."

"Garth, it's uninhabitable. Not even a witch could live here." He shakes his head in disbelief, more at himself than Garth for even humouring him by using the word witch.

"What if she has put a spell on the house to make it look uninhabitable to lure in unsuspecting victims?" Garth steps back. "I think we should just go home."

I am behind him, rolling my eyes and preparing myself to lay my hands on him to influence his conscious again.

"Oh no you don't." Al renders my need for intervention redundant, pushing past him and taking charge of the key. "You are not bottling out on me now, Garth, not after the song and dance you have made about it. Anyway, if you are right about Dee showing us this place she is stood with us and she wouldn't let you walk into danger, would she?"

I am and no I wouldn't.

"She is and no she wouldn't."

Twenty-Two

After it happened

Al turns the key. It gives a loud clunk. The door moves with a groan, slightly ajar, releasing a musty smell. Giving it a strong shove with the flat of his hand, with a creak and a billowing dust cloud it draws back fully. They step inside.

"Al, it smells."

"Garth, it's called damp. Hold your nose."

"It's massive. This must have been the dining room."

"How do you know?"

Nodding towards the back wall, Garth replies, "I'm guessing the kitchen is beyond that serving hatch." He shrugs. "It's just a hunch."

"That makes sense. I can see your logic."

Garth makes his way around the hole in the floor, which opens up the cellar like a wishing well. "Think of the entertaining we could do in here. It would be amazing."

"Easy, tiger. Let's not get ahead of ourselves. A look inside, you said. There is no way we are buying this heap of rubble."

"Al, it's gorgeous, only five minutes from the motorway, commuting would be a doddle. Give me one good reason why we can't buy it."

Frowning, he replies, "I think you've actually lost the plot. I married a loony. Mum and Dad had trouble adjusting to the bride they expected being a groom. They are going to flip when they realise I married a loony groom." Walking over to Garth he takes his hands in his. "Garth, come on, you have got your head in the clouds as usual."

"I'm thinking outside the box, you always say you love this about me."

Placing his hands on Garth's cheeks, he replies, "I adore this about you. Your enthusiasm is enthralling. This, though, well this is ludicrous. One thousand steps too far."

"You haven't given me a reason."

"Garth." Al searches his eyes beseechingly. "You're really serious. You're not even pulling my pisser."

"No," he says seriously, adding, more cheekily, "but I will, if it will persuade you."

"Cheeky," Al laughs. "Seriously, babe, I can give you a hundred reasons starting with the gaping void inches to our left and the one above us. We can see the sun from here."

Garth laughs. "We've talked about how lovely it would be to have a sun room, if we didn't live in an apartment, that is."

"A weather-proof glass one, yes. Nothing was ever said about actually having the sun directly in the flipping house."

"Come on." Leaning forward, kissing Al's nose, Garth leads him by the arm. "I want to see the rest of it."

They cross into the lounge. I am waiting for them.

"This is stunning."

"Garth, there is fungi the size of dinner plates growing out of the walls."

"It must be about thirty foot long, stretching the entire length of the cottage. That fireplace, you can stand all six-foot-three-inches of you in there and the rest of your football team. Look at the thickness of that beam separating the room into two areas. Al, it's gorgeous, close your eyes for one second."

Al follows his instruction. Garth follows mine, closing his own eyes. Placing his hands on Al's shoulder, I do the same to Garth, and feeding from my inspiration Garth relays it back to Al.

"Imagine an original vintage Chesterfield sofa in burgundy opposite the fireplace, a Chinoiserie style standing lamp on one side, a roaring fire in the fireplace and candles on the thick oak mantle. Imagine Christmas here, three hanging stockings, a glass of sherry, a mince pie and a carrot on the 1960's Ercol coffee table. Me, you and Freya curled up under thick woollen blankets, singing Christmas carols and drinking cocoa; Freya's piano on the wall behind us with pictures of her riding her pony standing on top of it. In the room over there," he says, flaring out his arm, indicating the other section of the room, keeping his eyes screwed firmly shut. "Beyond the beam, a library with floor-to-ceiling bookcases, a mahogany 1940's desk with a green leather top and a high-back green leather studded chair on wheels, french doors leading into the garden. Wouldn't it be lovely?"

Al steps back, breaking the link between them, rubbing his forehead. Garth gazes at him expectantly. I stand back and watch, hoping I have done enough.

"Where on earth did that come from? I was flipping there, Garth, living every second of it, visualising it all." The flat of his hand is over his forehead and there is an expression riddled with self-doubt on his face. "I think you have turned me mad. How did you do that?"

"Not the foggiest idea. I felt it too, though. This house is meant for us."

"I think," he says slowly and cautiously, "you may be right. Blimey, I don't believe I said that. It's mad, insane. We don't even know if it's for sale."

Stepping forward, I place my hands on Garth. "It is for sale with the estate agent in the village."

"How do you know?"

"It just popped into my head. It's a hunch, I think."

Shaking his head Al says, "This is mad." Taking Garth's hands, he asks, "Can you do it again?"

"Can I do what again?"

"Make me imagine our life here."

"I'm not sure I know how. It just came to me last time."

"Try, please."

Garth places his hands on Al again. Playing my part the three of us link again, shutting our eyes. The images flood from me into Garth again. "You're stood at the pot sink, which is full of soapsuds in the kitchen. Freya is knelt on a stool helping you wash up. You have flour on your faces and in your hair, you're laughing. I'm opening, by its coiled steel handle, one of the three small ovens of the cream range, which has a flat black hotplate top." He laughs. "I'm scolding you about the broken thermostat. 'We really should get it fixed,' I'm saying. You reply, 'You wanted to keep the original features. They don't make parts for ranges that old. Next you'll want to fix the hairline fracture in the sink.' Freya says, 'I like them, they make the cottage feel really old, I like old things.'"

"Wow! How on earth…"

"I keep telling you, I don't have the foggiest."

"Come on," Al says, pulling Garth by the wrist. "I want to see the kitchen."

In the kitchen, Al stands facing it. Garth pressed against his back, his chin on Al's shoulder and his hands stuffed into the front pockets of Al's jeans. "I don't believe it. It's just not possible," he says. "How could you have known?"

"It's a bit rustier than my vision, though, hey?"

"It will clean up, Garth."

"Maybe it was just a lucky guess. All cottages have ranges, don't they?"

"Not all exactly like this, though, like you described. How would you know about the broken thermostat? Have you been here before? This wouldn't be a conspiracy, would it?"

"No. I have never been here before. I told you, it must have been a lucky guess."

"How do you explain the pot sink with the hairline fracture?"

"Not a blooming clue."

"It was no lucky guess, babe," he says turning round, wrapping his arms around his neck. "It's fate like you said initially. We were meant to come here. We were meant to discover this house. It's Dee."

"Now who sounds mad?"

"If we are mad, so be it. I've never felt this energised. Let's do it. I'm a surgeon. You are top of the nursing game. We'll sell our apartment easily. Money isn't a problem. We'll move back into your flat whilst we do the renovations, then we'll sell that too if we have to, the lease is up next month for the tenants anyway. On the way in I saw some thatched roofed cottages, this cottage will look charming with a thatched roof."

"Can we have roses around the door?"

"Yes, we can have roses around the door."

I'm smiling. My Garth is getting his happy ever after; he is finding the end of the rainbow, with a little help from me, unbeknown to him.

"Could it really be Dee?"

Yes it's me. I wish you could hear me.

"What do you mean?"

"Could she really have brought us here? Is it really possible that she gave us those images?"

I did and it is.

Al reaches a thumb up to Garth's face and wipes the tear from his cheek. If I could cry I would join him.

"Garth, I'm a surgeon, a scientist. I don't believe in ghosts, but this, I just can't explain it."

"Maybe it is possible she still loves me, still supports me."

Garth, I do on both counts and always will.

A hand on his forehead, Al replies, "After today I'm sure anything is possible."

"I love you, Dee." Garth blows a kiss that floats through the air to me like a delicate petal torn from its flower in a gust of wind.

I love you too, Garth. I catch his airborne kiss and return it with one of my own.

"Come on," Al says, shaking Garth slightly, "Do you think you would know how to get to this estate agent in the village?"

"No." I stand beside him placing my hands on him again. "Hang on. Yes, yes I do. It's left out of here and right at a cenotaph of some Victorian missionary worker who was from here. It is back to back with the post office."

"How on earth do you know that?" Al shakes his head. "Never mind, don't answer that, I already know the answer. Come on, I'll race you to the car."

I beat both of them. In a flicker I'm sat in the back seat, waiting for them. *What took you both so long?*

Twenty-Three

After it happened

Glorious shards of sunshine are jutting through the sky slicing into the ocean like shards of colour loaded crystal causing a prism effect of rainbows to bounce out as far as the eye can see; it's like the sky is the ceiling of a cave and the shards of light are crystal stalactites. It is a beautiful morning and I am drinking it in from my beach hut terrace with James by my side, hand in hand, the warmth of the sun on my back. Summer mornings are my favourite. I love experiencing them.

Summertime can be all the time, if I want it to be. Simply by the power of my imagination, morning can be all the time, if I want. If I want, all the time can be Christmas time or every day could be my birthday if I chose it to be. It could be Christmas and my birthday on the same day, if I really wanted. Whatever I choose to experience, summertime, Christmas time, my birthday- all three at once- it does not dictate the order of the day for anyone else here with me; our existences are no longer impeded upon by the actions or desires of others.

Although it is a summer morning for me with relentless hot sunshine, it is a winter afternoon for James with relentless fluffy snowfall, which does not melt under the intensity of my sun. Wearing his snowsuit, goggles and carrying his snowboard under one arm he is pumped full of energy, he is buzzing with anticipation as if on the brink of an extreme adrenaline rush. I'm wearing my favourite gold Roman sandals and a hessian dress, light and floating in deep crimson. Despite our contrary choices in weather we are together, enjoying each other without experiencing the identical sensory experience of the other, unless we choose to.

Speckled with skiers and snowboarders, he describes the snow-covered peaks and steep mountain descents. They sound as magnificent as the pictures of Switzerland Garth and me used to drool over in his garage as teenagers. He tells me how, when they reach the bottom of the snowy peaks, some of the skiers high five or body slam each other and others, those who are choosing to ski alone and not part of a group, fist pump the air. Dancing and fluttering down from above him like a cotton wool shower he describes the thick fluffy snowflakes falling around him. Holding hands with giggling girls and expertly ice skating he describes the animated snowmen, waving, smiling and full of life. I immediately think of Christmas Eve when Garth, the girls and me would crowd around the TV under blankets eating Polly's homemade marzipan chocolates and drinking my homemade gooseberry wine watching our favourite Christmas Eve programme. He describes the penguins waddling and flapping, wearing ice skates and woolly hats, circling the perfectly smooth and rounded igloos that the little boys have built on the frozen ocean. He points into empty spaces and describes the things around him, things I don't as yet see. He explains how shards of light enter one side of the huge ice sculptures and exit at the opposite side cutting straight through them like swords. He lists the diverse sculptures born from individual imaginations: an elephant with a harness on its back full of delighted children, a family of giraffes standing tall with leaves falling from their mouths, a huge dolls' house with its front open so that all the rooms and their furnishings can be seen and played with, a giant tiered cake stand full of cakes made of ice and a giant fruit bowl full of every type of fruit conceivable to the imagination also made from ice.

Over there, just on the edge of the frozen ocean is a snowman. This one isn't skating around the ocean on one foot waving and smiling at me. He pauses, from feeding me the information telepathically to drink in the scene, throwing back his head in laughter enthralled by what he can see. *He's huge with two massive snowballs for his body and one for his head.* James is positively childlike and full of glee. *Two sisters are decorating him.*

What are they like, the sisters? I enquire, sending the thought into his conscious mind.

He describes every intriguing little detail of them to me. I feel the grip of the scene that he describes drinking me in as if it were a painting with supernatural sucking-in powers.

Deciding to experience it myself my eyes close and I let what he describes fill my imagination. Fading out, my experience of a summer sensation transforms into his winter wonderland. I open my eyes. The scene has changed. Once swishing around my legs, in the gentle summer breeze, my crimson dress has evaporated.

I'm wearing chocolate cords, a thick red jumper decorated with little white polar bears and a thick white woolly matching three-piece set of scarf, mittens and hat. My beautiful Roman gold sandals have gone. I am wearing red wellington boots decorated with tiny white love hearts over several pairs of socks despite the fact I could chose to feel warm without them if I wanted to. The people, whose desire and imagination had tuned into the same frequency as mine, an intense summer day, have now all disappeared. They have not gone. They are just now on a different channel. They are still available if I choose to go back to them. It's simply the same principle as switching a television channel from one programme to another programme. I could just as easily switch back again and the original programme would still be there waiting for me. It would be slightly moved on from where I had left it but it would still be there. There is no-one around me now in their swimwear, shorts and t-shirts playing in groups with beach balls. They have been replaced with the people James described, the people who want to experience a winter day. I can see the skiers and snow boarders that are making the steep cliff descents appear polka-dotted. I can see the children skating on the endless frozen ocean holding hands with animated snowmen. I can see the penguins expertly skating around the boys and their igloo construction sites and I see the huge impressive ice sculptures.

The two sisters that James described to me come into my vision now. They are Japanese and here on their own, waiting for their parents to join them. They have been here for a long time, much longer than me. One of the sisters is six years old and the other one is two years younger. They tell me that they had never experienced snow until they came here. Now they play in the snow a lot. I crouch down with them helping them to unwind a thick lime-coloured woolly scarf almost as long as a rail track. They explain that their parents are elderly now and almost ready to join them. One of them tells me that their mum has not driven a car since the day of the accident.

They are both wearing Eskimo-like clothes, thick and warm in bright colours and with vibrant pattern detail. They are the kind of costumes I only ever saw in travel brochures. Their pigtails hang out of their hoods when they bend down to pick up the things they have gathered around the snowman to decorate him with. The snowman, standing at least six times taller than them, towers over them. I watch as the older one lifts a purple silk top-hat from the ground and levitates high into the air, her little legs dangling underneath her, until she reaches the top of him. She places the hat on his head. Floating back down and resting beside her sister, she smiles at her and her sister smiles back. They say something to each other in Japanese. I never learned the language but I know that the younger one is telling the older one how good the snowman looks in his top-hat and that she wants to decorate him with something next. The older one is encouraging her to do so. I watch and smile as she lifts up the scarf that we unwound. Climbing up a spiral staircase made of snow blocks, which appears in front of her and runs up the side of the snowman, she trails the scarf behind her. Once she reaches the top of it the spiral staircase moves around the snowman allowing her to wind the scarf around his neck. When she has finished the spiral staircase transforms into a slope that she slides down. We stand back and admire him. James comes in closer. I suddenly realise I had forgotten about him, I feel his energy swirl into mine. We listen as the two sisters' talk to each other again in Japanese. They are deciding what to do next and the older one suggests they give him some buttons. Large gleaming gold buttons suddenly appear scattered on the ground around him. One by one the buttons lift off the ground and drift into their hands. They throw them like discs towards the snowman and they secure themselves neatly and in a uniformed, equally spaced, line down his two bellies.

It is now that I notice their dogs, two wolf-like white-grey dogs with pale blue eyes sitting obediently just behind the snowman with their front legs stretched out in front of them. Their heads are resting on the snow-covered ground between their paws. They tell me that they are the girls' guardians and came here the same day as they did. They explain that they will move on once the sisters' parents arrive to relinquish them of their duty. They remind me of my two minders, with their sheer white coats, when I first came home and who accompanied me to my own funeral. The only difference is mine were baby polar bears and not dogs.

Twenty-four

After it happened

I may not possess emotions but I am an intelligent entity, more intelligent now than I ever was when I was confined within a body. I understand emotion from a detached perspective, in an academic model. Grief, I'm aware, is a hounding mob of emotions: anger, resentment, sadness, loneliness, confusion and guilt. I know that they are all intent in sticking their penknives into the stomach of their chosen target. I understand, despite not being able to feel them, that these minions of grief strengthen its endeavour to abduct its victim. In Garth's case grief, the head of the mob, converts my bedroom into a cell and keeps him prisoner there.

I'm here now, reliving the memory of it; Rita's memory.

Leading up to my attic bedroom, in our shared house, Rita sits on the top step of the staircase. She rests the back of her head against my bedroom door, her feet rest flat on the fifth step down and she is gazing out of the skylight, above the stairwell, wishing me here. I'm the only one who can get through to Garth, the only one he will listen to, she is thinking to herself. Hovering in front of her, I want to make my presence known. It would help her to know that I'm passing back and forth through my bedroom door, I am with her, I am with him and then I am with her again.

In darkness I'm hovering above Garth's curled up body, hidden under blankets on my bed. Sometimes he hides in different places. In my wardrobe under my mountain of coats, huddling in the corner under a pile of dirty clothes I never got around to washing or in the corner alcove behind a thick purple velvet curtain concealing some of my things. He hides as if the heavy chest of drawers barricading the door is not sufficient walls of defence against the enemy, his friends who try to coax him back into civilisation on an hourly basis.

"I wish you could hear me, Dee."

I kneel in front of her, on the sixth step down. *I can hear you, I'm right here.*

"You caused this."

I know.

"How could you leave us? How could you abandon us? How could you abandon Garth?"

You'll understand one day.

I am unable to give tangibility to my answers. I can only be here, which is of little use or comfort to her.

"Why can't you help us? Why can't you give us a sign?"

I've tried coming to you all in dreams, bringing you messages. I came to Garth in a dream. He sees it only as a dream and nothing deeper. He doesn't realise that it is really me, none of you ever do.

Aryl is where I take Garth in this dream sitting, as we always did, in a cranny of his thick gnarled body, I am between Garth's legs with my head laid back on his chest. He speaks first. "I miss you so much."

I know you do, I am sorry for what you are going through. I never meant to hurt you.

"I can't stomach it, Dee. I can't eat. I don't know when I'm sleeping or when I'm awake. I have blocked out the world. Shut myself away from it. I just want to be in darkness."

I know, Garth. You must stop it. You must push yourself through it. There is a future out there for you, a life you must lead. There are journeys for you to go on. You are forgetting all the people you still have around you, you are letting everyone pass you by.

"There is no future without you, Dee. 'Together, forever and a day,' isn't that what we said?" He breaks off for a moment. "That means your end is my end. When life ends for you, when forever comes for you, it should come for me."

No. Garth, this is not true. My path is not your path. We were foolish to make this pact. I was never going to be able to keep the promise. You are missing so much.

"No, I'm not."

Yes, Garth. I plead with him. *You are. You're missing so much.*

"What am I missing exactly?" His tone is harsh. He is annoyed. He thinks that I am trivialising his feelings.

You are missing the day.

"I don't understand."

No. You don't, but you will. It will become clear in time. You have to live your life first.

"Dee, you have to stop talking in riddles and explain what you are blathering on about."

I try to inject humour. *Garth, I'm a spirit person now. Spirit people do not blather; we speak on the higher plane of truth only.*

"You are really annoying me, Dee."

We said, 'Together, forever and a day'. The forever has been on that life. There will be another day. Another day we will be together again.

"And a day." Garth repeats this over. "And a day." It slowly sinks in. "I will see you again another day, another day we will be reunited."

Yes, Garth. Look over there.

Looking at a patch of grass, lit up by sunlight filtering through Aryl's outstretched branches, he sees a young man and a little girl jousting playfully with sticks. He thinks of a knight and a princess, in a fairy-tale and familiarity hugs him.

"Who are they?"

They are your future.

Too quickly for him the dream fades. He wakes up with an empty feeling. To him the dream is not real because there is instant recognition and instant acceptance. He presumes that meeting me in a real situation would be more confusing. He'd question me and feel anger towards me. The truth is when a spirit person comes to you in dreams it is soul-to-soul communication. The soul of the dreamer leaves their body and astral travels with the spirit person. Recognition and acceptance, therefore, are instantaneous and because it's soul-to-soul communication it is also emotionless, confusion and anger are annulled. Garth's soul has left his body in dream state and astral travelled with me many times, but when his astral cord, which connects the soul to the body until the time of returning home, pulls his soul back into his body physical logic resumes and he rejects all possibility of our meeting being real.

Rita, I've given you lots of signs. You have missed them all.

Ignoring me, she speaks through the door. "Garth, this really can't carry on, sweetheart. Everybody is so worried. You're not the one who died." Regretting her words the instant they leave her lips, she bites on her bottom lip. "I didn't mean that, sweetheart. Not the way it sounded anyway. I just meant you have your life ahead of you to life. You should do that to the full, shouldn't you? For both of you, you and Dee, don't you see that? You must get on with life. People need you. People rely on you."

Silence.

"Priya and Polly need you."

Silence.

"Your mum and dad, they need you."

Silence.

"They come with Dee's mum and dad, making the four-hour round trip every day. They can't bear to come up here."

Silence.

"Dee's mum and dad, they need you too. They said you had been such a tower of strength to them this last year."

At the time of this memory I have been gone a year?

Silence.

"Is that why you have suddenly locked yourself up? Is it because you have been so strong this past year? Did you bottle it all up for that long? Keep it to yourself for everybody else's sake, for a whole year?" She fights back the tears, pressing the heels of her hands to the filling bags under her eyes. "You didn't have to. You could have spoken to someone."

Silence.

I'm glad that I have no sense of smell or taste, sitting on my bed next to Garth's curled up form. In all of the time he's been held prisoner by grief in my room he has not washed or changed. The need for the toilet has not even been enough for grief and its mob members to release him, forcing him instead to use a bucket in the corner of the room. When grief is sure the coast is clear the bucket will go outside the door and one of the girls will dispose of it. They also leave him food and water outside the door, sometimes grief allows him to eat and drink what the girls leave him, other times it doesn't.

Sensing Rita is about to give up I'm immediately with her, hovering at the top of the attic staircase. An idea occurs to me, a way I can make one last attempt to get them to recognise the signs I've been trying to give them. Kneeling on the sixth step just below her feet, I place my hands on her. Filtering into her imagination I feel the vision transmitting from me to her, recognition faintly stirs in her eyes. She is receiving. "There are two other people who need you too. You don't know them yet. They are your future husband and child, a daughter." She makes an odd face at herself, confused as to how that notion just popped into her mind.

Silence.

"He is stunning, Garth. Everything you have ever wanted. A knight in shining armour and not a court jester in tin foil like some of the men you have brought home." She chuckles to herself, processing that her dig at his taste in men is exactly what I would normally say, rather than something she would say. She is sublimely unaware that it is me saying all of it, channelling through her. I give her more. I'm not giving up on them, and this has to work. "Your daughter is so cute, Garth. A real cherub."

Silence.

"Dee doesn't want this, does she? She wants you to get on with your life and go get your dishy knight in shining armour and live happily ever after with your Snow White daughter."

Twenty-Five

After it happened

Shocked by her abnormal poetic and deep eloquence, unaware I have been broadcasting through her as if she is a radio, Rita lapses into complete hysteria, at herself.

Ear-splitting screeches chime out of her. Alarmed by the sudden siren Polly and Priya come out of the lounge, two floors below the attic. They quickly ascend the first-floor staircase and arrive at the foot of the attic staircase. Craning their necks upwards to get a better look, they exchange puzzled glances at seeing Rita in fits of hysteria pushing back against my bedroom door, kicking her feet out on the stairs, holding her stomach and screeching in a soaring pitch. Her laughter is thunderous, and neither she, Priya or Polly hear the footsteps padding across the floor of the room behind the door Rita is leaning against or the sound of the chest of drawers being dragged back from the door or the clicking sound of the lock turning.

Flying backwards with the sudden thrust of the door being pulled away from her, Rita rolls into the room. She promptly slaps a hand over her mouth and nose to protect her senses from the stench. Squinting in the light that filters in from the skylight above the bedroom door, Garth stands over her. Pale and drawn, his eyes are framed with deep purple rings, his hair is stuck to his head with a thick layer of grease and his face is barely visible due to thick stubble. A shadow of his former self, a healthy, glowing, well-trimmed and pruned fashion frontier, his baggy filthy sweatpants and grimy white t-shirt are a distortion of his usual attire.

"Look at the state of you. You look like a cave-man and you stink like an old wellington boot, get in the shower you smelly bugger," Rita cries out in laughter.

Saying nothing, Garth picks up a baseball bat, the one I kept by my bedroom door in case of night burglars. He lifts it onto his shoulder. He steps over Rita and charges down the stairs barging past Priya and Polly. Flipping herself onto her feet, Rita follows him. Polly and Priya join in her pursuit. We all follow Garth down the three staircases to the ground floor kitchen and through the patio doors at the back into the back garden. Bolting down to the bottom of the garden, Garth reaches my vegetable patch, which in my memory Polly has taken over pruning, planting and harvesting. He arrives at my huge terracotta pot of herbs. He pulls back the baseball bat in both hands, roaring like a lion, his face reddening, and his jaw clenching. He swings it forward with all his strength into the pot, which bursts like a pumpkin. With no regard for the injury the flying shards of glass could cause him, next he smashes my glass boxes of tomatoes to smithereens.

"We should stop him."

"Yes, Polly, we should stop him."

Polly starts forward but Rita grabs her by the wrist just as Garth begins tearing down my runs of broad beans. "No, leave him. Let him be angry. Let him get it out of his system. In fact, I've got an idea. Priya, fetch the garden hose."

"Come on," Rita says, catching Polly by the hand and dragging her forth. "Let's join him. I think he has hit upon something very therapeutic." Then she winks. "Get it? Hit upon."

Polly rolls her eyes but follows Rita's lead. They set about sabotaging my carrots. They ferociously pull them out of the ground; Rita and Polly start throwing them to Garth who whacks them with the baseball bat, launching them into space. Carrots are flying high into the sky like little orange space rockets, one after the other, soaring high and then looping before starting their decent back to earth. Everything else I have worked hard to accomplish: my terracotta pots of herbs, my broad bean runners and my glass boxes of tomatoes, smashed to pieces all around them. I laugh as Garth is laughing, like he used to; laughing frenziedly like a mad man as he beats carrots to death with the baseball bat. Rita catches sight of Priya trudging over with the hose coiled over one arm. She and Polly go to her. I stay with Garth, who is now beating my potato patch so hard with the baseball bat that potatoes are spontaneously shooting up out of the ground and somersaulting in the air, as if trying to escape some terrible earth monster. Priya sets the hose down on the ground and the three girls uncoil it, connect it to the water tap and holding the nozzle

Rita charges forward at the helm, the other two supporting the rear.

"Oh, Garth!"

He looks up and freezes in fear. Me too. For a moment I forget that I'm not alive and therefore not in danger of the cold drenching he is about to receive. "Shower time, you smelly pig!" Polly shouts.

"Twist it and hose that bitch down, Rita," Priya, uncharacteristically using coarse language, instructs.

Rita twists the nozzle and jolts backwards slightly as the first rush of water fires out of it and hits Garth square in the chest, causing him to fall backwards. He tries to get back on his feet but they slip and slide underneath him. He is defeated and rolls around on the floor under the drenching water. Eventually, Rita manages to twist the nozzle back again, having struggled for quite a while to the point of becoming quite concerned she will never be able to turn it off again. Garth staggers towards them, soaked through, covered in mud and with bits of vegetables in his hair.

"You cow bags."

It is the first time he's spoken to them in all the time he has been hiding away. They are relieved, all running at him and jumping on him, hugging and kissing him as if he has just returned from a long expedition. It is definitely a tear-jerking moment. If I were able to cry I would.

Garth never feels this bad about my death again; grief has decided to release him; now Garth will move on and time will take the place of grief to support him like a parole officer re-integrating him back into civilisation.

Later in the evening, after Garth has a proper shower and a shave, the girls have fumigated my bedroom, which will be his room from now on, and taken down the blankets he nailed to the skylights they all sit around the dining table with mugs of hot chocolate and marshmallows. I remember being part of that once, dunking my marshmallows in peanut butter grossing, the other four out. With them, I listen to their light-hearted banter, the talk of memories, and my peanut-butter-coated marshmallows fetish getting a mention from Priya, which causes the other three to cringe and stick out their tongues. They talk about what to do now with my vegetable garden. Polly suggests that they restore the vegetable garden to what it was as she had become quite accustomed to the bean bakes, potato curries and carrot soups she had been making on a regular basis. When she sees his face change to one of slight regret, Polly reassures Garth that she isn't angry with him and completely understands why he would be angry with me and want to get back at me. Garth joked that it had nothing at all to do with revenge and me but simply that he couldn't take any more of her hippy cooking. They all laugh. Just before he looks at his watch, sees how late it is and suggests that they all go to bed because they have an early start ahead of them fixing my garden in the morning, Garth looks at Rita thoughtfully. She feels like she is under a microscope and becomes self-conscious, wiping her hand over her mouth in case she has chocolate and marshmallows around it.

He finally asks, "What does he look like?"

"What does who look like?"

"My knight in shining armour, what does he look like?"

"Your what?" Priya asks.

"I'm lost," Polly chips in.

"Rita said she could see my knight in shining armour and a little girl, in a vision. It reminded me of a dream I had with Dee in it. It's how she got me to come out of my room. What did he look like?"

All eyes are on Rita.

"Well," she says, shrugging. "Like all knights in shining armour. He looked really very shiny."

The laughter resumes, continues all the way up the stairs and even after they have closed their bedroom doors and climbed into their beds.

Twenty-Six

After it happened

I am perching on one end of a huge rock on the beach that is jagged and irregularly shaped. I am looking out over the liquid charcoal ocean, my feet dangling. The sun leaks into the sky and into the dark ocean and they both become streaked with ribbons of bright colour. I can just about make out the dark silhouettes of a school of dolphins on the horizon, chatting to each other and playing gaily. Jumping over each other and splashing each other with their fins, behaving like children in a paddling pool. Breaking away from the school, a female dolphin swims as close to me as she can. I lift my rock with my thoughts from the beach and drift it towards her until it hovers over the ocean just in front of her, close enough to touch her silvery grey skin.

Hello, I'm Dee.

Hello Dee, I'm pleased to meet you. I'm Safriap. It is a very common name for dolphin girls. Do you live on the beach?

I do.

I live here in the ocean. In the physical world I lived in captivity. I was not born a captive. I was born in the ocean and then separated from my family as a young dolphin. I did not meet them again until I came home, and they are behind me now.

In the physical I was a captive too, captive to a demon. Like you I am free now. Was it terrible for you being in captivity?

Oh no, it was not terrible. I don't resent it. I was well fed and well cared for. I had my own carer. We loved each other very much. My coming home devastated her. I still visit her now, swimming around with her in my old tank. She doesn't see me now, though.

No, my friends don't see me either now. They will again one day, though.

Yes they will, Dee. In the physical I was a tourist commodity and I enjoyed being with the children who came to see me to have their photographs taken with me.

I was a commodity, too, in the physical. I intrigued many people also. We called them doctors. I liked children but I never had any of my own, though. I left too soon.

There was emptiness in me in the physical despite my comfortable life in captivity. I learned to live with it. I missed my family. This is the worst thing about not being bred in captivity but being placed there after experiencing a free life and being taken away after experiencing my family. I wouldn't know any different if I had been bred in captivity. I was also unable to have children of my own, like you.

How did you come to be in captivity?

I was struck by a boat and suffered severe injuries to my fins. I was washed up onto the shore and rescued by humans. I never made a full recovery. I was always very weak, swimming slightly lopsidedly, which is why I was used as a petting exhibit. My rescuers decided that I was too vulnerable to be back in the wild. They never used me for breeding because they felt I was too delicate even for this.

It must have been hard for you, learning in the physical.

It's what I chose before I went there. Just like you, you chose to have a demon and be a commodity, just like me. When I am ready to leave home and be born again I will still choose to be a dolphin. There is much more I can still learn as a dolphin that I didn't learn before. Will you return to the physical?

I will go back but I am waiting for my friends and family first.

I understand. I wouldn't have wanted to go back before my family joined me here. I must go back to them now. They are calling me.

Yes, I can hear them. Thank you for sharing your story with me.

You are welcome. We are friends now. I will come to you again.

Yes, friends, I will like that.

Safriap turns away from me, nose-dives back into the charcoal ocean and swims away to re-join her family, waving her tailfin behind her.

James imagines himself with me. He visualises me on my rock in my red satin maxi dress, a red rose in my hair, my curls blowing in the night breeze, sunset wrapping itself around me like a multi-coloured blanket, Safriap swimming away from me breaking the stillness of the charcoal ocean. My rock draws back from its position over the ocean, floating backwards with me knelt on it facing forward, stretching out my arms to the sky. James is on my rock now and his energy is meshing with mine. It feels intense. I feel like I would do in the physical when I was completely naked with someone I was extremely attracted to, someone I hungered to be touched by, and they were completely naked too, stood behind me kissing my neck and caressing it with their fingertips.

Hello.

Hello.

I haven't spoilt your evening, have I?

No, you have made my evening. I'm glad you are here.

I wish it could always be like this, always me and you, always sunset.

It can always be you, here like this, with me, and always sunset.

I know. What shall we do now?" Your wildest dreams are my command.

James, you know that my wildest dreams are achievable by my own command.

Hundreds of white horses galloping down the beach past our rock, which is now floating above the beach, come to my mind; so it happens. Their hooves pound down on the sand, their manes and tails fly wildly in the rush of their gallop; some of them arch their necks, pointing their heads down towards the sand, others have their heads held high and their ears back. We are on the back of one of them. His name is Galion and he is magnificent, strong and gallant. Charging with his head held high, his long sheer white mane flies back like a freshly washed sheet on a washing line flapping in the wind. Compounds of sand fling up from his hooves as he charges forward. We have no saddle or reins. Faster and faster we charge, me sitting behind James. We are safe and secure; we are not in danger of falling. The beach fades away piece by piece, a rock is replaced by thick vines and undergrowth, discarded shells and wandering crabs are replaced by luscious green tropical plants with bright flower heads in purples, pinks, blues, oranges and yellows; thick green vegetation replaces the sand beneath us and a thick canopy camouflages the sky.

I close my eyes and let myself connect with him more deeply. Our thoughts blend. Galion disappears and we are stood hand in hand by a lagoon. Steam is coming up from its deep greenness. Giant flowers the size of car wheels with pink and yellow petals float on the water surface. Birds the colour of steel with blue tinges feed from the pollen of them with their long, thin beaks like knitting needles. We are naked now. James leads me into the lagoon and we swim through a waterfall into a cave behind, which is dimly lit by floating orbs of light. The walls and ceiling of the cave are encrusted in twinkling white-purple crystal. We swim deeper and deeper into the cave and it becomes narrower the further we go until eventually we pass through a bottleneck and into a small round cavity. Sitting on the ridge of this cavity is a huge oak chest with shiny gold clasps.

Open it. James transmits the thought into my conscious mind. *There is something inside for you.*

The lid springs open at my command. Inside it there is a smaller chest. The lid springs open revealing another chest, smaller than the first two. The lid of this one springs open revealing a fourth chest. When each chest opens the one inside it raises up slightly. Seven chests, all becoming smaller and smaller, open with my command until one, the size of a shoebox, is the only one that remains unopened. Levitating it out and into my hands, it opens at my command. A red glow emits from within it and lights up both our faces. From inside the chest, a thick gold rope with a heart-shaped ruby pendant, which would be too heavy for any physical being to wear as only a spirit person has the capacity to render a soul truss weightless, raises itself and hovers above us. One half of it lowers down onto my shoulders, sliding down my wet hair. It twists into a figure of eight so that the soul truss, the heart-shaped ruby, is in the centre of the two circular shapes. Then the second half lowers itself over James's head, resting on his shoulders. Sandwiched between us the soul truss begins to glow red and then bursts with a blinding red light that fills the cavity of the cave. It travels through the bottleneck and all the way through the main cave area colouring the waterfall that falls over its mouth as if red food colouring had been poured into it.

The soul truss binds us. It is the private earlier stage of two souls becoming entwined in a public declaration before a soul weaver and all our spirit friends and family.

Twenty-Seven

Before it happened

Dribbling maple syrup onto crumpets, I am standing in our kitchen and I do not hear or sense him, hooded and cloaked, sneaking up on me, as usual. Instantly he dissolves into a vapour and seeps into my pores like a deadly plague. I am not me anymore; I am him and he controls my body. He goes into the bathroom, he opens the mirror-fronted cabinet and it does not stick for him like it does for me. He grasps my bottle of antidepressants, a tub of paracetamol and some prescribed painkillers Rita has been taking for a twisted ankle. He tips the contents of each bottle one by one into my mouth and chews and swallows them for me. At the top of the stairs, in one final murderous bid, he flings me down them and I crumple at the bottom. His vapour leaves me then, leaves me to die alone.

His bid fails and he is filled with rage upon discovering I was found by the postman in time. He swears vengeance.

The next day I am sitting on the starched, tightly-tucked in bedding of the metal-framed bed, positioned under a thin tall window that has cream painted bars across it. Garth has just left. He hates walking down the sterile corridors filled with the sounds of shuffling and whimpering. The buzzing of the electronic doors makes him as skittish as a horse when a car backfires.

The hooded cloaked figure has been waiting under my bed for his vengeance and he seizes it now. Crawling from underneath it as undetectable as a black house spider on a dark carpet, he silently scuttles across my bed and once again his poison enters my bloodstream. Trailing the sheet from my bed like a toddler trailing their comfort blanket behind them, my chin resting on my chest, he moves me to the bathroom like a pawn in a game of chess. My feet never lift off the scuffed linoleum floor as if they are protesting against him and want to make his next move as difficult to play as possible.

Whistling, a young male nurse leaves the front entrance of the hospital and walks towards his car. He is thinking about getting home to his young girlfriend and his small child. He wonders what delights wait for him in the microwave; he hasn't had time to eat all day. He hopes it is his favourite of plump Cumberland sausages and thick slices of liver in thick onion gravy with mustard mash. Tossing his knapsack on the back seat, he drops into the driver's seat, turning the key in the ignition. He looks up briefly and for a split second he thinks he sees me hovering in the window. Shaking his head at himself, he puts it down to tiredness and promises himself he'll never take a double shift again. As he reverses out of his parking space, twisting his head to check behind him, I catch the corner of his eye. This time my swinging silhouette, in the frosted window of the toilet cubicle sinks into his mind. Slamming on the brakes he hurls himself out of his car. Sprinting back into the hospital, he slips on the linoleum floor of the hospital entrance and skids into the reception desk feet first with a thud. Hysterically, he announces the attempted suicide on ward twenty-four to a small group of nurses sitting around a table sharing sandwiches and laughs, like I used to with Garth and the girls. They quickly jump up, abandoning their laughter and sandwiches and urgently follow him to the lift. Picking up the receiver, the receptionist telephones ward twenty-four like the male nurse who has seen my silhouette shouted at her to do. After sixty seconds someone picks up. She counts each one in her head; *the longer it takes the less likely the person hanging in the toilet cubicle is to survive*, she tells herself.

Clutching a stitch and panting, the male nurse bursts into the bathroom of ward twenty-four followed by the harem of female nurses. He hurls himself at the cubicle door, which buckles and bursts open with very little resistance. Holding my body up he tells one of the female nurses to climb up onto the toilet seat and release me from the noose, which she does. My body flops into the arms that are outstretched, ready to catch me. Laying me out on the floor the male nurse attempts to resuscitate me. I'm not breathing. A female nurse mounts my body, straddling me as if I'm a horse. The sound of my ribs cracking resonates as she pounds out chest compressions, which are broken up by him desperately blowing his own breath into my mouth, hoping it will inflate my lungs.

Being in limbo, surfing between the two worlds, is not the same as being dead. There is no control, not like now. I am completely powerless in limbo, passing in and out of my own body in much the same way as someone passes in and out of consciousness. My spirit form is very weak. I spontaneously flicker on and off in random places, not using a thought process like I do now as a trigger. Once, towards the end of the period of being in limbo, I find I am stood beside my mum and dad in the doctor's office whilst they are being told that my chances of survival are very slim. If I do survive they should prepare themselves for permanent brain damage, she tells them. I can feel emotion in limbo and I scream out at the doctor, begging her not to let this happen. I don't quite understand what is happening; whether it is real or not. Being in limbo is very much like an extended dream: very sketchy, blurred and surreal, all at the same time. When you come out of limbo, if you go back into the physical as I do on this occasion; you don't remember being outside your own body, nothing is definite.

Flickering vulnerably, like a fading light bulb in a light socket, I appear in our house standing behind Garth. Everyone is sitting at the dining table looking bereft. "Is it wrong to want someone to die?" No-one says anything, everyone looks at Garth. "Not want them to die, exactly, but hope that they die because the alternative is so horrible. Hope that they die for their own sake."

Priya drops her head, avoiding any eye contact with him or the others.

"None of us want Dee to end up like that," Polly says, emotion quivering through her voice, which catches in her throat. "No-one wants her to be brain damaged."

"I keep thinking of one of my patients," Rita says. "She is only eighteen and she got hit by a car last week. A hit and run. She is completely brain damaged. Her head hit the windscreen and then the kerb after she hurtled over the car. She needs feeding through a tube. She wears a nappy. She can't communicate. She can't bath herself." Rita buries her head in her hands. "Yesterday, her parents brought in all her gymkhana rosettes. I couldn't believe that it was the same girl and that the lifeless limp body lying in the bed had only weeks earlier been cantering round on a horse, show jumping and winning first prize. I cannot stand the thought that Dee might end up like this. Obviously she feels like life is hell on earth, otherwise she wouldn't keep doing this. It really will be hell on earth if she ends up trapped like that."

Garth hangs his head. "I can't stand to think of Dee like that either. I can't stand to think of anyone like that, but our lovely, bubbly, outgoing, creative and independent Dee like that, nothing more than an empty shell, it's just unbearable."

"Please don't," Priya says. "I'm supposed to be on honeymoon. If she dies I'll be sharing my anniversary with the anniversary of her death. What kind of legacy is that? To know I was having breakfast with my husband the morning after our wedding feeling so happy and she was feeling so alone and miserable at the same time, it's crushing me, I feel so guilty. How could I not see it coming? I was too wrapped up in myself and my wedding, that's how." She flops her head into her hands and tears leak through her fingers.

Rita rises from her chair and folds her arms around her, moving through my twitching hologram to reach her. I put them through a lot, my friends and those I love. They always stand by me despite this.

Twenty-Eight

Before it happened

I did not know then why the cloaked phantom is so intent that I take my own life when I am in the physical. People wanted answers, they wanted me to be able to explain but I could not, I did not have understanding or the words. I do now; I know all of it now. I know that I wasn't unjustly plagued by a demon that attached itself to me. I know now that I was its author. It did not control me. I controlled it. All of his endeavours to destroy me were written instructions I had given him in my blueprint.

In the psychical there are very long periods of time when my misunderstood puppet interpreted wrongly as the puppet master leaves me alone. There are other times when, like I had dictated in my blueprint, it plagues me; times when I wake up in a morning and everything is pitch black despite a shining sun and a blue sky. Ever since I can remember it was like this; I always knew I was not like other people, at least not like the people around me, like Garth.

I am thirteen years old when Garth finds me in my bedroom laid on my bed, my mum's bottle of sleeping pills on one side of me and a bottle of my dad's malt whisky on the other side of me, both empty. Shortly after this, hoping to help him make sense of it, my doctor visits Garth in my parents' house. Mum is fussing about, in denial about the whole thing, pouring tea into everyone's cups, which no one drinks and placing custard creams on their saucers, which no one eats.

Except for Garth and the doctor, who sit on the couch, everyone else, his parents and mine, sit on dining chairs across the other side of the coffee table. Despite being the only child in the room, he's not in denial. Voicelessly, the adults around him sit and listen. They don't look each other in the eye. When I visit the memory as a tourist like I always am I read their thoughts. They are all thinking the exact same thing. They are all thinking that if they do not speak, if they do not look anyone in the eye, they can pretend that it is not real.

"I don't understand why she does it, doctor," Garth states. "Why does she want to die?"

Mum drops five lumps of sugar into her tea, each one makes a plopping sound. She doesn't even take sugar, none of them do, yet every time she hears something she doesn't want to deal with she plops another sugar lump into someone else's tea.

"She is not in control of her own mind, Garth, when she makes the decisions to die."

Plop.

"Is it depression? Is she mental?"

Plop.

"Will she do it again?"

Plop. Plop. Plop.

"We hope not. All we can do is monitor her. She will need help with counselling, support and medication. She is a deeply distressed young girl."

Plop.

The doctor draws closer to Garth, perching on the edge of the couch, turned into him, his hands are clasped together. "Garth, do you know anything about postnatal depression?"

Plop. Plop. Plop.

"It's what a woman gets after having a baby. They can go a bit nutty sometimes, can't they?"

"Well, 'nutty' isn't the medical term we use, but yes, you get the idea. Not all women get postnatal depression, Garth, just some."

"What has this got to do with Dee? You're not saying she's had a baby and not told anyone and now she has postnatal depression, are you? I'm supposed to be her best friend. How could she be pregnant and not tell me? Where did she have the baby and where is it now?"

Plop. Plop. Plop.

"No, she has not had a baby, Garth, but her illness..."

Plop. Plop. Plop. Plop.

My dad throws out a hand at this point, places it over my mum's, draws it back, puts it on his knee and clamps his hand on top of it, preventing her from emptying the entire sugar bowl into the doctor's cup.

"Her illness is similar."

"How can she have postnatal depression if she has not had a baby?"

Shaking his head, the doctor says, "It's only a comparison. Let me explain. Do you understand Garth, that a mum with postnatal depression has a fear of harming her baby?"

My mum's hand twitches in the direction of the sugar bowl but my dad's clamp is too strong, her hand barely lifts a millimetre from his knee.

"Yes, I think so. I have seen it on TV."

"Having a baby can be very stressful and the mum can suffer from a lot of sleep deprivation, which can mean she has certain thoughts, she considers things she wouldn't normally consider."

"You mean they think about harming their baby?"

"Yes, Garth, they think about harming their baby. You are switched on," he says, smiling and patting him on the head- rather patronisingly- I read from the back of Garth's mind. "For example a new mum might be woken by her baby screaming several times in the night for the seventh night in a row." He breaks off and surveys the faces in the room checking that they are still following.

"Go on, doctor."

"I don't want to cause any distress, Garth."

"You won't. I'm following what you are saying. I need to know what is going on in her head. I can't help otherwise."

"The baby's mum will start to wish for a peaceful night's sleep, just one. The constant crying and the yearning to sleep will alter her mind temporarily and she will start to think that if she places a pillow over the baby's face, it will stop crying." He stops, assesses Garth's facial reactions, concerned he has gone too far. When he sees that Garth is intently engaged, processing and formatting the information, he privately reflects how adult and hardy he is for a teenage boy, adding to his thoughts that Garth would make a valuable addition to the medical world.

"So she can sleep, you mean? She wants to stop the baby crying so she can sleep?"

"Yes, Garth, so she can sleep. She actually does not go through with it and in reality is not actually a danger to her baby, it's perfectly normal for her to have this craving to sleep and to think of the ways she can secure this sleep. Sleep deprivation is a form of torture; it has been used this way in wars, so the mum is very vulnerable and in that sense being tortured by sleep deprivation. The problem is she can't take her thought back and begins to feel she is a danger to her own child and this is what triggers the postnatal depression. She may feel like taking her own life, removing herself from the situation to protect her child. Some do."

"I understand all of this and it's a terrible thing for someone to go through. I don't understand, though, what this has to do with Dee. She doesn't have sleepless nights. She doesn't have a baby."

"Garth, do you remember last week in the queue for the school bus when Dee got really upset with the boy who pushed in?"

"Yeah, it was Michael Duncan." He laughs at the recollection of what I had said. "She said she wanted to boil his head and make soup out of it. She proper freaked out about it we had to get off the bus and walk home. I couldn't calm her down. She was hysterical." He pauses in thought for a moment, considering all the things the doctor has said to him and how this could apply to the theory of postnatal depression. "Hang on a minute. Are you saying that Dee wanting to boil Michael's head is the same as the woman you described thinking she could harm her baby? Is that why Dee tried to kill herself because she said she wanted to boil Michael's head?"

"Yes, Garth, that's exactly it. She thought it, like the mum with postnatal depression, so she thought she was capable. She thinks thoughts and actions are the same when they are not. She doesn't trust herself just like a mum with postnatal depression doesn't trust herself around her baby."

"That's stupid, she didn't mean it. Removing his head and boiling it, it's ridiculous. How could she possibly think that she was capable of doing it? How could she possibly think that she was able to do it, even? What was she going to cut his head off with, my nail scissors?" He laughs, shaking his head in disbelief.

"Garth, there are some things that cannot be explained. Not all illnesses have a cause but Dee clearly feels she is a danger to society. She has thoughts, which to you and me and other people are perfectly normal and rational but to her are dark and dangerous."

"She isn't dangerous, not at all."

"It doesn't feel like this to her. What she needs now is a lot of understanding and love from you, from you all. Do you think you can do this?"

"Of course I can."

"She may want to talk about it, she may not. You will have to let her decide this for herself."

"Whatever she needs, doctor," Garth says with all the seriousness and maturity of an adult and not a thirteen-year-old boy. "She is my best friend I won't let her down."

You never did, Garth. Then I leave the memory.

Twenty-Nine

After it happened

Venue after venue is rejected on the basis of blemishes of imperfection, deemed charismatic and charming by most other people: the ceiling, too high; the original huge fire place, too draughty; the paint on the frames of the huge windows, too cracked; the wallpaper, too light; the wallpaper, too dark; the function room, too square; the function room, too oblong.

"Don't you even think about it," Al warns, on the last venue we see, with a screwed up face and a rigid pointing finger, which makes Garth start in surprise, as if he has just noticed a spider in the bottom of the shower tray whilst he is taking a shower.

Whilst Al and Garth engage in a brief stare-off I watch the smouldering sexual tension between a young red coat and his pretty dance partner, the orphaned niece of a wealthy Lord who grew up in the stately home we are viewing. They are unseen except to me. They are dancing flirtatiously, messages of affection sent and received silently through their eyes, in the centre of the ballroom. Skipping and prancing, their dance looks complicated; the mind of the young woman tells me that practicing the dancing for her very first ball in her honour had been a fulltime occupation. Candles light the entire ballroom. They are burning brightly in elaborate freestanding chandeliers, they reflect in strategically placed large ornate framed mirrors. *There are at least three hundred candles burning*, her mind informs me.

The gold buttons on the man's red coat twinkle like his smile. The sumptuous smells of the supper from the dining room fills the air. *White soup and pheasant pie are my favourites,* his mind tells me that.

"I don't care what it is this time. I'm not having it. You have dragged me around every venue this area has to offer. There's the lake you want." He thrusts his arm towards the window. "It has a boating deck, like you want. The manager has said we can hire swan boats and sail them out there. The lawn is massive, plenty big enough for the one-hundred-and-sixty-six guests you are insisting on inviting. There is no problem and we're booking it."

Garth refrains from telling the Function Manager that the ballroom intended for their ceremony is spooky.

It's not just venues; I follow Polly, Rita and Priya all practically on their knees in Garth's trawl of every wedding fair in the UK, tasting cake and sniffing flower bouquets until they turn green at the mere sight of cake and flowers. Al leaves Italy, every tailor in the UK having failed to produce anything harmonising with Garth's image of the perfect groom's attire, slightly bereft and in need of a stiff drink. Garth leaves Italy extremely excited and glued to his mobile phone, describing to the girls, in high-pitched screeches, every detail of the silk-lined sleek velvet morning suits; his latest tic, on his to-do list. Sitting between them, in the taxi to Milan's airport, I read Al's mind. Thinking that Garth's latest tick is seventeen ticks not enough, he inwardly dreads the prospect of auditioning the seven-band-line-up scheduled for one hour after their plane touches down on UK soil.

"We have gone over budget." Garth is sitting at what, when he and the girls are gathered around it, he insists on calling the dining system. Beside him is a bottle of claret and a half-filled glass, with a stem as thin as a tulip stalk and a glass bulb as big and bulbous as a fish bowl. Al is sitting on the black leather sofa, which doesn't look much like a sofa to me. It's probably called something pretentious to license an expensive price tag. It's more like a very posh psychiatrist's counselling bed, very low down, supported by four short bowed-out stainless steel feet, with a very low back rest. There is a glass of water is positioned by his ankle and he is wearing smart attire, as always when there is a risk his beeper might bleep him to duty. He looks very dashing in a pair of oat-coloured trousers with subtle chocolate pin stripes, a crisp white shirt with the sleeves rolled up to his elbows and a waistcoat that matches his trousers. He has his back to the glass wall behind him, which offers them panoramic views over one side of the entire city from every point they stand in their penthouse apartment.

Al tightly grips the financial times in the middle; it bows towards him, opening up his vision of Garth's back. He is facing the glass wall that offers panoramic views across the entire opposite side of the city. "How over budget, exactly, is 'over budget'?"

Garth swivels around on the tall white and chrome swivel stool and observes him, holding a Parker pen in his mouth, sheepishly with big gooey eyes.

"Is it really that bad?" Al says. "It must be bad, the puppy dog eyes are out. You don't usually bring out the big guns unless you are desperate."

Placing his paper down beside him, he lifts his water and himself gracefully off the sofa and walks in barefoot across the dark wood floor to his fiancé. Sliding his left arm over Garth's chest he pulls him backwards, Garth's head rests against Al's chest. With his right arm Al steadily feeds himself a mouthful of water. Garth pushes his head further back into Al and gazes up at him, his puppy dog eyes intensified now that Al is at point blank range. "Is it working?" Unable to respond vocally, Al shakes his head. "We are up to forty thousand." Gritting his teeth, he adds, "Fifteen thousand over budget."

Instantly Al exhales and spurts a mouthful of water into Garth's face, like an elephant, spraying water out of its trunk. "What!" He screeches.

Garth, ignoring the water dripping from his glasses, meekly replies, "I'm sorry. I just got carried away."

"Carried away!" Al is still at a screeching pitch. "Garth, a hundred wild horses couldn't bloody carry you away this far. We agreed twenty-five thousand pounds. This is plenty, surely?"

Al reaches for Garth's bulbous glass of red wine and gulps it down in thirty seconds whilst Garth observes him in disbelief. "I can't believe you just did that, Al."

"You can spend our entire retirement fund on a wedding and I can't even drink a glass of your claret?"

"It's not that I object to you drinking my wine, more I object to you potentially driving and going on duty after drinking my wine. You are on call after all, don't forget." Garth stubs a finger at Al's forehead in an attempt to drill what he has just reminded him of into his head.

Al takes his finger and directs it to his mouth, nibbling on it tenderly. Then he reaches out and refills the glass, lifting it up and drinking it again. "Bugger being on call, it's me that will need medical assistance." He laughs, shaking his head. "Garth, you're a bloody nightmare. Really, you have spent this much? Forty. Thousand. Pounds. Seriously, it's a lot of money." He claps a hand to his forehead.

"I know. I'm sorry. We can afford it, with the donations from our parents and the money Dee's parents gave me, we are only putting in twenty-five percent anyway. I didn't use any of our retirement fund, the surrogacy fund or any other fund we have in our million zillion bank accounts. It is just money, which we have accumulated and not spent yet."

"It doesn't hurt to portion save, Garth. It is sensible financial planning."

"I'm not having a go at you, Al." Garth lifts his hand to Al's cheek. Al places a hand over the top of it. "I agree we should save. What I'm trying to say is I have been keeping a pot of money myself for our wedding, since about six months after we first met at the train station."

Al laughs. "You have been saving for our wedding for four and a half years, six months after we started dating?"

Garth nods solemnly, "Yes."

"Why on earth didn't you say?"

"I didn't want you to feel pressured, or think I was a weirdo."

Al chuckles. "Oh no, you wouldn't want that, would you, because finding sketches of our faces, in top hats, on post-it notes, stuck to the pouch of my boxers when opening my underwear drawer every morning, is no pressure at all and not at all the behaviour of a weirdo."

"That's not weird, that's just funny."

"I can't disagree there," Al laughs. "It certainly made the lads at football laugh."

"You didn't. I can't believe you told them!"

"You have not got a leg to stand on here." Al gulps at Garth's refilled wine glass then hands it to him. "Go on, then."

Garth sips his wine letting it slide down his throat. "Go on, what?"

"This wedding fund of yours. My dowry. How much is it worth?"

"Oh, it's worth just a few pounds."

"How many is a few?"

"Not telling."

"Oh yes you are." Al tickles Garth's ribs.

Garth giggles uncontrollably, sloshing wine over the dining system. "Stop! Stop! Stop!" he cries. "You'll ruin the dining system."

"I'm not stopping until you tell me. Come on, or the dining system gets it."

"Okay, I'll tell you once you have stopped."

"I'm not falling for that, tell first and I'll stop."

Still giggling and jiggling on his stool, Garth cries out, "Eight thousand pounds!"

Snatching Garth's wine again, Al gulps at it whilst surveying Garth for a moment. Watching him swill and swallow the wine, Garth eyes Al uneasily. "You've got to be kidding me, you little sneak."

"Al, I never meant to upset you. I wasn't sneaking around behind your back."

It isn't supposed to backfire like this. Al isn't meant to be angry with him. With his hands together like butterfly wings, Garth buries his face in them. I read the fear in his thoughts.

Al takes hold of him by the wrist. "Garth, come here." He pulls Garth's arms towards him, placing one on each of his own shoulders. "I'm not angry, just surprised you managed to keep it a secret for four and a half years, extremely impressive for you. You can't usually hold your own water. Why didn't you say anything?"

"I couldn't say anything until I had actually got you to propose. I mean, I was saving for a wedding that might never happen. What was I meant to say? You have to marry me because I have been saving for four and a half years?"

"It's like I've always said and will no doubt always say until the day you croak it. You are as mad as a hatter, completely crackers."

Garth loops his arms behind Al's neck, drawing his face closer to his. They kiss. "I love you."

"I love you too, Garth, even if you are borderline insane."

"I can make some cut backs. The main thing is us and the people who-." Wobbling with emotion, his words fail him.

"Hey," Al soothes. "She'll be there." Al places the flat of his hand on Garth's heart as if hoping to ease the pain he knows will be shooting through it.

"Will she? You're a scientist. You don't believe that any more than I do." His eyes are watery. "I'd pay forty thousand pounds just to have her at my wedding. Then I'd get married in jeans and a t-shirt."

They hug tightly; Garth rests his head against Al's chest. I come in closer, putting my arms around them, making it a group hug. Garth's daydream is wistful, which I access every morning on his way to work, of me wearing a full-length navy blue bridesmaid's dress with diamanté sprays at the bust. Imagining me standing, with a slight wobble, hindered by the copious amounts of champagne I have thrown down my neck and the ridiculously crippling stilettos he makes me wear, to give my speech, brings tears rushing to his eyes.

"I wish I could bring her back for you, Garth. I promise I'll never leave. You'll always have me."

"You can't promise that. That's what me and Dee said: together, forever and a day."

Swiftly, my hands on Al's shoulders, an image of two very old men sat in a park breaking bits of bread up and throwing them out to a hoard of ducks, quaking and waddling towards them greedily, reels into the forefront of his mind. A group of three generations are around them, laughing and chatting cheerfully. Shaking his head as if trying to dislodge sand from his ears he says chirpily, "I just get this feeling we will grow very old together and have a family, even see great-grandchildren."

"Where did that sentiment come from?"

Stepping backwards, I take my hands off Al. "I have no idea."

Something vibrates against Garth's inside leg. Smirking dirtily, he asks, "What's that?"

"My beeper." Flying a hand to his waistband and unclipping his pager, he inspects it. "There has been a motorway pile up. I'm going to have to go in."

Garth looks at the wine. "Bugger me."

"I can't, Garth, I don't have the time."

Thirty

Before it happened

In the physical, traveling was something Garth and I spend hours planning to do. It really excites me. We spend hours losing ourselves in travel books and atlases, poring over them, immersing ourselves in standstill sandy beaches of the Caribbean or in the wilderness and forage of the Brazilian rainforest.

Tacked with nails to his garage wall, covering the majority of it, we have a huge world map. It is besieged with pins and sticky labels pointing out and making notes on the places we want to see, like an intricate storyboard. Thick arrows in red marker are drawn onto it to show the directional flow of our trip. Starting in Paris we loop around Europe, enter Asia through Russia; sweep down through a selection of countries in Asia, pop out at the end of the Malaysian peninsular and go onto adventure in Australasia. The pink Cadillac adventure of Central America is what I get most excited about. Teasing me, Garth says I won't make it this far because I will be devoured by a pit of snakes in the Brazilian rainforest. Hours and hours, all through our GCSEs and A-levels, we sit on stools in front of the map, a mountain of travel books almost as high as the stools piled around us, discussing it.

"Do you think we will actually do it, Garth?"

Leaping down from my stool, I walk over to the map, my hands in the pockets of my hot pants, a former pair of jeans and jumble sale find, which I breathe new life into with a pair of scissors and textile badges.

I stand in front of the map and look up at it awestruck, chewing rather strenuously on bubble-gum and blowing big pink bubbles that pop loudly. It amazes me just how big the world really is.

"Why wouldn't we, Dee?"

"Money, of course."

"Money isn't a huge problem."

I turn my face to him. "Garth, we can't get by on, Skittles."

I wait patiently, for him to crunch and swallow the handful of Skittles he has just tossed into his mouth, for his reply. "No, but there is this little thing called saving. I already have a thousand pounds. How much have you saved?"

Tearing my guilt-laden eyes away from him back to the map, I bite my bottom lip. Loudly his stool scuffs on the concrete floor and then falls back, indicating he has removed himself from it with some force; angrily, even. "You haven't saved anything have you?"

He is angry. "I tried," I say, wringing out my hands behind my back. "I've saved a bit."

"How much, is a bit?"

"It's in my piggy bank." I move out of his reach just in case he decides to wallop me one. "Two pounds and fifty-nine pence?" I screw my eyes shut, preparing for an angry torrent.

"You silly cow, we emptied that yesterday for crisps and chocolate." Laughter sounds out of him.

"I've saved nothing then, sorry."

With a hand on his forehead, wracking his brain, Garth paces up and down. "We'll just use whatever I save. Let's face it, you are never going to save a penny. We can do Camp America in the USA and get bar jobs in Australia. In New Zealand we will work on a fruit farm or something."

"You will really do that for me?"

Putting a hand on each shoulder, he looks intently into my eyes. "I love you, don't I, you daft cow? Together, forever and a day, you and me that's what we said, isn't it?"

Unfortunately, in the physical we never realise our dream of travelling together. There is no particular reason other than the usual: we grow up. The responsibility of being graduates with a lot of debt to pay off, the need to get some real nursing experience before we take a three year sabbatical, at the cost of coming back and competing with a cohort of more recently qualified nurses, stands in our way. We cling onto the possibility of 'one day,' like we all do, as if 'one day' is a piece of drift wood in the ocean where we are stranded following a sinking ship disaster. Postpone for three years, we agree. Accept the jobs we have been offered at our placement hospital, move into a shared house with the girls, save for three years and then do it. Ironically, after I come home Garth finds my scrapbook under my bed, entitled 'Travelling dream'. Glued to the pages are cuttings from holiday brochures and magazines of all the countries we plan to see. Folded in the back are bank statements for an account with a balance of £2,000. "You silly cow, Dee Winters," he says sitting on my bed looking up at my skylight unaware I am beside him, nodding my head.

Garth goes on physically without me to do lots of travelling, most of it with Al. Let's save up loads of money and disappear off for three years to see the entire world, then come back and get proper jobs and be proper grown-ups, he doesn't quite manage. Segmenting it, he manages to see lots of the world. The dust of my leaving them settled Garth and the girls spend a number of weeks inter-railing around Europe. In Paris, sitting around a water fountain, just outside the Louvre, tearing apart and sharing a baguette and a lump of brie Rita, refers to it as an 'eight-week sabbatical'. Later in the trip, whilst eating pizza at the top of the leaning tower of Pisa, Garth vents his frustration at being on week eight and having to fly home in the next few days. In later years he will go further afield with Al and Freya when Allison decides it time she joins them.

In Northern Thailand, living amongst a native tribe on an organised tour, is my favourite memory of his trips. Untouched by civilisation and sanitation, they lodge with a woman who, at ninety-six years old actively advocates they indulge in her finest home grown opium, which they politely decline. He never knew worlds like it existed and finds the whole trip wonderfully eye-opening. He can't quite believe that four generations of one family live in a hut the size of the average living room, on stilts ten feet above the ground, with no electricity, no toilet and a cold hosepipe in a wooden hut shared between entire communities, masquerading as the shower.

Appreciation for the stilts instils itself in him during a trek through the jungle when he trips up on some jungle undergrowth and comes face to face with a very angry, brightly coloured snake. Fortunately, his well-equipped and fearless guide is able to seize it and launch it into thick yellow leaves with a swift flick of his wrist. I can't help but laugh standing beside Garth, on a fallen and rotten tree trunk, as he hyperventilates into a paper bag. Freya, only a toddler is in a pouch secured to the front of Al, who is combing Garth's hair with his hand. Discussing their shock, in their native languages, for the Englishman who almost had his face eaten by a poisonous snake, two-dozen tourists feverishly take photographs of him like frenzied journalists feeding off a big story. Calm and collected on the outside, Al's thoughts contradict this. He's never been so scared in his life, over and over one train of thought pounds at the front of his mind: *we could have lost him*.

Garth, ignorant as always, has no idea that the only reason the snake withholds striking at him is the fact of me being stood between them, protecting him. I distract the snake, enabling the guide's intervention; it's my eyes she makes the unbreakable link with.

Each time Garth heads off to foreign climes he has a brush with death. In the Maldives on his and Al's honeymoon it is a freak accident when the catamaran they are skimming the ocean on flips over and Garth hits his head on a rock. In a state of semi consciousness he sinks further into the crystal clear ocean. Brightly coloured tropical fish in canary yellow, post box red and peacock blue dart past him with the speed of arrows shot from a crossbow. More aware than he has ever been, he sees the mermaid swim towards him, her thick auburn curly hair flaring out and dancing around her face like seaweed. He takes in her silvery green eyes and matching tail swishing backwards and forwards, flicking in and out, and causing ripples in the water. During the countless times he recounts the story, usually after one too many glasses of wine to an enthralled audience he never connects me with the mermaid, which I find surprising because when our eyes lock, just before he is pulled to safety, I really think he recognises them as mine. Hallucination, induced by the bang on the head, is his real belief.

In Africa it's choking on a peanut that nearly finishes him off. A lion jumps onto the bonnet of the jeep they are touring the game reserve in. Roaring furiously and pawing at the windscreen angrily, he proceeds to eat the windscreen wipers, crunching them like brittle human bones. Inhaling one of the half-dozen peanuts he had thrown into his mouth moments before, as a result of his startled jolt, Garth begins to choke. Freya, almost a teenager now, looks up at Al, rolls her eyes and pulls the lollipop she has been sucking on from her mouth, which makes a sound like a plug being removed from its sink hole and coolly states, "Daddy needs rescuing again, Pa."

She inclines her head backwards at Garth sitting behind her who has gone a deep shade of purple; one hand is at his throat the other one is gripping the metal protection meshing on the window he's sitting beside. Looking at his husband and daughter hopelessly, eyes loaded, very dramatically, with final goodbyes. No-one other than Garth is panicking; the driver and tour-guide is too busy in the front seat brandishing a riffle at the lion, swearing at it in a thick South African accent, attempting to scare it off and save his windscreen wipers. Al pulls Garth onto his knee. Calmly, as if it's an every day occurrence, he performs the Heimlich manoeuver, thrusting his knotted hands into Garth's belly, causing him to heave and wretch until the peanut fires out and hits the windscreen with the speed and impact of a bullet, causing the lion to jolt and leap off the bonnet, running back into the wild. Casting a glance backwards, his hind legs jolt up and down and his tail sweeps back and forth, just to check he is not being shot at.

Thirty-One

The day it happened

Garth and Rita topple through the front door in high spirits and carrying lots of shopping bags brimming with glorious fashions, sublimely unaware that they will soon hate every single item of clothing and that they will never wear any of them because of the metaphorical blood stains each one will soon bear. It is easier for them to take it out on the clothes, to tear them to shreds, to burn them in punishment for what they have done. The clothes seduced them, elicited them away whilst the life ebbed away from someone they loved so intently. The clothes will become transitory of the anger they will feel towards themselves.

They discard their bags on the leather settees and wonder into the kitchen. Garth goes immediately to the kettle and flicks it on at the switch. Stooping below the worktop underneath the kettle, he opens the fridge and takes out the milk, placing it on the worktop beside the kettle. Rita goes to the sink and lifts herself on her tiptoes, pulling open the glass doors of the cupboard above it. She lifts out two mugs, mugs made to look like cans of baked beans, surviving relics from our student digs. She swivels around and their eyes meet. She sticks her tongue out at him and he pulls a face back, using his fingers to pull down his bottom eyelids and his thumbs to push up his nose. They both laugh and she joins him by the kettle, resting the mugs down beside the milk.

Once they have made their tea, Garth takes the chocolate digestives out of the cupboard above the kettle and they go into the lounge. I follow them. They sit across from each other at the round, white melamine breakfast table, and the wooden fruit bowl over-spilling with red grapes between them. Drinking their tea, they share the biscuits, passing the packet from one to the other. I sit on the windowsill with my legs dangling below me, my elbows on my knees and my chin on the heels of my hands, watching and waiting.

"I hate it when that happens," Rita says. "I'm glad it was you and not me."

"Fantastic," Garth says, furiously. "Just what I wanted- biscuit mush at the bottom of my mug of tea. I hardly even dunked it too."

Rita laughs. "A second too long and it's game over, sucker."

I laugh too.

"Oh well," Garth replies. "It's not the end of the world. I suppose it could be worse. It's just a biscuit. It's just a mug of tea. No one is dead."

"Yep," Rita replies dunking another biscuit, being purposely brief in doing so. "You still have your gorgeous loot." She inclines her head at the settees. "Over there."

"Ooooh!" Garth exclaims, sucking in his cheeks with overtones of camp. "I can't wait to start the fashion show."

Rita lifts her mug up, nods her head and before she takes a slurp of tea says, "We'll just finish these then we'll get cracking with a fashion parade."

"You have got to help me decide what to wear tonight. I'm still undecided between the skinny red jeans and the navy blue ones."

"What footwear are you thinking?" Rita asks, lifting her mug to her mouth and taking another slurp of tea.

"Doc Martens, I reckon," Garth replies, surveying her over his glasses. "The purple ones."

"In that case," Rita replies, resting her mug on the table and reaching out for a grape, "it's got to be the red skinny jeans, babe." She plucks a grape from the plump bunch and pops it into her mouth.

"I was also thinking the David Bowie frill-fronted shirt."

She nods and swallows her chewed grape. "With the rosary beads, I reckon." She plucks another grape and hovers it in front of her mouth. "Loads of mascara too babe."

"Yeah, I reckon. What about the leather waistcoat?"

"Definitely. You'll look mega sexy. I might try and hump you myself."

"Don't you dare," Garth says, shuddering at the thought. "You have put me off my biscuit now," he says, laying down a half-eaten chocolate digestive.

"Charming! It is a good job I'm not easily offended."

"Yep, skin as thick as a rhino. That's you, Reets, and with a backside to match."

"Cheeky bitch!" Rita exclaims, plucking another grape and hurling it at his forehead.

Once again the room is full of laughter; mine is loudest but is the only one not heard.

Rubbing his forehead, Garth says, "Do you think Dee will like the jumper?"

Rita lifts herself off her chair and saunters over to one of the settees, delving deep into one of the shopping bags. She pulls out a mohair jumper. It is tight fitting, horizontally striped, all the colours of the rainbow, with elbow-length sleeves and a plunging V-neck.

"I think she will love it. She will probably wear it tonight with those chocolate cords of hers."

Garth rolls his eyes. "She lives in them."

Simultaneously they both say, mocking me, "My fifty-pence charity shop bargain, these are, so don't take the piss, dickheads."

You're not funny, either of you.

The room fills with laughter again. Rita comes back to the table and sits down opposite Garth.

"So?" She smirks.

He smirks back. "So?"

"Who will it be tonight?"

"I don't know what you mean, Reets."

"Oh, come on. You, dear boy, are the biggest tart going. No man is safe. Polly has been distributing the flyers all day. 'Watch out, Garth's about.'"

Rita and myself cackle.

"You are so mean."

"You know that it's true, babe. Whether it is husbands, sons, brothers, boyfriends or dads. No man is safe," she says. "Granddads, too, if last Friday night is anything to go by."

"That's so out of order. No way was he old enough to be my granddad."

"He was forty-five. It's not that far off the zimmer frame, babe. That's old enough to be a granddad even if not yours. It's a twenty one year age gap in any case, yuk gross."

"Get stuffed," he says back. "At least I'm getting some action. You know what they say: use it or lose it. Is Polly still not putting out?"

Another grape somersaults through the air across the table and connects with Garth's forehead.

"Owww," he says, rubbing the spot it hit. "You can dish it out but you can't take it. That's not very sportsman like, you know."

"I'm not a sportsman."

"Well, you're not sporty, I suppose."

"Owww, stop it."

The room fills with laughter again.

"Do you think we should wake Dee up?"

"I don't know, Reets. I hate to think of her sleeping all day."

"The doctor said it's to be expected, though. It's the pills."

The elephant is in the room. Their eyes break apart. Rita's eyes fly to the shopping bags and Garth's eyes rest on the fruit bowl. Silence hangs between them briefly before they pull it together.

"We'll give it another half an hour and then take her up a cup of tea and some cheese on toast. She'll like that."

Garth's eyes come away from the fruit bowl and hold Rita's again. "And the jumper, too. She is going to love it."

"The jumper, too. She is going to love it."

I do love it.

"So?"

"So?"

"You know."

"Seriously, Reets, you are insatiable."

"No, that's you, which is kind of my point. If I'm going to have to listen to your headboard bashing away at my wall all night I'd like a heads up on who it might be. Excuse my choice of words, 'heads up.'"

"Ha-ha, very funny," Garth laughs and pauses before adding, "Well, I was thinking."

"Oh no, I don't like the sound of this."

"You don't like the sound of what?"

"Deviousness and cunning in your tone of voice, like you're planning something you are not entirely convinced is a good idea, which means it won't be a good idea."

"I was thinking Mike."

"Bingo."

"What do you mean, 'bingo'?"

"I mean Garth, that I am right, it's not a good idea."

"Why?"

"Oh I don't know, perhaps because of Bethany, his poor girlfriend."

"That didn't stop him fooling around with me three Fridays ago."

"I'm telling you, babe, you'll end up burned."

"Oh it was just a little-."

"Stop!" Rita throws her hands up over her ears. "I don't want to hear it."

Garth stops talking and waits for Rita to let her hands fall from her ears.

"HAND JOB!"

"I said I didn't want to know!" she says, plucking another grape.

"Owww, stop it."

Rita places the flats of her hands on the table and lifts herself up. "Right, you start the cheese on toast and flick the kettle back on, babe. I'll go to the toilet. Then I'll come back down to help and we'll wake Dee up."

Garth picks up the two empty mugs by the handles with the same hand, chinking them together. He picks up the half-eaten packet of chocolate digestive biscuits in the other hand and starts towards the kitchen slowly. Losing himself in a daydream, hoping Mike will wear his PVC trousers again with the Velcro fly. Rita sprints to the door in the corner of the lounge and is already halfway up the staircase when I remember. I suddenly remember why that all the time I have been sat on the windowsill watching, listening, laughing, that my friends have not included me.

All of the windows in the house clench all their strength and cling to the window frames with their entire might, desperate to save themselves from imploding and filling every room with high-speed airborne shards of glass when Rita's blood curdling scream rings out of her; the toothy sinister grin and tortured staring eyes of my frozen expression, like that of a mounted fox in a taxidermist's waiting room, submerged in water, is what welcomes her to the bathroom.

In an instant Garth knows what her scream means. He's had enough experience. Slipping from his grip, the mugs crash to floor, cracking apart on impact; the fragments and splinters bounce up in slow motion. He takes in every detail as the pieces break away from each other. He swerves his body, stumbling on his ankles. He nosedives to the floor, throwing out his arms to stop himself. His palms hit the floor and he bounces himself back on them. Regaining himself he charges forward his elbows angling out behind him. He climbs the stairs, taking two at a time, using the banisters on either side to pull himself up. He reaches the top and flies into the bathroom, where his ears detect splashing noises and retching, which he knows is coming from Rita. The instant he sees Rita cradling my head to her chest and pushing her feet against the bath panel in an attempt to pull my body onto the bathroom floor he doubles over, gripping his abdomen as if he has just received a swift blow to it.

"Get her out, Garth! Get her out!"

"I think it's too late, Reets."

"No, it's not. Get her out. Get her out!"

It is Rita. It is too late. Garth is right.

"IT'S TOO LATE, YOU STUPID COW!" Garth screams at her. He darts to the toilet and on all fours retches into the toilet bowl, his whole body rising and falling rapidly.

"We shouldn't have left her!" she screams. "Why did we do that? Get her out, Garth. Why won't you help me get her out? You bastard!"

It's not his fault. It's nobody's fault but my own, Rita.

Garth's vomit hits the back of the toilet bowl hard with a rushing sound. Still on all fours and retching, he turns and makes his way to Rita, trailing vomit across the floor, his eyes watering and red. Lifting one arm off the floor and extending it, he grabs Rita and tugs her to him. Her body leans towards him with little resistance and she unlocks her grip on my head. My body slides down the slope of the back of the bath and sinks back underneath the water's surface. My hair, as if unaware that its owner has died, swishes and swirls around my frozen expression as if belonging to a dancing mermaid and not a dead body.

"She's gone, Rita. It's too late. I'm sorry, sweetheart, but it is."

I'm sorry, too, for both of you.

Holding each other, they rock back and forth, sobbing uncontrollably, until a passer-by, chilled by their hysteria spurting out of the window like blood from a stab wound anxiously, telephones the police.

Thirty-Two

Before it happened

Once, I visited my mum and found her perched on the arm of the sofa alone in the lounge staring blankly as if her head had been hollowed out and was an empty vessel, at the oil painted canvas of a vase of flowers that I had painted. I sit beside her, neither of us feeling the icy chill that whistles down the chimney. I eye the patchwork woollen blanket over the arm of the sofa and wish I could pull it around her shoulders. I sit with her until light turns to darkness and then to light again. Finally her heavy eyelids droop and close. Then I step into her dreams and meet her.

I am walking down the driveway of my sixth-form college.

"Hello, dear."

"Hi Mum." I take the lemon-flavoured ice-lolly she is holding out and flash her an appreciative ear-to-ear grin. I begin tearing the paper from the sticky ice-lolly, my mouth watering and my taste buds dancing in anticipation of its tangy zingy flavour. "Thanks Mum, you're the best."

Tucking a thick-coiled spring of hair, bouncing between her eyes, behind her ear, she chuckles. Prettiness is something I inherit from my mum. We are duplicated in many ways, right down to our marquee bras and small-waisted jeans. Just like me, my mum is small and petite everywhere but the bra department and has thick autumn-coloured hair and sprightly eyes. The same cute button nose, complete with a spattering of freckles like someone has gathered a dozen freckles in the palm of their hand and gently blown them onto our faces, is something else we have in common.

She looks beautiful in this memory. Catching the June sunshine we had that year, her skin glows healthily and she is picture perfect of a summer goddess, wearing a 1950s style white summer dress with strawberries printed onto it, a simple gold coffee bean pendant around her neck and a straw hat with a large brim and a red ribbon tied around it, knotted into a bow at the back. "I hope you're feeling green fingered and ready to forage the meadow. Janet said it's particularly exquisite this year. Mavis and Erin will be green with envy at class tonight when we turn up with the best flowers and knock the petals off their summer bouquet, which will not be as beautiful as ours." She smirks, wickedly.

"Mum, for such a 'mousy woman', to quote Mavis, you do surprise me sometimes. That's very underhand of you."

Mavis and Erin lived five doors down from us and like mum and me were another mother and daughter duo attending floral arranging classes at the local community centre. Every Tuesday evening, the evening of the classes, they would time the opening of their front door to miraculously coincide with me and mum being inches from the step outside it. Dramatically, in the manner of an A-list celebrity relishing a paparazzi moment, the door would thrust back and they would buoyantly appear on the top step, ornamented with an armful of immaculate and stunning, bright and sweetly perfumed flowers. Mavis's eyeballs would slide down the ridge of her nose to regard Mum, myself and our home grown offerings with utter distaste. Her offensive eyeballs and equally offensive nose were quickly joined by the full complement of her derogatory tuned tongue. "Ciara, your pokey little back garden does not bless you with the best conditions to grow flowers in. It's no wonder they are all wilted. You poor thing, you must be so disheartened. You do try, dear, but nothing ever seems to work for you, does it? You poor, poor thing I'm sure you will get something right one day."

"I know," Mum replies. "She has it coming, though." Bowing down, Mum lifts a wicker basket sitting by her ankles. We walk to the meadow behind my sixth-form college, slurping and sucking noises from our ice-lollies punctuating the silence.

The meadow is full of vibrant colours and sweet scents. "It's beautiful, Mum. I can't believe this is just behind my sixth-form building, hiding behind all the thick leafy trees and I never even knew it existed, amazing."

"It's just like 'The Secret Garden,'" Mum replies in her whimsical way, another inheritance she passed onto me. "Come on." Quickening her step, she calls over her shoulder, "Last one to get there smells like Dad's old socks." Skipping ahead of me, the skirt of her dress blowing about above her knee and the basket swinging over her arm, I hang back briefly; as a spirit person watching the memory replay I know that carefree days like this are numbered and once I'm gone she'll never know happiness like this day again, at least not whilst she is still in the physical.

Reaching the little wooden fence around the perimeter of the meadow, she throws a leg over the first wooden rung, ducks her head and manoeuvres her body underneath the second run. We, my physical self and I, stand and gaze at her and the beautiful meadow, a medley of flowers all different shapes, colours and sizes. White butterflies flutter just above the flower heads and the sound of bees feeding on the ripe pollen hum above the flowers.

"Come on, slow coach."

I run to the fence put my foot on the first wooden rung and hoist myself over the fence, straddling it. Mum's eyes fall on a patch of tall and deep crimson blazing stars, which stand about three feet high. She is pointing at them, and my eyes follow the direction of her finger. We exchange gratified smiles. Delving into her basket she retrieves a pair of bright red secateurs. Adopting an alien tone and speaking as if she has swallowed a floral arranging thesaurus, she says, "They will make an excellent vertical contrast to our flower arrangement." It's as if, all of a sudden we are back in class, and my mum is trying to outsmart Mavis in the class know-it-all competition. "Look how beautiful their wide leaves are and how vibrant they are in colour."

"Mum, I hardly recognise you. Who has been giving you sarcasm pills?"

"It must be the ice-lolly."

Mum snips five tall stems one by one and hands each one to me, which I place in the basket. Straightening up with a hand on her back, she wipes her brow with the other, which she then converts into a shield over her eyes and searches the meadow again for another patch of treasure. I come here often now and watch my mum knee-deep in these deep crimson blazing stars, a vacant expression on her face, standing here showing no more animation than a scarecrow, stuck and frozen in time. I will try and call out to her but the breeze is never strong enough to carry my voice.

"Wow, look at those." My eyes fall on the very pleasing sight of bright yellow flowers growing on the top of tall stiff stems. "They're beautiful, aren't they Mum?"

"Betty taught us about them last week. Do you remember?"

"Of course I do. They're cockscomb, aren't they?"

"Very good, yes they are. Do you remember what she said- sorry, what Mavis said about them?"

"She almost wet herself, Mum. She said-." I clear my throat and then put on my best stuck-up-cow voice. "'The cockscomb, also known as the celosia cristata, is perceived by many to be the most superior fresh and dried cut flower.'"

Mum laughs. "You know what that means, don't you?"

"Yeah. She is going to be well pissed off."

Mum gasps at my inappropriate language and is about to address it when I say, "Sorry I mean peed off."

Mum bites on her lip, re-considering the intended bad language lecture. Instead she hands me the clippers. "I think five long stems should do. They will look stunning next to the crimson."

"Look over there, Mum." As we walk towards the cockscomb I point in the direction of some baby's breath. "We so should get some of that."

Mum nods. "Yes, darling, and we should also get some of that pink cosmos, some of those tall daisies, a sun flower or two." Her fingers dart about the meadow. "And, definitely some of that Good Friday grass and some of those red and white gladioli'."

I put on my best Mavis voice on again. "'The gladiolus symbolises the birth flower for August and is also frequently named the sword lily, which is due to the fact that it possesses sword-shaped leaves.'"

"'Stupendous, Mavis. You are quite the flower connoisseur,'" Mum mimics Betty. "'One will find oneself unemployed if one doesn't watch out.'"

"'Not at all, Betty. My inspiration is you.'"

Gesturing to our mouths with two fingers we lean forward as if about to throw up.

After our fruitful forage, Mum and I walk the mile up the winding lane to the bus stop. "Mum?"

"Yes?"

"How come there are so many beautiful flowers in that meadow? How come it looks like a garden?"

Mum rolls her eyes. "Really, Dee," she says, half laughing and shaking her head. "For someone so intelligent, your lack of observation skills surprises me quite a lot."

"Huh?"

"Didn't you see the ruins dotted about the meadow?"

"You mean the old crumbling barns? Yeah, I saw them, but what do a handful of derelict stone barns have to do with the flowers?"

"They are not old derelict barns. That's what. They are the remains of cottages belonging to a former medieval community. It is a conservation site. The flowers are from the gardens of the cottages. It's not that well known about, a closely-guarded secret."

"It really is a secret garden."

"Yes, it really is."

"Hello, Ciara. That's a lovely dress you are wearing. I'm sure I gave one exactly the same as that to the charity shop last week. Come to think of it, didn't I see you heading in that direction on the high street yesterday?" She regards Erin over her shoulder with a smirk. "Well, waste not, want not. It's a bit tighter on you than it is on me, but you can always slim into it."

Erin's giggles filter out into the street from behind Mavis. I want to smack her in the gob. They are right on cue just as we arrive at their doorstep. Mavis's eyes draw to our basket. "What pitiful offerings have you managed to dig up this time, my dear?"

We wait for the noise like something is lodged in her throat and the hand that flies to her chest as if suffering a heart attack. Staggering backwards, she grabs the doorframe to stable herself.

"What's wrong, Mavis? You have turned a very funny colour."

"You do look a bit peculiar, Mavis."

Established around us, curious as to what the kerfuffle is, is an audience of would-be flower arrangers, all heading in the same direction as us: the community centre.

Mavis flings a finger at us. "Damn you, Ciara! Damn you and your deranged daughter!"

Slamming the door on our resounding laughter, Mavis doesn't attend the class that evening or any other evening for that matter, and she or Erin never bothers us again.

Thirty-Three

After it happened

I'm sat on the toilet seat watching them. They have filled their huge square bath, which Garth refers to as the health spa jacuzzi, half-full of lukewarm water. Together they lay Freya out on a blanket on the slate floor and tentatively undress her. Gingerly, Garth undoes the buttons of her tiny peach woollen cardigan, which my mum has knitted for them. Struggling to get a firm hold of the tiny buttons with his big clumsy fingers, I detect his stirring frustration. Garth, gently, a petrified expression cemented on his face, lifts her tiny wrinkly body with two hands. One hand is underneath her nappy-padded bottom and the other is supporting her soft hairless head. His fingers spread themselves over her back like support beams. Al coaxes her tiny flaring arms with their tiny sprawling fingers out of the sleeves of her cardigan and it falls away from her. The arms dangling down behind her like wings clamped to her back by Garth's huge-in-comparison hand.

Laying her back down softly, Garth places his hands on his knees, arching over her and smiling down in awe at his miracle baby daughter. Al reaches out a hand and begins stroking the nape of Garth's neck. The two of them, bursting with love and pride, watch her little chest rise and fall, listening to the soft, almost undetectable noise she makes whilst she sleeps.

Garth, choking at the throat with emotion, turns to Al. "Isn't she beautiful? Can you believe she is ours?"

"She is the most beautiful thing I have ever seen. Honestly, I can't believe she is ours. It's the most amazing thing. It's so unbelievable."

"Isn't it? I keep thinking I will wake up and find it's all just been a dream, a beautiful wonderful dream that in a waking moment could be snatched from us. She is just so perfect. I couldn't bear to be without her."

"She is better than perfect."

Garth laughs. "I love her so much it hurts. I understand now why people risk their lives for their children. I would die for her."

"Yes, I would."

Garth turns to Al then and cups his face in his hands. "Al, do you know something?"

"Maybe, what is it?"

"I love you so much, I feel like the luckiest man alive to have you and Freya in my life."

"Garth, I'm just as lucky and so is she, we're all lucky to have each other. I have an amazing husband and now I have an amazing daughter too and I love you both more than anything in the world."

"I hope we are a family forever. I couldn't bear to lose either of you."

"We will be, I've told you before." Al leans in and kisses Garth full on the lips, his hands resting at the sides of Garth's stomach. "You won't lose either of us.

I'm not going anywhere and neither is Freya. Everything will be okay."

I can read Garth's thoughts and he is thinking of me. He thinks of how I died at such a young age and he is paralysed with fear that the same fate might bestow Freya. What ifs, run rife like wild horses through his mind, the dread of what could happen pounding against his brain like their hooves against the earth. I want to be able to reassure him that Freya doesn't have an abrupt ending or any life-changing difficult lessons for her life written in her blueprint. Allison has chosen to experience hard physical lives in the past to bring home those lessons to help her in her healing and teaching of others here. In this life, as Freya, she has not chosen such a path; she has chosen to learn the lesson of the lucky to experience the kind of life where everything comes easily and is gold plated. Despite knowing it all, the bright and long future that awaits her, I can't reassure Garth; he will have to wait for time to unfold.

"But Dee," Garth says with watery eyes.

Al flies a finger to Garth's lips. "Hey, Shhh. Babe, Freya is not Dee. What happened to Dee is terrible but it doesn't mean it will happen to Freya."

"But no-one can guarantee."

"No. No-one ever could but scaring yourself with what might happen in the future does no good whatsoever. It will destroy you. It's not good parenting. Just enjoy being her Dad and don't think about that ever ending."

Garth kisses him and then turns his attention back to Freya. He gently pulls apart the press-studs on her baby-grow covered in tiny rag-dolls and on the matching vest underneath it. Then, in the same way as the cardigan, the two proud fathers remove both of them in a joint effort and wrap her in a warm dry towel.

"You get in first," Garth says to Al, "and then I'll hand her to you."

Al pulls his jumper over his head and tosses it onto the floor beside him and then removes his jeans and boxer shorts and climbs into the bath, sitting at one end of it cross-legged. They don't need to argue, like they did when they lived in Garth's flat, about who gets the taps in their back because the taps of this bath are in the middle, which is one of the grounds of reasoning Garth gave for bullying Al into buying the penthouse. Garth leans over the side of the bath, kneeling and holding out Freya in both arms. Al takes hold of her by the middle, lifting her out of the towel she is wrapped in and bringing her close into him, he cradles her against him. Garth undresses and climbs into the bath at the opposite end to them. I watch the love and happiness wash in their auras as Al holds Freya and Garth gently smothers her soft delicate skin in a thin layer of baby wash and then gently rinses it off with his hands by cupping and dipping them into the bath and scooping up water, gently pouring it onto her body. Every now and then her face screws up with the sensation of the water or she opens one eye and regards Garth suspiciously; sometimes she will let out a short, sharp cry, which reminds Garth and Al of a kittens meow.

"I wonder what her future will be like."

"Whatever she makes it, I suppose," Al replies to Garth's question.

"Yes, but I mean fate. I wonder what fate has in store for her."

"Fate?" Al jeers. "You have your head in the clouds sometimes, Garth. There is no such thing, life is only what you make it."

I laugh to myself. *You're wrong Al, so wrong.*

"There bloody is," Garth replies defiantly.

"Language, you have a baby now. You can't go about swearing." Al pokes fun at him again.

Garth gasps and slaps a hand over his mouth. "Whoops, I can't believe I did that."

Al laughs again. "You are so easy to reel in. Like a fish to a maggot."

"You're a twat," Garth says, instantly realising what he has said, his hand flies back up to his mouth and he gasps in horror again. "I'm so terrible. My child is going to grow up swearing like a trooper, isn't she?"

"Probably, if your potty mouth is anything to go by."

Garth dips his fingers in the water and flicks them out, spraying water at Al. It splashes into his eyes but also catches Freya in the cross-fire. In shock, her arms uncurl and shoot out, her fingers and toes flaring out wide and she lets out a piercing cry. "Shhh, Shhh,"

Garth soothes. "I'm so sorry, baby." He strokes her hairless head gently. "Daddy didn't mean it. I'm so sorry."

"You big meanie," teases Al.

"It was your fault."

"How do you figure that? I didn't ask you to flick water into the eyes of your husband and two day old baby daughter, did I?"

"Okay, I feel guilty enough about it," he says. "You don't think I've hurt her, do you? I can't have caused her any long term damage, psychologically I mean?"

Al gives a half laugh shaking his head. "As a surgeon at the top of my game I can categorically confirm that no, Garth, you have not done our daughter any permanent damage from the droplets of water that landed on her face." Al observes him for a moment. "Don't look so worried all of the time. Garth, you are going to make a fantastic dad. The best dad, she couldn't wish for better."

No, she definitely couldn't. That's why she chose him.

"Thanks, but you are forgetting something."

"What?"

"You are her dad too. You might be better than me."

"Garth, it's not a competition. We are a partnership, equally top dads."

"That's something we need to talk about you know. We should have talked about it already, I can't believe that we haven't."

"What do we need to talk about that you haven't already talked to death about, I can't imagine?"

"We haven't talked yet about what our daughter is going to call us? I can't believe I haven't brought it up sooner."

"Neither can I. it definitely wasn't on the e-mail you sent me with the attachment: a list of topics to discuss before the birth." He laughed, remembering his utter dismay at opening the three-page document. "Erm, let's see," Al brings the arm that he isn't using to cradle Freya up towards his face and places his forefinger on his chin, regarding Garth with a look of concentration. "Hmmm. Ahhh. Yes, I've got it. It wasn't easy but I have come up with something. What about 'Dad'?" he says, changing his look of concentration to one of self-importance, which of course as usual is aimed at mocking Garth.

"Ha blood-" Garth stops himself from finishing the word.

"Ha-ha," Al points an accusing finger at him. "You just can't stop yourself from swearing can you?"

"I never actually swore, though, did I?" he says, which prompts Freya to open one eye and regard him suspiciously again. They are still all oblivious to my presence on the toilet seat, laughing at the scene.

"Do you think she might be clean now?" Al asks. "It's been about twenty minutes and I don't know about you but my knackers have shrivelled like prunes."

"Ha-ha." Garth throws out an arm extended with a pointing finger. "You swore."

"Oh fuck," Al says slapping his free hand to his forehead.

In unison they both declare, "She is doomed, her..."

Al breaks off allowing Garth to continue. "Her first word is going to be a swear word, isn't it?"

"I think it might be," Al agrees.

Thirty-Four

After it happened

Passing Freya to Garth and standing up, rivulets of water rolling down his body, Al climbs out of the bath first, stepping onto the slate floor, crossing the room to the heated towel rail. Reaching for one of the white fluffy bathrobes, drawing it around him, he ties the belt at his waist. Taking Freya's hooded cream towel embroidered with a tiny teddy bear in one corner, one of the things Priya gave them in a huge basket she called a baby hamper, he returns to the side of the bath. Raising himself on his knees and holding Freya's tiny body in both hands, Garth moves her towards Al, who is extending out his arms. Garth lowers Freya into Al's towel cradle gradually and cautiously.

"Got her?" he asks urgently, locking his eyes with Al's for urgent confirmation.

"Yes, I've got her."

Falteringly, overwhelmed by apprehension, slipping his hands away from the underneath of Freya, Garth reluctantly relinquishes responsibility of her. Pulling her in close to him, Al recalls guardianship. Wrapping it around her and folding it so that it is over-lapping, as if she is a birthday present, a very precious and delicate birthday present, Garth encases Freya in her towel. Turning, Al begins to walk away, snuggling his precious bundle close to him. Garth feels the separation stabbing underneath his rib cage even though it is to be a very brief separation. Without the need for caution, he swiftly stands up causing tidal waves to crash against the sides of the bath. Following Al's wet footprints like a footpath he makes his way to the heated towel rail. Reaching for the second white fluffy bathrobe and pulling it over himself he ties it at the waist and follows Al out into the apartment lobby.

Waiting for them in the nursery, I'm sitting on the handmade rocking horse, side-saddle, in the corner of the spacious room that has two large picture windows overlooking a courtyard, which sits in front of a narrow boat-lined canal. Laying Freya down on the top of the handmade changing unit, Al steps back, allowing Garth access. Hand in hand, Al stroking his thumb over Garth's hand, they stare down at her. Everything in the nursery is handmade: the rocking chair, the changing unit, the cot, the book case, the toy box, the rocking horse, the wardrobe and chest of drawers. They are all skilfully crafted by the talented hands of a local carpenter that they randomly, or at least they think they randomly, discover on a country weekend break at a health spa they are on with Jo-Jo. It is all solid oak and decorated with carvings of bunny rabbits in various poses and in various sizes. Some gaily hopping, others are crouching in grass or berries and others munching carrots. The designs were Allison's idea. She sketched them all in her higgledy-piggledy house on the beach by the window that looked out to the sea. Then she showed me them before she became Freya. I gave the ideas, laying my hands on his shoulders, to the carpenter two days before Al and Garth 'took a wrong turn,' and 'accidentally' stumbled upon his cottage and workshop.

Allison, like her nursery furniture, chooses Jo-Jo to carry her also. When Garth and Al filter through the photographs of potential surrogates, which they print from the Internet, Allison and myself are there stood on the opposite side of the dining system, our backs to the skyline, looking out at the one behind Garth and Al. As they lay Jo-Jo's picture down on top of the pile of possibilities, we combine our strength and cause a gust of air that causes all the pictures to become airborne and flutter back down landing on the kitchen floor. Every single one of them face down except for Jo-Jo's, her teeth framed in bright red lipstick and as brilliant white as her three-storey seven-bedroomed dream house in California, dazzling their eyes. They lift her up and rest her in solitude on the dining system, staring down at her, scrutinising every inch of her face, her kind eyes locking them into an instant contract; they know instantly she is the one who will carry the egg from the donor clinic, which will be inseminated by Al. Jo-Jo falls head over heels in love with Al and Garth seconds into their afternoon tea in her orangery on her sprawling lawn when they visit her. The three of them feel it instantly: they are the perfect union to create a baby and complete Garth and Al's family. Sitting with her husband and teenage twin sons, later that day, on their terrace by the swimming pool, she describes every detail of them with fondness. As cute as teacups, she calls them.

After softly patting Freya dry, Garth takes charge of getting her ready for bed with Al assisting him by passing the things that he needs. Laughing at them, the scene reminds me of watching them at work together in surgery. Only now roles are reversed, as

Garth becomes the surgeon instructing his surgical nurse, Al. Garth asks Al to pass him something. Al passes it to Garth. Garth applies it.

"Pass me the pink baby-grow." Al passes the pink baby-grow with white hearts on it and Garth passes it back. "I didn't say anything about hearts. I want the plain pink one."

"What difference does it make?"

"It just does. It's like you asking me for a scalpel and me handing you the surgical scissors. It's just not what I asked for."

Al rolls his eyes, dutifully passes the plain pink baby-grow and wisely chooses not to say what both he and I are thinking, that a baby-grow is hardly equivalent to lifesaving surgical equipment. Both move fluidly, with precision and with fixed looks of concentration just like in the operating theatre. Then, when she is ready for bed and they have tidied up around her, they pick up the conversation from where they left it in the bath.

"We still have to decide what she is going to call us," Garth says, in a low voice, dimming the lights and flicking on the night light that instantly starts throwing star-shaped lights onto the walls and ceiling-another gift in Priya's hamper.

"I thought we had?" Al says, squeezing Garth's shoulder affectionately with one hand whilst slipping the other hand inside his robe, resting it on the flat of his stomach, Al initiates his thumb in gently stroking the hair around Garth's belly button.

"No, we haven't decided yet."

"Dad," Al blurts. "It's a no-brainer considering we are both men."

"Yes, but don't you think she might get confused? Don't you think there should be a distinguishing name for each of us?"

"You are not seriously suggesting she calls me Dad and you Mum, because I think that will cause her more confusion than calling us both Dad."

Garth sharply jabs his arm back, digging Al in the stomach with his elbow. "No, I do not want her to call me Mum. I just want to spare her the embarrassment of shouting out Dad in the supermarket and having both of us turn around and say 'Yes darling'."

Al raises his eyebrows but only I see him do this. "It's unnecessary worry again but if it makes you feel better I don't mind being Pa. It's rather masculine and strong don't you think? You can be Dad or Daddy. Daddy is better for you, I think. It's safer, softer."

"Oh charming, what does that say about me?"

Al steps away, rips open his robe and begins beating his chest with his fists. "Me Tarzan, you Jane," he says in an overtly masculine exaggerated tenor.

"You're a pig," Garth says, shooting him a glance over his shoulder. Then lowering his eyes, adds, "And, I disagree with you. I don't think you're Tarzan, at all. I think Tarzan would need a much bigger loin cloth than you."

"You've never complained before." Al pulls his robe back across him and ties it again. Closing the gap between him and Garth, he wraps his arms around Garth's waist from behind him and nibbles softly on his ear. "Daddy says that you are more nurturing. You are a more overtly loving and a more giving person than I am. You just gush it, don't you? Love, I mean. I'm more the hunter-gatherer, the gatekeeper of our daughter's purity, sniffing out rogues and dealing with them before they defile her."

"Oh no, that's the way it is going to be, isn't it?"

"What do you mean?"

"I mean you are going to have the poor girl in a chastity belt until she is thirty. Can you pass the milk?"

Al reaches for the milk beside the baby monitor, grasps it in his left hand and passes it to Garth. Garth settles down on the rocking chair with Freya, clean and warm, nestled in the nook of his cradle, contently sleepy. He takes hold of the bottle. "Lid off please."

Al places one hand over Garth's to help keep the bottle steady whilst he uses the other one to twist the lid off and then he places it on the top shelf of the bookcase next to the original and complete collection of Beatrix Potter story books, which they buy from the antiques shop next to the joinery they commission the nursery furniture from.

"Come on, darling," Garth says softly as he coaxes the teat of the tiny bottle into Freya's mouth. Her tiny lips part just enough for him to gently persuade it into her mouth and then she suckles hungrily. Sitting on the shag pile carpet, draping his arms over Garth's legs, Al takes hold of one of Freya's tiny feet in his hands and begins stroking it.

"I can't believe she is so tiny," Al says. "Perfectly formed yet so incredibly tiny. It's really amazing. I mean, I have seen plenty of babies in my line of work but when it is your own its mind blowing. Somehow I just can't comprehend that this tiny little human being will evolve and grow, continually developing her entire life."

"Yes, it is amazing. So tiny and destined to be all grown up one day. Honestly, though, I thought she would be smaller than seven pounds eleven. Jo-Jo hardly put on any weight at all," Garth replies.

"True."

"Have we decided then?"

"Decided what, Garth?"

"Have we decided on our names?"

"Garth, if you don't know either of our names by now there is nothing I can do for you, but I have friends who can."

Garth gives him a gentle kick. "You know what I mean. Are we decided that you are Pa and I'm Daddy?"

"Oh, that's what you meant. Yes, I'm agreeable to Pa and Daddy."

"Are you sure?"

"I'm sure."

"Are you sure you are sure?"

"Yes, Garth, I'm sure."

"Good. That's settled, then. Just one last thing."

"Honestly, what on earth is it now?"

"Beethoven."

"What?"

"Priya did it for us. He was in the hamper. She swears it's why her three boys always got straight A grades."

"Garth, as generally is the case you have completely lost me. Priya did what for us? Put Beethoven in a hamper? But how did he fit into it? Not to mention how she managed to resurrect him from the dead. It's like I always said: remarkable woman that Priya is."

Garth giggles. "You're a silly fool. It's a CD. It's in the baby bag down there." Garth nods his head at the brown leather bag, a present from Rita and Polly, beside the chest of drawers. "She gave it to me at the baby shower last week, in the hamper."

"And, dare I ask, what does this have to do with straight A grades?" Al having retrieved the CD from the bag, waves it in the air.

"Priya said that when she was carrying her first, a woman on her fifth pregnancy at the same antenatal class as her told her that playing classical music whilst a baby sleeps increases their intelligence. She said she did it with all three of hers. Priya, not the random woman she met at antenatal classes. And, well, you know all of them are total brain boxes."

"Actually, I think my mum said something about playing Pavarotti when I was a baby."

"Well, that proves it, then. Classical music must work if your mum played it for you. You're a total egg-head."

Al starts laughing. "Your mum obviously didn't play you any classical music when you were a baby, then. Not if you don't even know the difference between a classical musician and an opera singer."

"I hate you."

"No, you don't."

"Yes, I do."

"No, you don't."

"Yes, I do."

"Yes, you do."

"No, I don't."

"Ha-ha! Got you. Every time, every bloody time you fall for it. Hook line and bloody sinker."

"Oh shut up and put the CD on."

Thirty-Five

After it happened

When James and I choose to experience Africa, we find ourselves instantly sitting on a red blanket spread out on golden coarse grass; our imagination is our airline that travels quicker than the speed of light.

Behind us stands a single row of trees with thin trunks and bright green leaves. Behind them stretches a bumpy and uneven expanse of sand, splattered with clumps of grass. We are looking out over a huge motionless watering hole, which wildebeest drink from, hippos play in and crocodiles sleep in, all in perfect harmony like all spirit beings; no-one is under threat or in danger, there is no hierarchy, no food chain. Beyond this are acres of endless golden grassy planes, brilliant sunshine bathing them in sheer light. Giraffes saunter around, spirit beings just like James and I, picking leaves from the trees and chewing on them lazily. Hyenas, with absolutely no threat to the baby giraffes or us, roll around playfully, pinning each other to the ground in the tall grass nearby. We sit side by side, playing with a pack of lion cubs that climb and roll over us, pawing gently at our hands like human babies. They came home because of starvation after the lioness. Their mum, shortly after giving birth to them was killed by poachers. Here now, she lies out in the sun beside a tree stump, stretching and washing herself, occasionally gazing, with no air of concern, upon her young cubs playfully mauling James and me.

Instant gratification is also what happens when we choose to experience India. The sky is a sheer and cloudless blue with one perfectly rounded and intense sun burning a bright light on everything, as far as our eyes can see, as if it's all underneath a huge intense lamp, just like when we are in Africa. It all appears as a world under a dome of sunlight, like a snow globe with a casing of light instead of glass or plastic.

Congregating in huddles like families are leafy trees, crouching low. They look almost like bushes, their short trunks almost completely hidden by their overbearing canopies. James says that they remind him of people wearing huge wigs, as if intending to attend a seventies party. I laugh at his silliness but, looking at them again, I find myself agreeing.

In a valley at the bottom of one of the gently sloping hills is a wall-enclosed village. Some parts of its walls are crumbling and there are children sitting on the stray rocks, wearing white cloth gowns and turbans. Close by to them there are two billy-goat kids with their mouths fixed to the grassy ground, munching noisily. Weaving down the valley and curling around the wall is a wide south flowing twinkly silvery-blue river. Pungent smells fill the air, wafting over the horizon and through the trees, carried on the gently flowing breeze. I breathe in deeply and let the tang of fresh herbs and spices fill me: ginger, paprika, garlic, saffron, coriander, lemon grass and chilli. They are all dancing in the energy around us. I recognise them all. There is also the smell of burning wood from the many fires that burn inside the village walls; thin ribbons of smoke, lots of them, from different positions and angles inside the village stream up to the sky like delicate spiral stairways.

On a sandy track, sitting together on the back of a large grey elephant, we watch the people around us, spirit people, who once lived physical lives a long time before me or James.

The elephant, Celia, is a spirit being indigenous to India and this village we are seeing now; she lived to serve tourists, just like Saphriap, my dolphin friend. At home, in the spirit world, she desires to continue doing so to spirit people whom are tourists. They dial her up with their imagination, like James and I have done. She tells us her life in the physical was good, she enjoyed being with humans and was treated well. Her masters gave her the opportunity to breed and to keep her young with her. When she tells me this I feel my dormant sympathy for Safriap return. They feed her well and don't over work her. Her enclosure is large and well maintained.

From the south-flowing river shrill and high-pitched laughter filters out from a large group of children playing there. They are shouting to one another, splashing each other with water from the river and diving from rocks into it. Some of them swing from ropes hanging from the branches of the trees, on the riverbed, stretching out across it. Just like they do in the physical, the branches croak and creak even though the children are weightless.

I look over and connect with a young boy who is stood slightly back from the rest and looks nervous of the water. Intrigued by the stranger who has arrived in his village when he notices me, he considers me exotic.

I have never seen others like me, except my villagers.

Have you always lived together? Did you all come here at the same time?

Yes. We all lived here together, in this village, by this river, in the physical. Then, the river was very volatile. She could be very dangerous if she got angry. One day she got very angry and her belly swelled. She didn't like the rain because it bloated her. She took her anger out on my village and all of my villagers.

Is this how you came to be here?

He nods at me. *The rainfall, it kept coming and coming. My villagers, and me we prayed to it, we asked it to stop. The river, she was getting angrier and angrier with every day. One day she ruptured in anger and tore violently through our village, ripping apart our houses as if they were made of paper. They flattened and washed away to nothing.*

You must have been very frightened.

It happened suddenly. There was no time for fear. We were submerged in dense muddy water, unable to see anything. I could feel the soft small hands of my little brother and sister. I held onto them tightly. We could not scream; when we opened our mouths the angry rushing water filled us. We could feel other people, horses, goats, chickens and elephants swirling around in the water with us. I used to watch my mum swirling clothes around in the water at the riverbank to get them clean; it was the same for us. Me, my brother and sister, the animals and all the people of my village- we were the clothes swirling around in the water, being cleaned, becoming new again.

You were reborn.

Yes. When we stopped swirling and I opened my eyes everything was the same as it had been but better, much better. The river was not angry, she was gentle and calm and the rain did not bother her anymore.

The little boy turns his head towards the sound of his name being shouted by his friends, coming from the river.

I think they are shouting at you.

He smiles and nods his head then he turns to face me again. *I like you, lady. You are a very nice lady but now I must go and play with my friends. I hope you enjoy your stay. Come back soon.*

Then he runs off in the direction of his friends, his astonishingly white crisp robes flapping in the wind in his hurry to reach them. He looks back once, waves and smiles brightly and then he is gone.

Thirty-Six

After it happened

Today is the day. James enters my aura. I am stood on a finely-covered-in-grass, wafer-thin peninsular of a chalky white cliff. It juts out as far as an airport run way over the ocean. Seagulls swoop above me, ducking and diving and calling out to each other. The sweet smell of heather carries in the breeze I have commanded. On top of the cliff on the other side of the ocean, sitting on a rug of tall grass, is a sheer white lighthouse propelling a powerful far-reaching spotlight. Celia, my Indian elephant friend, is visiting and stands beside me, her trunk lolled over my shoulder like an embracing arm. We watch Saphriap soaring out of the ocean into the air and then nose-diving back into it, performing with her family like trapeze artists under the lighthouse's spotlight.

Yes, James. Today is the day.

We connect as one, our channels of thought blending into each other like the converging of two streams merging into the same river. Materialising first is a giant bamboo platform floating in the middle of the ocean, despite the impracticability of its size and weight. Saphriap and her family swim in circles around it, singing gaily, splintering the clear ocean with slaps of their fins, sending crystal sprays and droplets high into the air. Glinting gold, engraved with the sacred symbols of home, the ceremonial rostrum appears, reflecting rays of the lighthouse's spotlight, which bounce off it in shafts of light as touchable and glistening as the steel of a newly born sword. Celia disappears from beside me and reappears wearing white and gold embroidered armour on the platform standing behind the ceremonial rostrum. In a coat of gold encompassing the entirety of her robust body, the soul weaver appears sitting on top of Ceilia, a gold turban sitting on top of her rotund head, concealing her thick ebony braided hair. Chunky wooden beads are threaded around her neck, which remind me of conkers; large, lopsided and with a shiny chestnut veneer.

Floating in mid-air, in two rows, large white burning candles appear from nowhere marking out an aisle from one end of the floating bamboo platform to the ceremonial rostrum. With iridescent complexions, their souls freed and limitless like mine and James's, our friends and the family members we have here with us, appear either side of the candles; James's on the left and mine on the right. In the centre of the aisle a pale green stalk with a pink tip begins to slowly grow. It twists and turns on itself, opening up slowly and sprouting appendages. Gradually it gets bigger until eventually it is a towering tree with an ash white trunk and far-reaching branches arching over the entire platform, creating a canopy of blossom; the whole thing is unobtrusively lacquered with glitter.

Polly and Rita, wearing floor-length, off one shoulder, royal blue dresses in material as delicate as the petals of flowers emerge beside me; they are here with me now, limitless and freed souls, at home and no longer amongst the living in the physical. Only Priya and Garth of the five of us remain there now. Their hair is held up on both sides with ornate gold and diamanté clasps, there is a thin gold strap belt around their waists and glinting gold cuff bangles at their wrists. They hold my hands and we revolve in a ring-a-roses circle, throwing back our heads and laughing in carefree celebration.

James's energy withdraws from mine; he evaporates, coagulating on the platform next to Danny who had written in his blueprint that he would not survive his skiing accident like he had survived his fall into the quarry the day James and I were reunited. They both wear royal blue suits, sheer white shirts, gold waistcoats, gold cravats and a white rose buttonhole.

Instantly the clothes I had been wearing transform. I am standing in a champagne-coloured mermaid tail dress in taffeta with an open back. A train spills out behind me like a puddle of fondant icing in a circular shape, framed with ivory pearls. My hair has plaited itself curling on top of my head like a crown. Ornate pearl, diamanté and silver hair pins decorate it and a champagne-coloured thin veil falls gracefully down my back, spilling over the train of my dress. Polly stretches out her arm and hands me a bouquet of white roses.

My grandmother, my mum's mum, emerges from the sky in front of me stepping out of a cloud, as if coming through a doorway. Running her finger from one side of my neck to the other her pearl necklace, the one that my mum had placed on her neck the morning of her funeral, appears pearl by pearl in the wake of each finger stroke. Before walking back into the cloud and coming out of another one at the bamboo platform she touches each ear. From the tip of her finger develops a silver clasped pearl drop earring, which attaches to my ears.

From the pink-tinged sky flies a huge masterful and strong Pegasus. Landing in front of us and acknowledging us, he stoops down, his wings stretched out, which seem to me to be never ending. He tells us that his name is Oreo. There is a glass carriage in the shape of a domed pavilion, gilded with gold and covered in tiny lights, like a lantern, on his back. We close our eyes and instantly transfer from the cliff peninsular into the glass carriage on Oreo's back. Swiftly, we cruise smoothly through the sky, circling the large bamboo platform below us and then, with a whooshing, we descend towards it. He vanishes into thin air as quickly as he had arrived, taking Polly and Rita with him, leaving me outside the bamboo platform, which is now a dense container of light, shutting out the pink sky, the dark shimmering ocean and me. Hovering above the ocean, on the verge of the bamboo platform and a wall of light, my puddle train spills out level, like I'm stood on an invisible floating platform.

I have never seen anything look as beautiful as you look now, Dee.

Thank you, Saphriap.

Floating into the light, leaving the pink sky, the dark shimmering ocean and Saphriap behind me I arrive beside Polly and Rita on the platform and we glide towards James, passing through the trunk of the blossom tree to reach him.

We assemble on this glorious day to share in the soul entwining of these two pure-of-soul spirit people. Raising her arms up level with her shoulders, tilting her face upwards, the soul weaver closes her eyes. She towers above us all sitting on Celia's back. *When two souls are entwined they intensify each other's energy, existing in unison as one. The truss between them is infinite for all of their time on the home plain. It is a truss, which is fierce to all trespass and indissoluble to any outside force.* The soul weaver pauses, opens her eyes and looks deeply into everyone in the congregation. *The souls who are on this day to be entwined will each now make their declaration before the entwining will commence.* She closes her eyes again.

James and I turning into each other, looking into each other's souls, simultaneously make our declaration.

Let our souls be entwined for infinite time. From this time forth we exist as one, not as two. No other shall trespass upon the union we shall share. We shall forth be one soul, one entity, one pure and powerful existence.

Opening her eyes and fixing her wide eyes on us the soul weaver entwines us. *Then let it be so. Your souls are ever-more entwined.*

She raises her arms into the air and closes her eyes summoning a cyclone of blossom petals with a deep inward breath. They engulf us, swirling around us, encasing us in a petal tornado.

It is done. You are now as one. The soul weaver lifts her arms and tilts her face again.

The congregation applauds and cheers and then, they instantly melt away leaving James and I on the bamboo platform alone. We elevate high into the sky as if a huge spring has uncoiled beneath the platform launching it into space. Suddenly we find ourselves amongst the planets of the universe, travelling through space until we reach our tropical sky island. A private place where waterfalls flow backwards, the rivers run above us, the water is the colour of pink flamingos, purple horses drink from it and push-me-pull-you fish with two heads at each end swim in it; just another personalised world we dream up together where we will stay until we decide otherwise.

Thirty-Seven

After it happened

Guilt builds a very comfortable nest inside Garth when he places the receiver down on the phone beside his bed after taking Priya's 7am phone call. Through a mega phone whilst doing its morning exercises on his insides, guilt shouts, "'Thirty one and in the bin.' That's what you said and now Priya is devastated because her adulterous husband has gone, he's gone to his whore." Garth tries to tell guilt that Priya and he are now fifty-one so technically he isn't responsible for tempting fate.

Polly, Rita and I are all stood beside Priya in the hallway of her modern four-storey canal-side town house when Garth arrives and she opens the door to him. She is still in one of her full-length silk nightdresses, the previous day's make up smudged over her face and a serious case of bedhead. This is so unlike her even for this early on a Saturday morning,

"The nasty sod, I can't believe Mr Green is a two-timing swine. How long has it been going on, Priya?"

I can't believe he is still calling him Mr Green after all this time, Polly tells Rita and me.

Garth struts through the front door, thrusts a bunch of garage-purchased carnations into her hand, takes her by the other hand and strides towards the kitchen.

"I don't know," she sobs. "I had no idea. I'm fifty-one Garth, too old to start again and too young to be in the bin, no use to anyone."

At Priya's words guilt suddenly jumps out of its nest inside Garth and spears his insides. He winces. When they arrive in the kitchen Garth pulls out a chunky farmhouse pine-dining chair from under the round farmhouse style table, instructing Priya to sit on it. Polly, Rita and I gather around it too, sitting on the other chairs.

"You are not in the bin. Don't ever think like this. It's him that should be down on himself, the little weasel. Listen, I'll put these into a vase." He takes the flowers back from Priya. "And I'll stick the kettle on, then you can tell me all about it and we'll hatch a plan to take the bugger down by the balls."

"Thanks but I think I'm in need of something stronger than coffee, to be honest."

Garth, who, unnoticed by Priya, is also carrying a petrol station issue carrier bag, sits it on the kitchen side and delves in, pulling out a bottle of brandy. "Who said anything about just coffee."

"Right, here you go." He joins Priya, surrounded by the three of us, at the kitchen table and hands her a coffee laced with brandy. "It's time to stop feeling sorry for yourself now and get down to business. Tell me everything and don't leave anything out. I need every detail if I'm going to help you plan a strategy."

Priya starts from what she believes to be the beginning. "He has been very distant for years ever since our Samuel moved out. You know, less affectionate towards me, spending more time in the shed than with me, finding excuses to eat his dinner in his study whilst working instead of in here with me. Then he started working away a lot. Financial conferences at hotels, he said."

Priya sheepishly explains that she thought he was finding it hard to adjust to an empty house, that she naively hoped things would get better with time. Telling Garth all the ways she had tried using to put the spark back into their marriage including art and cookery classes for couples. She shakes her head. When it didn't work she told Garth she just accepted that it happened to all married couples who'd been married thirty years. When Garth asked why she hadn't confided in him before, she broke down with her head in her hands and said she thought he had enough on his plate with the whole Polly and Rita tragedy. Garth held her hand, kissing it lightly and looking over at Mr Tuna Rita and Polly's cat, which Priya adopted after the tragedy. He thanked her for being so considerate but reminded her that it was only the two of them now; they had to stick together.

"What has changed then, exactly?"

"I waved him off at 7a.m. yesterday morning and he said, 'I'll be home by seven.' I replied, 'I have two lovely pieces of cod, which I'll breadcrumb. I thought we could have fish and chips and share a bottle of wine. Maybe we could watch one of the old home movies of our holidays in the Dordogne with the boys?' He smiled at me, it was the first time he smiled at me like that in three years and then he kissed me on the lips. I can't even recall the last time our lips even touched."

"Then what did he say?" Garth leans his elbows on the table and rests his chin in the palms of his hands. "What happened next?"

"He said, 'I can't wait. I'll pick up a bottle of Sauvignon Blanc on the way home and I'll see you at seven.' Priya drops her head into her hands. "I'm a fool." She hits her forehead with the heel of her hand over and over. "A stupid old fool, I deserve to be abandoned for a woman half my age."

Garth raises an eyebrow, pulling her hands away from her face before she turns herself into the elephant man. "Come on Priya you are more intelligent than this. Stop blaming yourself."

Rita, Polly and I move into her aura in an attempt to calm the erratic waves around her.

"So go on, what happened? How did you find out about his whore, the dirty bugger?"

"She rang me at eight-thirty. I'd already had two gin and tonics. The fish and chips were ruined and I knew he wasn't coming home, not for supper anyway."

"She rang you?"

"Yes, she rang me."

"Why the hell did she ring you? What did you say?"

"I said, 'Hello Julie, how are you?'"

Garth has just taken a mouthful of his brandy-laced coffee, which he promptly spits back into the cup. "You know her?"

"Yes, of course I know her. You know Freya's boyfriends, don't you? In fact you know Julie."

"She is one of the boys' girlfriends?"

"She was."

"Whose?"

"Sam's in their last year of high school. You remember, she is the one I caught in his bedroom."

Garth instantly remembers the day years ago when he, Polly and Rita- whilst they were still alive- had come round for coffee. Momentarily Priya left them sitting around a half-demolished coffee cake in the kitchen. She strode into Sam's room carrying a washing basket of ironing, having no idea that due to Sam's successful phantom burglar routine he had sneaked Julie into his room. Sam was lying naked on the bed, his arms behind his head, his eyes screwed shut, groaning and moaning and thrusting his head from side to side. Julie's head of thick blonde hair bobbed up and down at his crotch. Priya didn't disturb them; the grunge music they were playing at full volume disguised the bedroom door opening, her gasp of horror and the sound of the falling laundry basket. The look of violation on her face and the laundry basket full of jumbled clothes when she returned keeps Garth regularly amused, not that he would ever confess this to Priya.

"He has been having an affair with a girl who is not only the same age as his youngest son but also gave said son his first nosh at the age of fifteen? The. Dirty. Little. Bastard."

"I wish Dee, Priya and Polly were here."

She is unmindful of our hands sitting on top of hers. *We are here.*

Garth pats her hand. "I know. I do too, all the time."

"Sorry, I don't mean that you are not good enough. You have been a gem racing over here to rescue me."

"It's not a problem," he says with a smile. "Go on anyway, what did she say, this Julie?"

"Julie said very calmly, 'Priya I think you should know something. I've been having an affair with your husband. We are in love and he is going to leave you for me and Tyler.'"

"Who is Tyler?"

"Tyler is their two-year-old son."

"You mean her son from a previous relationship?" Garth looks at her expectantly. "Priya, tell me that's what you mean."

"No. I mean their son," she says more composedly. "My husband has a two-year-old son by a woman half his age who, well, you know. I could lose everything, Garth. He earns all the money. I don't even have my own bank account. They are all joint accounts. I haven't got a bean to my name without him."

"That's job number one, then, Priya," Garth bluntly instructs her. "Let's get on the internet. We are going to take him by surprise, hit him where he's not expecting it."

Sitting in the window of the newly refurbished wine bar and restaurant, Priya gulps her large glass of chardonnay, nervously darting her eyes around the other tables trying to detect any potential members of the fraud squad undercover, and preparing to make a run for it if she does; Polly, Rita and myself cackle when we read this unhinged notion from her.

Slightly slurring and with a lopsided face, Priya is feeling the effects of Garth's alcohol remedies. "How long do you get for stealing thirty thousand pounds? Five years? Ten years? Oh gosh, Garth, we can't do ten years in prison- they'll be handing us both our bus passes with our parole papers. I wonder if they will let you come to a female prison with me on account of you being a gay?"

Garth laughs ungraciously with the lack of inhibitions. "Priya, you are being totally neurotic about this. This is what has just happened and I want you to listen to me very, very carefully because this is the last time I intend to say it. If I have to say it again I am going to beat you to death with this." He lifts up the empty Chardonnay bottle, their second one, and brandishes it at her. "Right, here it is in plain English. Your husband is a lying cheating bastard who has had the best thirty years out of you and then dumped you for a younger model who has not only had his child but has a sexual history with your youngest son. You, in the first steps to moving on and rebuilding your life, salvaging what years you have left, have opened a bank account and transferred half of your joint savings, to which you have equally contributed to for thirty years, into them. It's not stealing if it's a joint account. The end." They both take large gulps of their drinks, then Garth adds, "Plain enough for you?"

"Yes, very plain."

"Got it?"

"Yes, got it."

"Good." Garth looks at his Rolex watch. "Oh shit, we have to be back at yours in thirty minutes."

"Why?"

"Because that is when he is coming."

"Who is coming?" Priya's voice is high with terror and she sloshes wine all over the table with a slight flaring of her arms. "Garth what have you done?"

"I've told Mr Green we'll meet him back at the house."

There he goes calling him Mr Green again. It doesn't suit him trying to be young and cool.

"Garth, why on earth have you done that?"

"Because we are going to rub Deep Heat all over his-."

"No, no, no!"

"He deserves it."

"Absolutely, not. The whole embezzlement scandal I can just about cope with, if I try really hard, that is. But now you're talking about sadistic, GBH! They'll throw away the key!"

"Oh relax, silly Priya," Garth waves a hand at her, which causes him to over balance on the very tall stools they are sitting on and slip under the equally tall table they are sitting at. Once he has composed himself and is stood at the table, resting his top half on it for stability, he brandishes a finger at her. "Do you think I am really that evil?"

Priya slumps with relief. "For a moment I actually thought you were serious. If it's not him, who is it?"

"The locksmith, to change your locks, if that isn't completely obvious."

"What locksmith?"

"The one I phoned whilst you were in the loo."

Polly, Rita and I watch in amusement as they engage in a rather comical stare off, their eyes rolling around drunkenly. "Garth, it feels too extreme. He is not going to try and take the house off me."

"Priya, there is only one reason young girls go for old wrinkly men. I have seen Mr Green in the shower on that god-awful camping holiday last year. Tinned prunes are less shrivelled, if you follow my drift. It's Mr Green's money this whore wants." Garth wiggles his little finger for visual effect.

Priya screeches, which causes a blonde businessman in his early twenties, wearing an expensive shiny silvery suit, to slosh red wine down the left side of his previously gleaming white shirt. Polly rushes to calm the anger misting in his aura, placing her hands on his shoulders.

Priya taps Garth's arm. "How often exactly did you check out my husband's penis?"

"Not that often really, once or twice but I'd hardly call it a penis, babe. It was never out of pleasure; more morbid curiosity like when you rubber-neck at accidents on the motorway- you're fully aware you are going to see something gruesome and should save yourself the counselling bill but you just can't help yourself."

Priya screeches again and the poor man in the expensive suit sloshes a matching red wine stain on the right side of his shirt.

"You're terrible, Garth."

In one day, a few waves of Garth's magic wand, some invisible string pulling from three friends behind the scenes and lots of alcohol consumption and Priya's life is repositioned. Positivity for the future is beginning to familiarise itself with her. On top of the bank account and lock changes including the garage, so that Mr Green's other woman can't get her hands on the twenty-thousand-pound motor home they bought last year with Priya's redundancy pay out, Garth has also set up a profile page and photograph on several dating sites. Under strict supervision he has coerced Priya into messaging several men, who Polly,

Rita and I have already got to work on, and will be messaging her to arrange dates very soon. They have also indulged in mild sadomasochism, taking scissors to all Mr Green's suits, burning them along with his work files and papers on a bonfire in the back garden. Finally, the icing on the cake of recovery is ordering three, outrageously sexy and sleek dresses intended for when the dates start rolling in, which they will.

That night Priya dreams that Mr Green and his mistress have a row, an almighty row because she discovers there isn't as much money as she was led to believe. "The bitch has cleared you out. She's even changed the locks." She dreams of a bottle blonde, tangerine tanned woman screaming furiously, clawing at her hair and flying at Mr Green baring teeth and nails savagely. The dream ends with Mr Green standing on the street in just his shirt and underpants, looking up at the front room window of a council flat desperately trying to catch his belongings as they are hurled out of it.

Thirty-Eight

After it happened

"Have I missed anything?"

"They've just hung the bunting from the tree, James."

"This cottage really is stunning. They really are lucky you showed it to them, Dee."

"Thanks, Polly. I'm very pleased they took my advice and bought it."

"They have definitely breathed new life into the old place."

"Hang on a minute, James," Rita informs us. "We all had a hand in it."

We all laugh.

"It's definitely a beautiful home. Knocking down walls to open up original light and airy rooms, rebuilding chimney breasts to restore open fires, uncovering centuries-old beams, cast-iron fireplaces and ceiling cornices has really brought charm back," James thoughts proudly tell us. "We definitely did an excellent job, quite right, Rita."

"Every day a brand new discovery, the antique silver in the attic- 'a gift from above'- Al said."

"He didn't know he was right, though, Dee."

"No, Polly. They never do."

Polly laughs. "Garth's face of disgust at the thought of Victorians scooping out the marrow of bones and slurping it down their throats when Al explained what the set of Victoria silver marrow scoops were was hilarious."

"His disgust soon turned to delight at the auction. He seemed very pleased with the eighteen thousand pounds all the treasures in the attic earned them."

"He was indeed, James."

"We can't really blame Al for saying, 'I told you so. I bet you're glad I made you get them back out of the bin now.'"

"We can't blame him at all. They would have been lost forever if Polly hadn't brought the vision of them, in the bin, to Al's dream."

"I'm always happy to help, Rita. I love the outside of the cottage best. It really is magical. Tiny windows heavily hooded with ivy and vines. The front lawn brimming with country garden charisma, little wooden tables scattered here and there covered in candle wax."

"Cute garden gnomes hiding behind the sundials, which you guided them to in the attic, James."

"You know I like sundials, Dee."

"Don't forget the antique clock faces and mirrors, old bookcase displays of antique medicine bottles and the huge wooden chests as planting boxes. These were my ideas."

"Yes Rita, we know."

"The inside is every bit as charming as the outside, James projects into our conscious minds. It's everything you showed them it could be, Dee."

"What is happening now?" Rita diverts from the conversation

The four of us are sitting around the stretch of trestle tables in the centre of four apple trees, which have been linked together by fabric bunting. The tables are covered in a white tablecloth and will shortly be laid with plates full of sandwiches and cakes. We watch as Garth and Freya decorate the tables with a procession of different coloured helium balloons down the centre. Weighted with silver boxes, each balloon has a different letter, on the front and back of it, in glitter, spelling out, 'Happy eighteenth birthday Freya.'

"Garth is growing old gracefully, don't you think?"

Polly nods her head. "I like his slightly lined skin. It's still so soft."

Rita laughs. "Surprising of someone who has had so many tropical holidays."

"His salt and pepper hair makes him look like a charming English gentleman."

"It does, James."

"I think it would suit me too."

I nod. "I think so too, James."

Instantly James's hair turns black and becomes flecked with silver springs, just like Garth's.

"I'm glad that with age he has become more refined."

"Me too," Rita agrees. "Jeans and a white shirt certainly cannot be accused of making him look like a gothic transvestite like the mascara and skin-tight clothes he used to wear."

We all laugh together then turn our attention quickly to Freya.

"Isn't she beautiful?"

Polly is not wrong; Freya's beauty is just how Allison wrote it in her blueprint, overwhelming. Showcasing her shapely legs is a pair of white skimpy shorts. Her knees are tinged with red juice from strawberry picking with Al this morning. Clinging to her torso is a blue halter-neck top with horizontal white stripes, which Rita thinks is too tight. Materialising one around her own neck, Polly has fallen in love, with the large gold chain hanging to her bellybutton, a large gold heart pendant swinging at the bottom of it. Slightly cocked to the left, in line with a long sweeping fringe, on top of her head is a white sailor's cap, the rest of her waist long hair is knotted in line with the nape of her neck and tossed over her left shoulder.

Glancing at Freya's wrist Polly smiles brightly. "It's so lovely that Garth gives her a charm, for her charm bracelet, every birthday and labels the box, 'Lots of love Aunty Dee x.'"

"He has done ever since I guided him to do so for her first birthday. He'll never stop."

"You would never guess Garth is not Freya's biological parent, would you?"

"No, Polly, you wouldn't."

"They don't look alike."

Everyone but Rita laughs.

"No Rita," I state flatly. "His nature, personality, mannerisms and his vivacity for life and people has transferred to her as a result of his nurturing."

"Her habit of biting down on her lip and playing with her ear whenever she contemplates something comes from him too, doesn't it, Dee?"

I nod at Polly and smile. Rita is about to comment that Freya's intelligence and study ethic are inherited from Al, his smile and height too, when Freya and Garth draw us in with a conversation of their own.

"I still think I'm too old for a tea party. I haven't had one since I was nine."

"Nonsense. You are never too old for a tea party."

"I would have preferred to celebrate by going to-."

Garth shoots her a disdainful look. "There is plenty of time for pubs and clubs. You wouldn't deny me making a fuss of you on your eighteenth birthday, would you?"

"I never mentioned the pu-."

"I read your mind. Fathers are good at this."

"But-."

"No buts, sweet pea. It's all arranged, everybody is coming. We can't turn Jo-Jo away from the door when she has come all the way from California, just because you want to go to the pub can we?"

"I never said anything about the pub."

Garth isn't listening and presses on. "She gave life to you. The poor thing went through hell on the cold floor of that DIY store. We both did." He looks down at his hands. "My poor fingers have never been the same since."

"So you keep reminding me every time I want to do something you don't agree with. You know, anytime I show free will or an independent mind. And," she laughs, walking towards him, "I never said anything about the pub. Of course I want to be here with you and Pa and everyone else. I am just pointing out that it is very reminiscent of when I was nine years old. That's all." She shrugs and then places a hand on each of his shoulders, kissing his forehead.

"There is no point arguing with him." Al comes into the garden carrying a huge cake; each of the two tiers smothered in chocolate and piled high with deep red juicy strawberries. "The birthday party is really for him because he's in denial about his age and doesn't want to acknowledge you are eighteen."

"Al, stop!"

This is meant to safeguard the cake but it backfires. Wobbling, the cake has an uncertain fate as Al staggers backwards, startled by Garth's sudden outburst. We all watch him dance around trying to regain balance. Garth's eyes are firmly screwed shut, covered by his hands and Freya makes dramatic fear-loaded sound effects and jerky body movements.

"Shall we, Polly?"

"I think we should, Rita."

They disappear from around the table with James and me and reappear behind Al with their hands on his shoulders, steadying him, thwarting an upside-down-on-the-decking fate for the cake. Garth opens his eyes one at a time, finding Freya with an expression of relief and Al frozen to the spot with an expression of terror, the cake in one piece firmly balanced in the palms of both hands.

"Don't move an inch," Garth says in a tense tone. Al opens his mouth and Garth flies a hand in the air. "Shhh! Don't even speak. Stay completely still."

Garth is scared that the vibrations of moving too quickly or too heavily might overturn the cake's balance, so he tiptoes cautiously towards Al. When he is in front of him he slowly reaches out with both hands and firmly takes hold of the base.

"Slowly step away from the cake."

Al lets his hands fall from under the cake base and backs off slowly.

"Get the doors."

Slowly Garth makes his way inside calling out behind him, without twisting around even an inch, "Fridge door."

Al, with a quick hop and a skip, makes his way across the quarry tiled floor, original tiles each one taking Garth and him an hour to scrub clean and restore when they moved in, arriving at their sixties remake fridge ahead of Garth. Several bottles of champagne rattle with the judder of the door being wrenched open. Easing his way over it's as if Garth is walking a tight rope. He gently crouches low. When he reaches the fridge, he places the cake on the middle shelf. Gently closing the door, he rises and turns around pressing his back against the door; he spreads his arms across it. Closing his eyes he breathes a sigh of relief. Al begins to tiptoe backwards towards the door.

Without opening his eyes Garth senses his retreat. "Where on earth do you think you are going? I'm not done with you yet. You come back here right now."

Al turns and runs out into the garden. Garth chases him, leaps from the balls of his feet when he is close enough and flies at his back, wrapping his arms around his neck and his legs around his waist. Al leans forward, buckling under Garth's weight. Running with the awkwardness of an ostrich, his gangly legs banding about clumsily, Freya steps out of their path, her dainty hand loosely over her mouth and nose she giggles at her parents' childish antics. Suddenly Al trips on a rock and darts forward, we all laugh at the panic registering on both of their faces. Al doubles over, nose-diving to the ground. Garth slides head first off his back as if it is a slide. The top of his head hits the grass and his body backflips over. He lays out flat on the lawn. Swiftly he covers his eyes and cries out in panic. Al hurtles forwards towards him, unable to put the brakes on himself; he lands on top of Garth.

In the commotion none of us hear the slam of car doors, the crunching of gravel or the sound of the gate latch. The congregation of guests, with armfuls of gifts wrapped in brightly coloured paper and tied with ribbons, watch in silence until Jo-Jo at the forefront of the congregation, slightly ahead of Priya, speaks. "Awww, you guys. You're as cute as tea cups." She throws out her arms, her two adult sons pulling back their own children; fearful they are about to get walloped in the face by their grandmother. "Come here, all of you, and give the surrogate a great big juicy hug."

Soon the garden is filled with sounds of popping champagne corks, cheerful chatter and lots of laughter: mine, James's Rita's and Polly's being the loudest but of course the only laughter that is unheard. Just before we leave I go to Freya and whisper in her ear, *Happy eighteenth birthday, darling. I'm sorry you don't remember meeting me as Allison on the higher plain. We will meet again one day, though, when you come back.*

Thirty-Nine

After it happened

James's mum, unimportant and fragile-looking, wearing a blue rain coat, a transparent plastic rain cover tied like a scarf over her head and tan coloured tights, has been studying the poster intently.

Emotion and logic are battling, each one desperate to defeat the other; the firing of their pistols gives her a headache. Emotion plays on a tiny fragment of hope, pleading with it to force her to push the heavy stained glass door open and go in. Logic cleverly acts out a role-play, echoing her husband. 'It is a ridiculous idea. No good will come of it.' Edging forward slightly, she throws her shoulders back, holds her head up high determined to go in. Triumphing over logic, emotion is preparing for its victory dance. Logic senses defeat and draws itself up to its full height, relentlessly firing bullets of doubt at emotion, blowing holes into it. Instantly, her foot draws back, her shoulders slouch and her head bows.

This morning she served her husband boiled eggs and toast, longing as always for the days of serving two plates of boiled eggs, tight pains wrung out her insides like a wet rag. "It's nonsense." He regarded the boiled eggs with distain; she noticed and wondered if the distain was for her, for the eggs or for both. "Its mumbo bloody jumbo, Frieda." Sensitivity abandoned him. "He's gone. Nothing and no-one can ever bring him back," he said.

Malice seized its opportunity. "There is no love like a mother's love. You couldn't possibly feel the same pain that I'm feeling. You didn't love him, like I did."

The stool abruptly scraping across the tiled floor, the front door slamming loudly and the irate roar of his car engine spoke his anger for him.

"Popcorn?"

"Garth, this is not the cinema. Put it away, right now."

"Are snacks not allowed at séances, then?"

"No, they are not and I keep telling you it is not a séance."

"If it's not a séance, what is it? Dee would think me bringing popcorn was a hoot."

"Dee's not here."

Mum, yes I am.

"If Dee is not here why are we here? I thought the general idea of coming to a séance was to talk to Dee?"

"She will be here when the medium summons her."

"You didn't answer my question."

"What question?"

"If it's not a séance, what is it exactly?"

"It's a psychic night. Simon Thomas is a psychic medium."

"What's one of those when it's out of bed?"

"He can make contact with the dead."

"He talks to the dead?"

"Yes."

Garth grins. "And summons them here to talk to us."

"Yes."

"So the key elements of this evening are a psychic?"

"Yes."

"Who speaks to the dead?"

"Yes." My mum twists round in her chair and hisses, "What is your point, Garth?"

"It's a séance, that's my point, you daft bat."

My mum is about to retort when the meek shaky voice redirects her. "Excuse me, I'm so sorry to interrupt. Is it okay if I sit with you?"

Garth and my mum both look up at the frail woman her tan tights crinkled at her calves simultaneously thinking the same thing: is this throwback one of the dead?

Garth gestures at the seat on the other side of him. "Of course it is."

Shimmying sideways in the gap between Garth's and my mum's knees and the chairs in front of them, she eventually gets to the seat, a little pink cheeked, and sits beside Garth.

"Popcorn?" Garth asks James's mum.

She waves a hand. "No, thank you, dear."

"Suit yourself, I was just being polite."

"Oh sorry, dear. I didn't mean to offend you."

My mum reaches out and clips Garth's ear with the back of her hand.

"Owww," he cries, rubbing his ear. "I think I'm a bit old for a clip around the earhole."

"You are never too old," she says looking, at him intently, exactly like she used to look at me whenever I did something wrong. Tearing her glare away it softens with kindly eyes. "Ignore him, love. He likes to wind people up."

Shabby-looking, heavy purple curtains made from velvet draw back to reveal a scuffed parquet stage. Frieda instantly recognises him from the poster. She stares at the tall, gaunt man standing in the middle of the stage. His arms are spread out like the Angel of the North and he is drawing breath in and out deeply through his nose. "Good evening, ladies and gentlemen I am your clairvoyant for this evening, Simon Thomas. I will be joining the two worlds together, the spiritual and the physical to bring you messages of love and hope from loved ones in the unseen world."

How theatrical, Garth thinks.

"In just a few moments my guides will reunite you with your loved ones."

Poignantly, with an air of nostalgia and a pensive expression, he draws breath deeply and becomes statuesque again. Garth leans towards my mum and whispers. "What's he going to say next? 'Is there anybody out there?'"

My mum rolls her eyes and ignores him.

"Yes. They are all coming through to me now. There are so many spirit people wanting to connect. You are all loved dearly." He opens his eyes. "I have a Mary, or a Mavis. Maybe it's a Margaret?"

Garth leans towards my mum again. "You have got to be kidding. Talk about three chances?"

"Can anyone take this?"

Several hands rise into the air. Garth leans into my mum again. "That figures."

"No." Simon puts a finger behind his ear as if straining to hear. "She's not Mavis or Margaret, she's Mary. Come on, sweetheart, tell me again." He pauses and listens. "She is coming through stronger now. A lovely woman, very family orientated. She is wearing a tweed jacket and pork pie hat." He points at a woman in the congregation. "She is placing a pot of homemade gooseberry jam on your knee. It's in a small round jar with white fabric covering the top and secured with a green ribbon tied in a bow. Do you understand this?"

"Oooooooo," she fervently replies, her eyeballs bulging in curiosity, stretching the edges of their sockets. "That's my Aunty Mary. She wore tweed and pork pie hats all of the time. She was a journalist for Agriculture and Horticulture. Her gooseberry jam was amazing. It's my favourite."

"Okay my love, I would like to work with you. Is this okay?"

She nods emphatically. "Yes."

Garth thinks that if she nods anymore her head will dislodge from her neck and roll under the chair in front of her. He gives a little giggle at the image. Simon looks wistful and gazes into an empty space. He laughs to himself. "She has quite a sense of humour, your Aunt Mary."

The woman's face glazes with a layer of cheerful nostalgia. "She definitely did." Simon continues the reading by giving the woman an accurate memory of falling off a bolting pony at Mary's livery stables as a child, an accurate song that Mary used to sing to her and the accurate month in which Mary passed over including the fact she passed of a brain tumour at fifty seven. "I'm going to leave Mary's love with you. I have got something of a queue here. Is that okay for you, my love?"

Awe and gratitude roll around in her eyes. "Yes. Thank you so much."

"You are welcome."

"It's a fix," Garth tells my mum.

Garth, no it's not. Just wait for your turn.

From the glass standing on a table beside him, Simon takes a drink of water and surveys all of us in the audience again, thoughtfully considering his next move before he continues delivering messages.

Garth flicks his eyes at the Rolex watch on his wrist, last year's birthday present from Al; he can't believe how quickly forty-five minutes have passed. Simon has now given lots of messages including messages from a greyhound named Sausage Stew telling her owner that she is racing again. A message from a woman to reassure her sister that the baby her daughter miscarried last week arrived safely. A message from a man to his wife, to tell her it is time she cleared out his wardrobe but not to get rid of his leather jacket and motorbike helmet, as she must keep them for their grandson Vinnie.

Frieda starts rising from her seat.

Simon points towards her. "James says stay."

Frieda freezes, looking positively petrified, crippled by the spotlight and wanting more than anything to dart out of its fierce glare; she has nowhere to go and everyone's eyes burn into her expectantly.

Garth sits on the edge of his seat looking back and forth from Frieda to Simon and back again; he reaches for his popcorn and eagle-eyes them whilst shovelling handfuls of popcorn into his mouth.

"J-J-J. James is my-my-my-."

I'm her son, I drowned and I have a daughter called Lucy.

Simon clears his throat. "He is your son, he drowned and he has a daughter called Lucy."

Frieda drops back into her seat.

Tell her I still love boiled eggs. Tell her I'm with her all the time, Dad is wrong.

"He says his Dad is wrong, he is with you all the time."

You left the eggs out.

"Okay please be patient, James." Simon redirects his focus from James back to Frieda, "He still loves boiled eggs."

Through heavy sobs, Frieda snorts a sort of laugh. James gives Simon some more information, which he relays to Frieda. "James wants you to know that he is with his soul mate. He would like to introduce you to her." Simon breaks off, listens patiently to what James tells him pulling a surprised face by my sudden appearance beside him. "This is a new scenario for me. Can anyone take a young woman, who says her passing is her own fault?" A lump forms simultaneously in my mum's and Garth's throats and they look at each other in bewilderment, hope and fear coiling internally. "She is in her early twenties and she comes through with James, wearing a nurse's uniform. She says that she and James have guided both of their families here to unite them. She and James feel you can help each other."

Mum raises her hand. "I think she is my daughter."

I'm Dee.

"Dee." Simon states confidently.

"Yes."

"Then I'm with you, can I work with you?"

Breathlessly, Mum answers him. "Yes. Yes, you can."

"Dee and James come together, they are a pair."

"I don't understand." Frieda and my mum look at Garth. "They didn't know each other." Flitting his head back and forth between Frieda and my mum, he clarifies. "We don't know each other."

James and I feed Simon the information, everyone in the congregation silently observes Simon's musing. "Yes, I understand," he repeats, increasing everyone's curiosity. "Dee and James passed in the same year. It was meant to be that way. They are eternal soul mates, they are happy and in love."

There are lots of puzzled faces. The man who received a message from his greyhound raises his hand. "You're not seriously suggesting that a ghost can fall in love with another ghost, are you?"

"Not ghosts, sir; spirit people. And it is possible. The spirit world is a mirror of our world, only much more wonderful. Spirit people have the ability to form relationships or reunite old relationships."

"Are they happy?"

Simon looks at me for an answer to my mum's question. *Yes, we are. We are very happy.*

Simon relays this and the congregation resound with collective- 'oohs' and 'aahs'.

"I just don't buy it," Garth says. "I was her best friend I'd know if she was still around us. I'd sense her happiness. I just don't buy it, it goes against science."

All eyes are on Simon, scrutinising him as if Garth has just set him a test.

Simon turns to me. "He needs more proof." The congregation watch as Simon listens to me noticing his responsive body language. "She wants you to know that her fish are with her. I understand you had a helping hand in their journey to the other side."

Garth throws a hand to his mouth and gasps; there is no way, Garth recognises, that Simon can know the fish story unless I have told him it.

"I don't understand this," Simon says. "But I am told it will have significant meaning to you. Dee has just said, 'Fish and Y-fronts don't really mix.'"

The congregation exchanges looks of puzzlement before erupting into unanimous laughter. The tears explode from Garth, my mum and Frieda too and the three of them hug and cry all other each over. It's the start of a lifelong friendship; just as myself and James intended.

Forty

After it happened

Freya passes through the open french windows of the country manor house leading from the function hall they are currently viewing. She is feeling suffocated. Waddling onto the white stone terrace, which is huge and almost the same size as the hall itself, James and I follow her. Polly and Rita stay inside.

Permeating out behind her, following her like the scent of flowers carried on a gentle breeze is Garth's voice. Without taking breaths he is barraging the event organiser, a young woman with blonde spiky hair and half-moon rimless glasses, with information. As she walks, the airy floor-length poppy red skirt, which she is wearing swishes against the flesh of her legs in the light breeze. One last backwards glance and she sees that the three men she loves the most in the world and Sarah, the event's organiser, are all standing in the same arrangement as she left them in like mantel piece ornaments. Sarah is holding her clip board with one hand, the bottom of it pressed against her stomach for stability as her other hand furiously scribbles down Garth's dictations and demands. Garth is stood in front of her with his hands on his hips, fervently talking away without a moment's consideration for anyone else in the room; Al is stood beside him with his arms crossing his chest and with a thoroughly bored expression on his face; he is completely surplus to requirements, unable to penetrate Garth's vocal torrent and contribute an opinion. Andy is looking around desperately trying to locate Freya who has abandoned him, scuffing the parquet dance floor area they are all stood on with the toe of his trainer. The three men form a semi-circular shape around Sarah, like a theatre audience.

Shaking her head and turning her face away from them, Freya redirects her attention forward and continues walking, sauntering past the terrace furniture, which is in clusters. High-backed chairs, in dark brown rattan with chocolate cushions, around square rattan tables topped with glass and all of them shaded underneath a huge chocolate parasol, which is held up by a thick dark wood pole with brass fittings. Once she passes the furniture she weaves her way around the huge stone urns over-spilling with brightly coloured and sweet smelling flowers, the sound of buzzing coming from them. She continues on, giving the Greek statues of half-naked men and women a wide berth for fear of bumping into them and snapping off a protruding body part. James and I exchange smirks as we both register that her mind compares the terrace to an obstacle course that leads her to ask herself if it is safe for Garth to be let loose out here on his own fuelled with champagne when it comes to the day of the event they are planning.

The three of us, Freya, James and I arrive at the edge of the terrace, stopping at the top of a huge stone staircase flaring out like a fan, descending down to the lawn. A huge stone lion sitting on its hind legs guards the terrace from unwelcome ascenders at either side of the staircase. Two huge urns overflowing with flowers sitting either side of the bottom welcome those descending the staircase to the beautiful lawns and gardens. Both the lions and the urns have witnessed many visitors, friends and foes, spanning over many centuries. Sometimes these friends or foes come back even after time has forgotten them. Freya, gazing at the far-stretching light-green-dark-green banded lawn drinks it in. She wonders to herself how many young lords and ladies have swum in the huge fountained lake in the centre of the lawn that, like a mirror, reflects the image of the manor house in all its grandeur, every spectacular architectural triumph replicated in the waters still surface. Something draws her attention to the left of the lake and as she turns her head, she wonders how many young lords and ladies have run naked through the hedgerow maze her eyes feast on. She chuckles, as James and I do, at the kinkiness of her thoughts as in her mind a collection of pink pert buttocks disappear into the maze; she is ignorant, like so many people in the physical world this happens to, to the fact that briefly she has activated a generally deactivated sixth sense and connected with historical souls attached to the energy that swirls around her.

The manor house listens to her thoughts. Stirring, the energy of the manor house begins searching through the shelves of its memories like books in a library. Although she cannot see it, her connection lost by her inability to recognise and exercise it, the energy of the manor house responds to her inquisitiveness. James and I watch a group of four superficially spritely young men swim to the edge of the fountained pond. They all look to be around the same age. As James and I ponder this we are granted the confirmation in our minds that they are an even split of seventeen and eighteen. They seem carefree, laughing and splashing, but this is far from the truth. The horrors that they have seen, the horrors that they have experienced grow and spread rapidly within them; unwelcome spoilers of beauty like ugly weeds in a beautiful garden. This is not a memory that the manor house considers one of its favourites; the memory makes the manor house's energy despondent; these four men are not examples of the privileged young lords it has known. The men clamber out of the pond and race competitively towards the maze. Two of them struggle to balance on their feet because of their missing toes, maliciously claimed as war trophies by the cold-hearted trenches. Another one winces slightly as he runs, the stinging of the mustard gas burns on the back of his body reawakening now that he is out of the water. Once they disappear into the hedgerow maze their laughter dies like they have seen many of their friends die.

Flattening down the back of her skirt, she lowers herself into a sitting position on the top step, putting her hands on her robust stomach and resting her sandaled feet on the step below her. Searching far and wide, her gaze is hungry. It finally rests on the church spire towering above the thatched roofs of the village beyond the lawn. In just a few short months' time, in this church the most important event of hers and Andy's lives will be taking place before they celebrate it here. Closing her eyes against the overwhelming fear this recognition brings with it, she brings her fingers up to her temples and begins massaging.

Rapidly, her thoughts turn back to skinny-dipping lords and ladies. She thinks of herself and Andy and all the skinny-dipping they have done. She recalls all the places they have done it in with a private smile. Far flung places where the ocean was as warm and frothy as a luxury bubble bath. Closing her eyes, she recalls the crash and splash of the waves, indistinguishable from the sky, rushing forward. She recalls the sensation of the wet sand squishing between her toes as she runs away from Andy and his splashing water at her. James and I can see the memories forming as pictures in her mind. The sky and the sea are blended together, appearing to be shimmering dark blue obis. The full moon illuminating and glowing, catching the naked skin of their bodies and making them blaze with radiance. The sound of her giggles, as Andy catches up to her and swings her back into the sea by the waist, burst out in our heads.

We, Freya and I, begin to relive the very first time we saw him. On all fours she claws her way to the top of Ayres Rock, its rust rubbing off on her skin, huffing and puffing with strands of her hair clinging with sweat to her face. She doesn't even have the energy to wipe them away from her mouth and eyes. She manages to balance on two feet, winching herself to half her normal height, bending over with her hands on her knees supporting herself. Gasping and wheezing she desperately tries to regain her normal breathing pattern. She casts a fleeting glance behind her; registering the pain that movement causes her. She can just about see the heads and bums of Ellen and Helen, contemporaries in the harsh world of junior doctoring, ascending the rock a lengthy stretch behind her. Reaching for her water canister that is strapped to her waist, she eases herself up to her full height and as she takes a gulp of water, her wilfully wondering eyes rest on him. He is stood on the edge of Ayres Rock using binoculars to extend his view of the rust-coloured emptiness that never ends, making enthusiastic and embellished noises to suggest he is blown away by the view.

"Wow, this is awesome! You can see for miles up here. This must be what it feels like to be a bird," he laughs. He is stood with the tip of his toes almost overhanging the edge, looking back at his mates who are metres away from him and clinging to each other. Standing beside them, I read from their thoughts that they are scared of becoming separated. They fear being carried right over the edge by a gust of precipitous wind, which is ludicrous because the air is stagnant and thick.

"You pussycats," he calls.

They all shake their heads at him and one calls back, "You won't be saying that when that Concorde of a nose of yours is inverted into your skull when you take a nose-dive and hit the bottom, mate."

"I'm a dare devil," he declares in a loud and bold voice.

"Daft devil, more like," another one of the four men huddled together calls out.

Freya finds herself listening to their conversation, unable to resist against the urge to paste her mouth across her face in a grin. He has a strong voice and a cheeky smile, which shows itself after he speaks, book-ended by deep dimples.

Forty-One

After it happened

His smooth charcoal hair topples in curls to his shoulders and a few random strands are braided and beaded, which she recognises as a souvenir from Indonesia. She had some too until the ocean of Bondi Beach claimed them. His face, I discover she is thinking with a private inward laugh, has obviously not seen a razor in all of the time that he has been travelling. Wearing jeans clinging to and cut off just below his thighs and teemed with a red vest, he is bizarrely co-ordinated with Freya's clothing colour scheme. Suddenly she hears the sound of her own voice, inside her own head, shouting out 'snap' like she would do as a little girl at the top of her voice every time she saw something that vaguely matched. It was a trait that drove Garth to the brink of a nervous breakdown; she'd be sat in the shopping trolley whilst he read the back of a product and she'd see another little girl in another trolley and shout out 'snap', causing him to lurch out of his own skin, throwing the product into the air, usually a liquid in a plastic bottle, which would somersault and then explode on impact on the floor.

Uncharacteristically, normally a stickler for subtleness and dignity, her eyes feed almost to the point of indigestion on the muscles of his upper arms and calves. Another private thought darts through her mind; she thinks it is no wonder he doesn't look encroached upon by the hefty rucksack he is carrying on his back, which she also tells herself looks, by the lack of cargo his mates are carrying, to be five men's worth of supplies. Resting her eyes on his calf muscle she hears 'snap' scream out inside her head again noticing the bandage that indicates his moped exhaust burn, like hers a Kho Samui tattoo, a souvenir from time spent in Thailand.

His metallic grey-framed visor sunshades are propped on top of his head to make way for the binoculars, which means she can see his astonishingly beautiful eyes, which grip her and refuse to release her. She considers how luminously green they are. Instantly she is sitting on the luminous pasture of The Green Lagoon in British Columbia, Canada, where she and the girls camped at the beginning of their worldwide exploration. If he had been with her she would have looked at the pasture and then at his eyes and shouted 'snap.'

He is about to shout something to his mates when his gaze wonders just beyond where they stand and he catches a glimpse of Freya. Andy realises, I read from his mind, that Freya is staring at him. She realises he is reading her like a book and that he knows it's a slushy love story. She is grateful to her already crimson complexion, the heat and the extreme workout the ascent up Ayres Rock has so generously gifted to her, because it masks her mortification that he has so easily perceived her feelings towards him. I read from him, his recognition of her beauty; a treasure all of the exquisite places he has visited recently have failed to unearth in comparison. I smile at the harmonisation of his mutual magnetism towards her eyes as she had had for his. He finds them as equally timeless as he found Tibet, and strangely, just as spiritual. Somehow he processes that they appear far wiser than her years, he sees their history is older than Freya's years and he finds this alluring.

"Do you see something you like?" He asks immodestly. "Because if you do, I don't come cheap."

For a moment Freya looks bashfully at her feet but only for a split second before fixing his eye again remembering what Garth has always taught her about never shying away from whatever or whomever she wants to achieve. Laughter bursts out of her and she doubles over, clutching her stomach. When she has regained herself, she speaks. "No it's quite all right, thank you. I hadn't meant to wander into the cheese aisle. I must have got lost. A big lump of cheese isn't on my shopping list today."

His four travel companions, still all clutching each other, unlike Freya's spontaneous outburst, intentionally burst into over exaggerated laughter. Rubbing salt into his wounds with a few high fives with big loud slaps of the palms of their hands, keeping one hand firmly gripped on another person to maintain anchorage. "Crashed and burned," one of them calls out.

"Hit and run," another one pipes up. "Wounded, much?"

Still grinning cockily, Andy says, "Eject, eject, mayday, mayday." He presses an imaginary eject button in the centre of his chest. He makes the whistling sound of a doomed plane nose-diving through the sky, followed by, "Boom!" and accompanying hand gestures to signify an explosion. Andy comically adds, "It's a good job I have my old faithful and trusty parachute with me." He taps the back of his rucksack and smiles.

Freya likes him; tall, strong men equipped with a sense of humour are exactly her type. Of course I knew this when I gave him the idea of staying an extra night in Australia so that his last day, the day of this memory, is Freya's first day; I can't take all the credit, though; I was merely carrying out Allison's instructions as they are word for word in her blueprint.

Freya makes an instant decision to play along; Garth's confidence and flare for theatrics is something his brush has painted her in a thick coating of, which complements the biology she has inherited from Al and of course the added additions that Allison scripted.

"Oh my, oh my," she cries in embellished damsel-in-distress overtones. "My plane is on fire. Whatever shall I do? I forgot to wear my parachute. I will surly die unless I'm rescued by a big strong handsome man who has a parachute and happens to be falling through the sky at this precise moment." She looks bereft with a hand at her forehead, arching her body backwards.

Andy's mates observe with their bottom jaws resting on the rusty top of Ayres Rock.

In a deep hero–like voice Andy booms, "Why, fair maiden, this is your lucky day." He clenches his fists and pulls them into his stomach causing his bicep and shoulder muscles to bulge and become riddled with thick veins. "Here's one big strong rescuer at your service."

"Oh, my hero!" she says dreamily, almost completely submerged in her role now. "Will you save me?"

"I sure will, fair maiden." He flies out his hand. "Take my hand and hold on tight. It's a long way down."

She steps forward and takes his hand, registering instantly how strong and firm his grip is. He gives a gentle tug and she is pulled forward awkwardly, stumbling over her balance. Finding one side of her head pressed up against his thick concrete torso, without thinking and in the heat of the moment, as if their role play has become a reality and they really are falling through the sky, she slides her hands over the ripples of his torso and around his neck. Holding on tight, she presses herself into him. As if they are both wearing Velcro, they connect at every inch of their forms.

"What the heck is going on?" Ellen demands. "Is this why you raced ahead, to bag all the fit men for yourself?"

She is ignored; Freya is lost in Andy and their enactment.

"What happens now?" she whispers in her normal voice. She is out of character now and so feeling the pinch of vulnerability is less inclined to release her hold on Andy, not that she even knows that this is his name at this point.

"We wait until we land safely and then you kiss me in gratitude for saving your life," he whispers back, craning his head down so that she feels his words rest on the top of her head. "Then I carry you off into the sunset, we live happily ever after and have ten sons, of course."

"Okay," she whispers into his chest. "How long will it take us to land?"

"It will be a while yet. Keep holding on."

"Oh, I intend to."

They have fallen in love at first sight. They, as Allison wrote it in Freya's blueprint, will have a long and wonderful life together, and will never fall out of love.

All three of us return from reliving the memory of the first time Freya and Andy met. Freya's thoughts briefly consider whether she regrets any of the choices she has made. She asks herself if she regrets leaving getting married so late. She tells herself that she never thought as a teenager that she would be thirty-three when she got married. She reminds herself that the years after meeting Andy sprinted by in the blink of an eye. They were twenty-three and stood on the top of Ayres Rock, falling in love. Then they were twenty-five and signing up to the forces, her as a medic and him as a pilot. The next she knew, several countries and years later they are back in the UK settling into countryside living and here now planning this elaborate event to pacify her daddy. Her thoughts tell us, James, and me that she doesn't regret a thing and would not change a single detail. Of course James and I know every single detail was never hers to change.

Forty-Two

After it happened

"So the cake will go..." Garth wanders into an expanse of the room on the far right hand side, walking between three sets of pillars. He stops in front of a huge semi-circular window overlooking the fields and moors to the side elevation of the estate. "Here," he clarifies, stretching out his arms and swivelling himself around on his heels. He beams at the other three people in the room who are stood in the middle of it. "I want it to go on one table, which will be covered in a white tablecloth, which will be covered with rose petals."

"How many tiers does the cake have?" Sarah asks not looking up from her scribbling hand.

"No tiers, just three variations of size. All iced in sheer white and then decorated with pink marzipan rose buds, and they will have pink ribbons around them."

"Sounds lovely," she says.

"It should be for nine hundred quid," Al chips in.

Andy shoots him an apologetic look, which Al returns with a comforting look. The look tells Andy that Al doesn't hold him responsible for any of this. Garth, observing Al's look meticulously, realises this and shoots a look of his own at Al. This look tells Al that Garth knows he is insinuating that he is in the wrong. Al in many private conversations has told Garth that he thinks he is going over the top and being too lavish. Al has reminded Garth often enough about the amount of money that he spent on their wedding, years earlier before they had Freya, and Al has tried to get Garth to see that he's being unfair thrusting all of this extravagance onto Freya and Andy.

Al feeling Garth's eyes penetrating him re-directs his own eyes from Andy and they meet Garth's. Briefly they engage in a determined stare-off. Each of them demands with their eyes that the other person submits.

Garth realising Al is not going to apologise for the look he gave Andy, rolls his eyes and transfers them from Al back onto Sarah. He presses on. "I would like them to be arranged in size order," he repeats. "Then over here on this side of the cake…" he walks into the space to emphasise where he means. "I would like the chocolate fountain."

"That is tiered," Al adds, looking at Sarah and feeling sorry for her poor wrist. "Five of them," he adds. "It's almost as tall as me," he laughs.

"Then here…" Garth leaps, in grasshopper fashion, to the other side of the cake table- or where it will be. "Should be the champagne cocktail fountain."

"That," Al says dryly, "also has five tiers and stands as tall as me."

"It's a good job this hall is so big," Sarah says, looking at Andy for confirmation. He gives her a wiry uncomfortable smile back.

Andy still, like Freya, looks exactly the same physically as the day they met. She is still tall and slender, with all the right curves in all the right places and with a sheet of glossy hair all the way down her back. Her complexion and skin is still rosy, youthful and supple. Andy is still toned and strong, he is still slightly unshaven and despite the silver threads, which are an obvious contrast against the vastly charcoal curls of his hair, there are no evident traces of age. His hair is shorter now and only reaches the bottom of his earlobes and his curls are more conservative, tucked behind his ears and the Bali braids have gone. Instead of contact lenses, which he was wearing the day they met, he now wears silver-rimmed square-framed glasses, which are very fitting of a physics and mathematics master of a prestigious country private school.

Al looks at him. "If this isn't what you want, speak out."

Andy shakes his head and in an unreadable way says, "Its fine, honestly. Whatever Garth and Freya want is fine by me. I just want them to be happy."

Polly and Rita read his thoughts and detect that he really doesn't mind. He doesn't feel railroaded by Garth's overbearing father-in-law routine. He doesn't feel oppressed. He wants Freya to be happy and she is happy if Garth is happy. He adds to his own thoughts, which Priya and Rita read, that besides this he genuinely likes Garth and so wants to please him as much as anything else, nodding his head as if to give his own thoughts substantiation.

Al looks around them as if only just realising Freya isn't actually here. "The thing is I'm not sure it is what

Freya wants. She said the same thing, but excluded herself and you from the equation. 'Whatever Daddy wants,' she said."

Andy dips his head and scuffs his feet. "It's fine."

I don't want to have this conversation; I don't want to have an opinion. Priya and Rita read from him.

"Oh grow a pair will you," Al says, slapping him on the back. "Man up and tell him to get stuffed." He laughs.

Polly looks at Rita. "He can talk; he should listen to his own advice and grow a pair too. He has never stood up to Garth, has he?"

Rita laughs and shakes her head. "No, he hasn't, you're right."

Then Rita is distracted, her attention focussing on the young nurse crossing the hall carrying a pile of blankets. Polly sees her too and watches her pass through the wall at the other side of the hall.

"Pal, she's some Filly ain't she? You're a lucky guy all right."

Both Polly and Rita follow the direction of the new voice. A young man, no older than twenty years, in striped pyjamas is sitting in a wheelchair beside a slim metal-framed bed. His left eye is covered with an eye patch, his right arm is in a sling across his chest and his left leg has been amputated above the knee. He hands the photograph he is holding back to a younger man, almost a boy like those from the lake in the grounds of the manor house, who takes it with his left hand, the only hand he has now blood-stained bandages covering the stump of his right arm. He stows it back under his pillow.

"Ain't she just perfect? Ain't she beautiful? I sure am a lucky fella."

Garth, who has ears like bats, hears every word that Al says to Andy despite his distance from them right at the other side of the hall. He comes over to them. "Oi you." He shoves Al in the shoulder, "Don't bully him. You're fine, aren't you, Andy, with everything?"

His voice disturbs the memory of the young war veterans and they disappear, Rita and Polly refocus on the formation of a present day memory.

Andy looks up briefly, gives a little nod and then drops his gaze again.

"Oh yeah he's fine," Al says, sarcastically. "And what do you mean by 'don't bully him?' I think you need to look closer to home for the real bully here, don't you?"

Outside on the steps, having been temporarily lost in her imagination Freya is dragged back to reality by the sound of the light-hearted bickering inside. She rolls her eyes and heaves herself up with one hand on her stomach, the other on her back and she starts back towards the french windows, manoeuvring skilfully past the obstacles she met on the way out.

"Al, why are you trying to cause trouble?" Garth accuses.

He lifts his arms out like wings and shrugs his shoulders. "I'm not. I just think that if Andy feels you are taking over, he should tell you."

"I don't," Andy says hurriedly. "I really, really don't."

Freya stands in the doorway, a hand still positioned on her stomach stroking it protectively. She watches them. I do too from the same position.

"He is taking over." Rita joins me, and her thoughts enter mine. "Like always."

Polly joins her by my side and we are all gather around Freya, encircling her, not that she realises this. "He's not taking over he just wants the best for his daughter," Polly's thoughts tell us. Then she turns to me. "He really doesn't mind you know, Andy. He doesn't care that Garth is pulling out all the stops."

I am about to telepathically answer her when Freya steps forward, passing through me, and our conversation.

Forty-Three

After it happened

"Play nice, you lot."

The three men in the room tear their gaze from its current focus and turn to her all of them beaming with love when they lay their eyes on her. Al is closest to her and moves in so that they are in reaching distance; he places a hand on the small of her back and kisses her cheek.

"Are you okay?" he asks. "I wondered where you had got to."

"I'm fine," she replies, smiling at him and kissing his forehead. "I just needed some fresh air, Pa. That's all."

"I don't blame you," Al says with a trace of laughter in his voice. "If the heat gets too much- get out of the kitchen, right?"

Garth is beside them now and places a hand on Freya's stomach. "There you go again," he says, addressing Al with slanted eyes.

"What?"

"You're causing trouble again. She didn't say it was because of me that she left, did she?"

"I never said you were to blame, did I?"

"You did, didn't he?"

Freya shakes her head. "In all fairness he actually didn't say that, Daddy."

"He implied it."

"I didn't," Al smirks.

Freya looks at him. "I don't know why you do it, Pa."

"Do what?"

"Wind him up."

"I wind him up because it's too easy, it's fun."

Garth snaps his hand off Freya's stomach and folds his arms huffily.

"Exactly," Andy chips in. "You'd think that because it is too easy you would easily tire of it and that therefore it wouldn't be fun."

"Never," Al says. "Not ever."

They all laugh, except for Garth.

"You don't think I have taken over, do you?" Garth asks Freya and Andy.

Andy comes in close to Freya and replaces Garth's hand with his own on Freya's stomach. They both look at Garth with sincerity in their eyes and in their smiles. They both shake their heads simultaneously.

"A deal is a deal," Andy says earnestly.

"Yeah," Al chips in. "You're the scorned fairy who didn't get an invite to the wedding. So you cast a spell on their first-born demanding its christening at your disposal."

Everyone laughs except Sarah and Garth. She has no idea what she would be laughing at so therefore restrains herself. Garth sulkily regards Al and is far from amused with this latest dig at him.

"Oh lighten up Daddy," Freya says, flying a hand out to his shoulder and squeezing it lightly. Then she looks at Sarah and recognising her confusion, decides to enlighten her. "Andy and I didn't get married in England; we got married on a beach in Hawaii, just the two of us. We actually didn't tell anyone, we just came home for Christmas two years ago and announced we had got married a month before."

"In grass skirts," Garth adds bitterly.

"Oh," Sarah exclaims, unsure of what to actually say. Looking at Garth's sulk-ridden face complete with protruding bottom lip and moodily folded arms tight across his chest, she is concerned with saying the wrong thing. She doesn't want to put a foot in her mouth and say something that might upset him further. "Well that sounds lovely, very romantic."

"That sounds lovely, very romantic!" Garth mimics her, rather rudely.

I feel sorry for Sarah and I wince as she does. I read her thoughts and she is cursing herself. I want to be able to tell her that whatever she chose to say Garth, a drama queen, would still have reacted this way simply for theatrical effect.

"I just meant that I would love to be able to marry my fiancée in Hawaii," she says weakly, hoping that her ill-chosen words have not lost her the biggest commission the manor house has seen in a long time, the biggest commission she has secured, or rather possibly in this case not secured, since she started working as the event organiser nine months ago. "It will just be the local registry office for us and one of granny's buffets in the local workingmen's club," she adds hoping, I read from her thoughts, to secure the sympathy vote.

Garth says, "I bet that you Sarah would invite your poor parents, though, if you did get married in Hawaii. Am I right?"

"Well, hum, er…" She looks at each of the four faces around her, feeling like a trapped and hunted animal.

"Poor girl," Polly communicates telepathically to those of us in the room that are spirit people. *She's really uncomfortable, and her aura is all-over the place, look at it?*

"He's only playing with her."

"I know that, Rita," Polly replies. "But still, he's being a big meanie."

I laugh and James does too.

Then our sub-telepathic conversation falls to the wayside as the physical conversation between the living people in the room recommences.

"Stop teasing her, Daddy," Freya says pushing Garth lightly on the shoulder.

"Don't you dare talk to me, Judas." He shoots up a hand twisting his face the other way.

"Oh." Sarah looks most concerned.

Then Garth cracks in laughter. "I'm teasing," he says reaching out and touching her wrist. "I'm over it now."

"Only just," Andy pipes up, looking up and smiling. Then he realises what he has said and quickly looks back at the floor to dodge the daggers shooting from Garth's eyes.

Al chips in. "He is right, you are only just over it and it happened two years ago. All we have had since is grief. Until this," he adds, stroking Freya's swollen belly.

Sarah smiles and cleverly attempts a diversion. "When are you actually due?"

"In three weeks," Garth answers promptly, stealing the words out of Freya's mouth, as she is just about to say them.

Freya nods in confirmation.

"And, the christening…" Sarah quickly flicks back through her notes. "Is the 28th of August? That's in eight weeks' time. So the little sweet pea will be very tiny then, won't it?"

"Very," Al adds dryly.

"Shut up, you," Garth demands.

"I hardly said anything. I only said, 'very'."

"It's not what you said, it's how you said it."

Al is about to retort and both Andy and Sarah are shrinking further into themselves when Freya doubles over, cries out in pain and clutches her stomach. Everyone, including those of us who are spirit people rush forward with shocked concern.

"This isn't meant to happen now." James's thoughts filter into Rita, Polly's consciousness and mine too.

"No, it's not."

"She is going to be overdue. They have to induce her. That's how Allison wrote it in Freya's blueprint," I inform them. "It's not happening."

"Free will," Rita's information arrives into our minds with an all-knowing tone to it. "You know we all have free will. The soul of the new baby may have decided it wants to be born now."

She is right, of course, in principle, wrong on the whole, though. Everybody does have free will and this can alter blueprinted events slightly although things usually find their way back on course if they are truly meant to be. Freya isn't about to go into labour the soul of her unborn child, whom we have all met, is not about to exercise free will.

Garth has gone drip white. "Freya, no, it can't be happening now," he cries.

"It's just a Braxton hick," Freya says waving her hand.

"That's what your birth mum said," Garth says. "I have told you-."

"Yes," Al says. "You have told them the story, several times over. Freya knows full well that she was born on the floor of a DIY store. We all know about the plight of your poor fingers after Jo-Jo crushed them. We certainly don't need to hear it all again now."

Al and Andy help Freya over to a high-backed velvet and mahogany chair. Garth stands in the middle of the dance floor with his hand slapped across his forehead muttering something about lightning striking twice. As Andy and Al help her to sit down she regards them both with a conspirator's look in her eye and whispers something to them. Then Al spins round and says, "She is fine, Garth, honestly. I think we should wrap it up here though and get off for lunch. You can confirm the finer details over the phone."

Garth nods, and thinks to himself that Freya and the baby should come first, and then he smiles at Sarah. "Is that okay? Can we wrap it up now and I'll phone you in the morning to go over everything?"

"Yes that's fine. Of course it is, just ring me any time." Then they all leave. Only Sarah and Garth are unaware that Freya has just faked the twinges as a ploy to escape. Al and Andy know because this is what she whispered to them. Of course I, James, Rita and Polly know because we read her mind.

Forty-Four

After it happened

"Did you remember to book the tickets for tomorrow night?" Rita asks over breakfast, cocking her head to one side, in the usual accusing way.

"Why do you always assume I will forget to do the things you ask me to?"

"Oh I don't know, Polly. Perhaps it's because your memory isn't just a sieve. It's a sieve with ten-pence-piece-sized holes."

"That's so unfair. When was the last time I forgot anything?"

Rita stifles a laugh to keep her toast from spraying out everywhere. "When have you ever remembered anything?"

"I always remember your birthday."

"I highlight it in your electronic Filofax, write it on the fridge calendar in red felt tip, set a reminder in your phone and laptop, and put post-it notes on the inside of the front door for a month leading up to it."

"I'd remember it anyway."

"No, you would not."

"Yes, I bloody well would."

"No, you bloody well would not."

"I remember our anniversary. See, that proves it."

"For the same reason," Rita's voice heightens a few decibels. "I go through the same regime for birthdays and anniversaries. You don't even remember the regime I go through to ensure you remember."

"You always make out like I'm the world's worst wife."

Rita makes a violin motion with her arms and then sticks out her bottom lip. "Oh did-dums, poor Polly."

Polly snatches up a piece of toast and tears at it with her teeth huffily, turning her face to the side and staring into space. After a couple of minutes of indulging Polly's tantrum, Rita presses on. "Well?"

"Well, what?"

"Well, did you?"

"Well, did I what?"

"Did you book the flaming tickets for the comedy club for Al's fiftieth birthday tomorrow night?"

"No."

"I flaming well knew it. I knew you couldn't be trusted, which is why I booked them myself."

"You did what?"

"Booked them myself and it's a good job I did otherwise Al's birthday surprise would be ruined and Garth would never forgive you."

"I can't actually believe it. I'm fuming with you."

"I've saved your bacon, bitch. A thank-you wouldn't go amiss."

"No, you bloody haven't saved my bacon you dipstick. You have wasted one hundred and forty pounds. Oh ye of little faith. I was joking." Reaching for her handbag on the back of her chair she opens it, fishes inside and retrieves six tickets for the comedy club. "There."

"Fuck." Rita stamps her foot. "I can't believe it. You owe me the money."

"Do I heck. It's your own bloody fault for doubting me."

"No, it's your bloody fault for being so useless so that I have to cover your arse, all the bloody time."

"How do you work that one out?"

"It's a fact."

"No, it's not."

"Yes, it is. You owe me the money."

"We'll see."

"We will."

They sit in silence for the rest of breakfast. Standing up first once they have finished, Rita pulls her gaping dressing gown tighter across her chest. Polly rolls her eyes at her and stands up too. Whilst she lifts up the breakfast crockery and heads for the kitchen sink, Rita heads upstairs to get dressed. In terms of fashion and style, two people couldn't be more different than these two. Rita is the kind of woman who showers once every three days and wears whatever she has taken off and thrown on the bedroom floor the night before. Whereas Polly requires the entire duration of washing up after breakfast to contemplate what she might wear, and then the entire duration of the shower afterwards where, shaving her legs into the bargain, she considers how she will wear her hair. This morning, a beautiful spring morning, the daffodils on the grass verge over the road, which she can see from the view of their kitchen sink window, inspire her to go with the little strapless, short A-line linen dress in yellow and a white neckerchief, tied in a knot at the side of her bony neck.

Minutes later Rita is back in the kitchen wearing a fitted white shirt with grey pinstripes, a pair of crumpled grey linen trousers, her short bobbed hair, to hide the fact that it needs washing as always is pulled tightly into a short ponytail, a straw trilby hat on top of her head and over her shirt a black waistcoat. Settling down at the breakfast bar with the weekend paper, something she always does to pass the time whilst Polly transforms herself, Rita gives Polly a little cough to prompt her. Polly, like she has all the time in the world and not fifty minutes until they are due to meet Garth and Al at the Easter fair, gazes idly out of the window at the rabbits playfully hopping about under the trees backing the daffodil-covered grass verge.

A few minutes later, realising the cough failed miserably, Rita says, "You really should get a move on Fanny Anne. We don't have long and you know what Garth is like if the schedule is breeched. If we are not there to see Freya in the over-thirteens Miss Easter beauty pageant, he'll never forgive us."

Polly rinses the last plate of the washing up under the hot water, places it in the drying rack, dries her hands on the tea towel, saunters through the kitchen into the lounge, out into the hall and ascends the staircase.

Forty minutes later, leaving only five minutes to make the twenty-minute journey, Polly slowly makes her way down the staircase, her eyes and hands giving full attention to the contents of her small leather satchel handbag, checking for her lipstick. Rita is beside the front door, the car in front of the garden fence has its engine already running; she is twirling the front door keys on her index finger impatiently.

"Come on Polly," she huffs, rolling her eyes. "You're a nightmare, no urgency about you. Just you go at your own pace. Take all the time in the world, why don't you?"

Polly poises halfway down the staircase, one of her newly-shaved legs bent slightly at the knee. Stuffing a lollipop, she had forgotten she had in her bag, into her mouth, which Freya gave to her on their last visit to Garth's and Al's, she sucks it hard for a moment, eyeballing Rita, then removes it from her mouth. "I have all the time in the world. It's not like we are going to die today. I have tomorrow, the next day, the day after and hundreds of days after that."

"We better bloody not die today," Rita says. "Who would feed Mr Tuna?"

You don't need to worry about Mr Tuna. He'll be taken good care of, Priya will see to that. I say without recognition.

Right on cue their white Persian cat, who is missing his left eye, saunters out of the dining room doorway, crosses their path, without acknowledging them and goes into the lounge. *Who would look after Mr Tuna?* they ask themselves silently. Rita marches down the garden path. Polly, sucking the lollipop again, saunters after her, her hips swinging from side to side, her flip-flops making slapping noises on the garden footpath. Mr Eldridge, their neighbour, alerted by the noise, looks up from his marrow patch.

"Ahoy there, Miss Polly."

The soft spot Polly has for him instantly swims in her eyes. Ever since Mrs Eldridge passed away leaving her husband of sixty years behind last year, Polly has taken it upon herself to play Florence Nightingale, regularly taking him around one of Priya's homemade cottage pies.

"Hello Thomas."

Registering that Rita is already in the car, looking at her expectantly, she bites her bottom lip. Going against her wish to stop and chat, she smiles at him sweetly, blows him a kiss and carries on walking, wondering, not only about who would look after Mr Tuna, if something happened to her and Rita, but who would look after Thomas also.

He'll go to live with his daughter and her family at the seaside, I call after her.

The conversation throughout the drive is idle. They chat mainly about the things Garth will be saying to Al about them being late and Polly texts Priya to tell her they are on their way.

The red light shows at a cross roads and they stop. Polly fishes in her bag for her lipstick with one hand, pulling down the sun visor with the other so she can inspect herself in the mirror. Withdrawing the lipstick from her bag, it slips through her fingers. Gasping in horror she watches it land on the floor between her feet and swiftly roll out of sight under her seat. Automatically, as if her life depends on retrieving the lipstick, she releases her seatbelt and lunges to catch it.

Lost in a daydream, hardly noticing Polly fishing around between her own legs, Rita passively registers the distant sirens of police cars and the whirring of a helicopter. The traffic light changes to amber, the sirens get slightly louder, Rita looks left then right. Unable to distinguish the direction they are coming from she shrugs her shoulders and tells herself that they are either invisible or nowhere near the vicinity. The green light shows itself. With Polly still fishing under her seat, Rita emerges. The car chugs forward and stalls with a miserable splutter. Rita secures the car. She revs the engine. It point blank refuses to restart. Intuitively she becomes aware of something on her left and turns her head. Piercing green eyes staring out of a black balaclava from behind the steering wheel of an oncoming car lock with hers; reaching for her seat belt clasp she unclips her own seatbelt and screams hysterically at Polly, "Get out!"

The sounds of crunching metal, piercing screams and breaking glass intermingle. Rita and Polly feel the pain of their bodies pounding against each other as their car repeatedly rolls over like a child rolling down a hill. With one last roll of their car the last physical experience they have is the almighty splitting sound.

For a split-second they revisit the shattering walnut shells Garth always showers his front room with due to his heavy-handed employment of the nut cracker at Christmas. Their skulls clout together and after the split-second vision of Garth shattering walnut shells their senses disappear into momentary blackness. Unlike me, they do not wait around once their souls leave their bodies; the ascent is immediate. They soar through the sky like birds. The wind is rushing beneath them. Higher and higher they lift. The carnage of twisted and crushed cars and discarded broken bodies quickly reduces to tiny specs in the distance below then. Eventually they are completely partitioned by the clouds. They continue rushing through the air like skydivers only travelling upwards instead of downwards, no emotion or fear attached to them.

Then there is a dazzling white light, from which I step forward. "Hello Rita and Polly, welcome home. I've been waiting for you."

Forty-Five

Before it happened

In the psychical world aggression, malice or violence are not features amongst the highlights of my character. This doesn't stop me thinking that they are, though, sadly. In the physical I am unable to rationalise my thoughts like Garth and other people are able to do. I never wish harm on people intentionally and, for this matter no more than anyone else. Everybody, even the Sunday church heedful, at some point over the course of life has that moment of wishing ill happenings to find their way to someone who has wronged them. That split second moment when one hopes they get what is coming to them. Especially towards the ex that has hurt them badly.

I can see this now that I am not in the physical and now I have all the answers, but I couldn't see this then. I have learnt it as a freed soul on my visits to the physical world and through reading people's thoughts. Anyone could easily become an ill-wisher towards others. I have, since it happened, sat on many buses undetected by the person next to me, reading their mind and its whirling with increasing frustration for the person behind them talking loudly on a mobile phone. My study subject sits silently stewing and comforting themselves with thoughts of grabbing the phone and ramming it down the throat of the offender. They not only manage, like I did, to restrain themselves from enacting their imagined violent reaction but they also manage to forgive themselves for it crossing their mind, which is where, in the physical, I differ from them. It's not just buses; I have stood unseen in supermarket queues, the annoyance of the person stood at the back of the queue blistering towards the ditherer being served, counting out their loose change and holding the process up. They stand fantasising about grabbing the back of their head and whacking it into the counter in front of them. Again, the passing consideration, part of human nature and the physical person's daily struggle with tolerance, does not hound them like it hounded me. I have read these thoughts in these scenarios, scenarios where people get frustrated and where their patience and understanding gets pushed a little too far. Time and time again I have visited and have learned. In circumstances like these I discover that, as a spirit person trespassing into their feelings, people's thoughts can trail outside the normal realms of their thinking patterns; they create spontaneous subconscious mind sets due to frustration that would never otherwise be formulated. The difference between them and me is their ability to forget it as quickly as they thought it. For them it passes through like a light snowstorm that is unable to settle, but for me, it's a snowstorm bringing everything else to a standstill, barricading relief.

Michael Duncan wasn't a very nice boy in mine and Garth's year; he was quite a bully, actually, feeding off of other people's vulnerability and fear like all bullies. When he pushes in front of me in a queue for the school bus that I have been patiently waiting in I feel he is insinuating he has hierarchal importance over me; that he somehow thinks he is better than me and deserves to be on the bus first even though I had been waiting for it longer. Naturally I hate him and want something bad to happen to him. Unfortunately for me, in the physical, it doesn't appear as rational as I can articulate it now.

In the physical, on the day this happens, I fixate, becoming stuck like a magnet to the front of a fridge. It possesses me, the desire to punish him, and I stare at him all the way through the bus journey, re-running the enactment of his punishment over and over in my mind. Rather abruptly and rather brutally and, without meaning to, I suddenly visualise Michael's decapitated head bobbing up and down in a huge pan of boiling water, onions and carrots bobbing about around him. Then I panic for his safety, I doubt my ability to restrain myself from exacting this revenge. I let out ear-splitting and unhinged screams so disturbing everyone on the school bus covers their ears with their hands. They all shout and jeer at me calling me 'deranged Dee' and 'crazy cow'. The bus driver has to stop the school bus on a lay-by where he deposits me and Garth and we have to walk the three miles home, hand-in-hand, me incoherently sobbing, and Garth fixing his eyes firmly on his feet.

It is horrifying and in the physical this is what I live with. It regurgitates in various forms at various stages of my twenty-four years of life. The image that I conjure up is so vivid that it almost becomes a memory of something I have actually done, not just imagined doing. On and off for days, weeks and years I see Michael's head in the pan bobbing up and down in my mind's eye. The fallacious memory torments my every waking moment-sometimes my every sleeping moment, too. It eats away at me so much that sometimes I almost feel the need to confess and to turn myself in at the police station for murdering Michael. In reality no murder has even taken place. Once, hoping to get it off my chest, I write it on a piece of paper in a science lesson. 'I have murdered Michael Duncan' My science teacher lifts it up from my desk and reads it right before Michael enters the room.

In later life, as a student, my Bank Loans Manager, when I want to take out a loan for a new car, is another in a long line of my illusory victims. I want to ram the stack of forms down the Loans Manager's throat. I now know, this is perfectly normal and not something that a person can be classed as dangerous and unhinged for or certified to the loony bin just as long as, of course, they do not follow through with the craving. This isn't something I realise in the physical. It's even more understandable, the desire to choke the Loans Manager with his own forms if the Loans Manager presents them to you with an echoing thud on the desk because he lets them free-fall the last six inches, making you jump and yelp like a startled puppy. More excusable is your desire to enact such torture if he adds the pressure of making you fill them out in block, black capital letters but only tells you this information after you have completed the first page in lower case blue-ink.

I am, like in the case of Michael Duncan, unable to rationalise these thoughts. I am unable to unravel them and separate imagination from actual action. Simply I cannot do the outwardly straightforward calculation that imagination does not equal capability, which leads to action and equals culpability. The way my cognitive process works in the physical, as written in my blueprint is, if I am capable of thinking something terrible it means that I am capable of doing something terrible. There is something amiss inside me like a loose wire or faulty connection in my brain. Never is it fully or logically explained in a way it can ever be fully accepted, understood or rectified.

I sit across from the Loans Manager my urge to do him a mischief not getting stronger but my guilt for having this one tiny thought that in all reality, though I can't see it, only lasts a second. The guilt of this tiny insignificant thought, this thought which everyone else has fifty times a day, swells and pulsates in the core of my brain like a nasty painful tumour. A simple thought borne of frustration will somehow manifest itself into a huge tornado inside my head. Inevitably I become incapable of thinking anything else; there will simply be no more space in my mind for another single thought other than the thought that goes around and around in my mind on a merry-go-round, laughing gleefully. *Dee, you're a danger to him. You're going to hurt him.* I am up and out speedily, like a wild charging animal, running into people, knocking them over, spilling things, ranting to myself. The situation escalates and I look madder and madder and more out of control with every second. I am running madly through the streets crying hard and shouting out loud at myself, "You're a nasty cow, Dee. You're evil, Dee." People stop and stare at me. Some laugh and point at me; these are usually groups of teenagers. Others turn away and hurry in the opposite direction. Mother's with small children pull their children closer to them.

Forty-Six

Before it happened

I visit these memories regularly so that I can read the thoughts of the other personalities in them. The irony is they never do feel in danger. The Loans Manager on the day I go to him for a loan actually thinks I am quite sweet and funny. Even when I run, it does not occur to him that he is on the brink of having his forms stuffed down his throat. He is never insecure about my presence; it is just me who is insecure about my presence in the bank with him- in the world with him, actually.

Mostly from the thoughts of those around me whenever I'm in this state I read concern for me. Many wonder what they can do to help and some don't even notice. Even those that do notice quickly forget me because other things in their life soon swallow me up. This is something else I'm unable to do in the physical, recognise my insignificance in other people's lives and I fail to recognise this as being a positive thing; they don't hate me or think negatively of me because they have their own lives to contend with. They don't have the time for worrying about me.

When I visit the day in the bank I watch it all from start to finish. It's a perfectly normal day in the summer. Garth and I are back from our first year at nursing college, my parents' house is empty and I get up late, feeling cheery. As my spirit self I watch my physical self from the corner of the rooms I potter about in, walking into the rays of sunlight that filter through the windows. Into the kitchen where I make a cup of tea and two slices of toast, which I butter and spread with a thick layer of Mum's homemade blackberry jam. Then I meander idly down the hall and into the lounge where I flick on the television and wander out again passing through a shard of sunlight disturbing particles of dust. One of me ambles up the stairs whilst the other one of me doesn't use the stairs at all. The ambling me dreamily eats a slice of toast with one hand whilst the other balances a small tray carrying the second slice of toast and the tea, which slides a bit, sloshing small amounts of tea onto the tray. On the landing she passes through me with no realisation and goes into the bedroom where, from the drawers and wardrobe, she lays out her clothes for the day. All the while I am observing her like some invisible super sleuth, completely undetectable. I sit on the toilet and watch as the other me showers and then dries off in the bathroom, brushing her teeth and applying her eyeliner and lipstick in the mirror above the sink. I laugh at her care-free nature, wandering from each room to the next, breezily and humming happily like a bird; I'm aware of how her mood will change direction like a monsoon later in the day and it seems a shame to me that this is the way she has to live, so temperamental and fragile. At this moment, she is not even dreading the visit to the bank and the appointment with the Loans Manager; rather she is excited to get her loan sorted out to buy a little run around car for her next year at college. When she is ready she leaves the house, skips down the path and then heads off out of the gate and down the back alley onto the main town street, followed like a dutiful puppy by me. She, my physical self, is uplifted, smiling and saying, "Hello, lovely day isn't it?" to the people she recognises including the vicar, who will take her funeral. The vicar stops and chats idly to physical Dee, unaware I am, as a spirit person, stood between them. Still humming happily as she walks, there is a spring in her step as she continues on her way after stopping to chat to the vicar. She boards the bus and sits down. I read her thoughts and they are merely idle thoughts about the glorious weather, the potential car that will be bought from the loan money and the things that she, Garth, Priya, Polly and Rita will do with in the car. She thinks about trips to the seaside at the weekends with a hot flask of soup in the winter and a picnic in the summer. She smiles at the thought of no more taxis for the weekly shops. She is delighted by the thought of no more being late for lectures and practical placements at the hospital because of unreliable buses.

As she walks down the main street to the bank, thoughts of their weekend trips to the beach come back to her and she pictures herself and Garth in the front of the car, the girls in the back, parked up in front of the promenade wrapped in blankets and holding hot soup in gloved hands, watching the unwelcoming steel-coloured waves crash onto the pebbles of the beach. She ventures into the bank with no apprehension in her stride. I read the thoughts of some of the people around her at this time. There is real resentment going through the minds of some of them. Most of them are wishing they are somewhere else, anywhere else. Thoughts of hanging out the washing or mowing the lawn are hovering like growing black clouds above everyone's heads, anything rather than the bank on this glorious sunny midday afternoon. Not her though, my physical self, she is quite happy to be here. She saunters inside and is greeted by a young man standing just inside the door. He doesn't want to be here either and is having, according to his own thoughts, a really rubbish day. That is until she turns up and then his thoughts tell me that he feels that his day is suddenly getting brighter. He is cute, short and slim with a square jawline and short spiked blonde hair. He fancies her. He is having thoughts about her, thoughts that won't plague or torment him later like they would do to her if their thought trains were transposed. Kevin, which is the name of the young man, politely and with a huge beaming smile, shows her into a little side room. It is a fish bowl, really. Glass fronted so that the world can glare at her and cast aspersions as to why she might be there. Soon after a large overweight man with double cheeks as well as double chins thumps into the room and introduces himself as Eric, the Bank Loans Manager. It's soon after this that her mind begins to whirl into its counterpart, the evil twin, with the irrational thought processes.

She knocks a woman off her feet as she races out into the street incoherently rambling and crying. Jenny is her name and she has come into the bank to pay some bills. She is slightly distracted by fishing in her handbag for the things she needs, which is part of the reason for her not being able to nose dive or swerve out of her way like several other people do because she isn't really looking where she is going.

She shouts out, "Hey, watch it, you bloody lunatic!" as her bag and all its contents clatter to the floor and spill out, a tube of mints rolling away never to be seen again. She staggers backwards into the man behind her. Her reaction is purely instinctive upon being impacted on without warning. There is a change in Jenny's thoughts when she sees Dee's face and sees that it is twisted and contorted with torment. Instantly she regrets calling her a name, which unbeknown to her is a name that only confirms Dee's insecurities: she's a lunatic.

After Physical Dee flees the bank I stay with Jenny. I want to discover once and for all if there is any long-term impact upon her life because of physical Dee, which is something she thinks about a lot in the physical. Dee, I mean, not Jenny. She has this overbearing ever-tormenting notion that by knocking into Jenny on her flight from the bank she somehow impacts upon her life forever in a negative frame. She gets it stuck into her head, like a nasty splinter on her brain, that Jenny resents being bumped into so much that somehow her life is never quite the same like an abused child who never goes on to live a fulfilled and functional adult life as a result of the abuse. This is how she sees herself: a malevolent deviant interfering and restricting other people's happiness, like an abuser.

She is wrong. Jenny suffers no long-term side effects. Her first thought after she wishes she hadn't called her a lunatic is sympathy. Jenny can see she is young and she feels concern for the poor girl who she assumes has been chastised, probably unfairly, by some mean jobs-worth of a bank manager. Then the physical me completely vanishes from Jenny's thoughts. I, the spiritual me, discover on following her home that, contrary to what physical Dee imagines, she does not rant and berate about her to her own family. Jenny does not, as Dee imagines on many occasions, say to her husband over dinner, "Guess what happened to me today? I was in the bank minding my own business and this evil girl who goes around boiling boys heads and suffocates bank managers with their own forms attacked me. I'm lucky to have not been hideously tortured."

Nor does Jenny develop post-traumatic stress disorder that becomes such a burden to her husband that he turns to the arms of other women wrecking the marriage, which because of bitterness sees their children living an unmoral life. It's a possibility Dee, as a physical person encased in a physical body, contemplates later that day locked in her bedroom with her thoughts tormenting her.

Until I come home I never understood that in the physical no-one was oppressed, harmed in any way or in danger of being harmed by me, the physical me.

Forty-Seven

After it happened

My Dad is standing in front of a trestle table full of fresh flowers that the woman, sitting on a deck chair in front of the caravan door behind the trestle table, grows in her own garden and then sells here, from a caravan in a lay-by. Her flower station is situated next to a red double-decker bus that has been converted into a roadside café and is frequented daily by burly truck drivers shovelling greasy breakfasts down their throats. He thinks about Mum and me as he chooses from the display unaware that we are both stood beside him, linking an arm each.

"Are they for someone special?" the florist asks, as if she is reading from an auto queue, whilst tying string around the daffodil stems he has chosen.

"Very special," he replies, smiling. "My wife and my daughter. It's my daughter's forty-third anniversary today and, well, my wife has always loved daffodils."

"That's lovely of you to think of them both," the woman replies. "And how many years have you been married?"

There is no hint of sadness or melancholy in my dad's tone or demeanour to betray the truth. "Sixty eight years now."

"Gosh. That's more than a lifetime for me," she says with genuine exasperation. "I only managed four years with my first and seven with my second," she adds, letting out a chortle. Then tapping the gold band on her left index finger she says, "Let's hope number three does better, although it's still only early days, two years. Your daughter has done well to make forty-three years. You must be very proud of her."

Dad feels something sharp pierce through his heart. "No, no she isn't. Married, I mean. She never married," his tone is solemn and he faces his feet when he speaks. "She didn't have the time to get married, really."

Not joining the dots the woman presses on. "Career-minded, is she? My sister is the same. She is in her late forties now and has no husband or children. I expect your daughter is the same, is she?"

"Hmmm," Dad says avoiding a lie.

"Is she forty-three then, your daughter? Is that what you meant by forty-third anniversary?" she half laughed. "That's what they say in France, isn't it? Bon anniversaire. My second husband was French. You don't look or sound very French, though." She chortled.

"No. My daughter is Sixty-eight at the end of this year. My wife fell pregnant almost as soon as we were married," my dad says absent-mindedly. "It's too late for her, now."

She doesn't reply. It isn't what he said, but how he said it, with macabre emptiness, that causes the chill to sliver down her spine like a snake; with a look of mystification at his cryptic, almost haunting, last sentence she eyes him with her big blue eyes.

He withdraws into himself for a few seconds, staying silent and staring wistfully into an empty space. Mum and I read that she is beginning to suspect something isn't quite right with my dad and without realising exactly why, sympathy and concern coils around her insides for the frail old man standing in front of her. She begins to weigh things up in her head and realises that they don't exactly add up. She has this sudden urge, which she inwardly questions, to come around the trestle table between them and hug him. He looks up at her and smiles. She registers the watery sadness in his eyes and then she knows.

"You poor thing. Your daughter is dead. It's the forty-third anniversary of her death, isn't it?" She stops herself from knocking the trestle table out of her way and rushing to him. "She must have been so young."

"Yes, she was twenty-four." Emotion gushes in his words like water from a tap. "My wife too she passed away in the same week twenty years later. It's her anniversary the day after tomorrow." They regard each other, words abandoning them both before my dad speaks again. "Well, I'd best be getting these daffodils to them. I'm meeting a friend at the cemetery."

The woman is holding tightly onto the lump in her throat. All she can manage is a nod and a weak smile. As Dad makes his way back to his car he is thinking about the men and women from bowls. Many of them are widows or widowers but they have children, grandchildren and great-grandchildren. It's when he sees them together that he feels most robbed. We try, Mum and I, but we can't comfort him in these times when he shuts himself away in the living room, turns the lights off, draws the curtains and lets the fuzzy white noise crackle between his ears.

He is waiting by the cemetery gates now. The sun has been strong since morning broke and its glare spangles off Dad's bald crown and makes the silvery shine of the white hair that grows at the back and sides of his head more bracing. Every so often he dabs his forehead with a handkerchief, which he folds up and puts back into the pocket of his cream chino shorts. His mood has lifted slightly, he feels close to us now. When he and Mum came here together I always came with them. I was alone and they were together. Now it's Dad's turn to be alone whilst Mum and I are together. It's what Mum said, when she refused treatment. She told him, holding his liver-spotted hand between both of her withered hands and looking deeply into his eyes with sincere regret, that it was time for her to be my mum again.

Doesn't he look dashing? Mum asks, dusting the shoulder of his navy blue golfer's polo shirt. *Still as handsome as the day I married him.*

Yes, Mum very dashing. Very dashing indeed.

Across the road he can see Frieda appearing at the top of the hill. She gives a little wave and a wide smile, bearing all her dentures. She is wearing baby blue pleated trousers and a white short-sleeved blouse with a fringe collar. Pearls are strung around her neck and a neat silver bob frames her creased face. She is carrying a basket looped over one arm, which contains four bunches of white roses, which she pruned from her own garden and tied with ivory ribbon, earlier this morning. Her purse, pruning scissors, a glass bottle of homemade lemonade, two plastic cups and two rounds of salmon and cucumber sandwiches in brown bread also sit in the basket along with a neatly folded cream cardigan. Standing at each side of her, as Mum and I stand at each side of Dad, is James and his dad.

Before the Simon Thomas psychic phenomenon, Garth, his mum and my mum came here together often. I laughed at his morbid fascination for reading the inscriptions on the gravestones around mine. One day Garth feels compelled by the woman in a blue overcoat shielding from the light rain under an umbrella that obscures her face. He can hear her sobbing intermingled with her one-sided conversation hunched over a grave, which is parallel and three gravestones back from mine. When she leaves he decides to investigate the grave.

"It must be her son."

"Garth, come away right now. What if she comes back and sees you reading her son's gravestone? I'll die of embarrassment."

"Nice choice of words, Mum," Garth laughs. "She won't come back. His name was James Oliver Hemingway. It says here that he was an only child, a postman and had a wife and child. She was called Lucy. The child, not the wife."

"Poor woman, that's terrible," my mum says as if forgetting she is in the same position herself.

"No more terrible than Dee," Garth reminds her. "He was thirty-two, same age as I am now. I'd have given anything for those extra eight years with Dee, wouldn't you?"

"Yes, yes I would."

"He didn't die long after Dee. He'd be forty now. That's still not very old, is it? I wonder what happened to him."

"Who knows?" his mum replies. "Anything could have happened. Now come away, Garth. It's not polite to read other people's graves. I really don't understand what your fascination is with it."

My mum backs her up. "I would be mortified if I came here and found someone snooping about Dee's grave with macabre fascination."

"Would you?"

"Yes, I would. It's my daughter's grave, and her death is not for someone else's entertainment."

"I don't think Dee would mind. I think she would see it as keeping her memory alive, not being forgotten."

They never saw Frieda again. Not until James and I engineered their meeting at Simon Thomas's psychic night and it wasn't until they were swapping numbers outside the community centre that Garth's mind jogged and he realised who she was. Frieda never visited the graveyard alone after that and after their first holiday together at the villa in Italy both James's dad and mine began accompanying their wives on the visits- something they had never done before. Twice a year on our birthdays, in the days before Rita and Polly's car accident, James's dad's heart attack, Mum's cancer and Garth's parents passing within weeks of each other, both of pneumonia, they would all come down in convoy carrying baskets of sandwiches, cakes, fresh fruity drinks and arms full of flowers and balloons. Freya, in my honour, would blow out the candles on my birthday cake and Lucy, James's daughter, would blow out the candles on his birthday cake.

Garth was right when he told my mum I wouldn't mind people reading my headstone. No spirit person does. There are many times when people stop beside my heart shaped gravestone, drawn to it as if it stands out amongst the others as being somehow more tragic. They all read my inscription. Those that are alone read it to themselves, those who are walking their dogs read it to their dogs and those who have human companions read it aloud to them. I don't mind, not at all. Neither does my mum. Sometimes people connect her grave to mine- it stands beside mine- other times they don't.

Forty-Eight

After it happened

"Good morning. Lovely day, isn't it?" Frieda beams, waving her hand high above her head.

"Good morning, Frieda. Yes, it is a lovely day. May I say, you look lovely- a summer vision."

"Oh stop that, you old fool," she giggles. "Have you been waiting long? Doris from next door popped by just as I was leaving the cottage and she kept me talking. I am very sorry."

My dad shakes his head. "Not long at all. Don't bother about it Frieda."

Frieda places her basket on the floor by his feet. Grasping each other by the elbows they kiss one another's cheeks. "How are you doing?"

"Oh, keeping busy, doing this and that book group, lunch club and Lucy popping around with the boys. They are coming along lovely now. They're getting to be so tall, just like James was."

Dad and Frieda begin to walk into the graveyard, myself, Mum, James and James's dad following behind them. "Well the boys will keep you busy with their mischief."

Frieda laughs. "Luke has discovered football in a big way. He still needs a bit of fine tuning but he has managed not to smash any of my windows unlike his granddad James who had broken my full set of ground floor windows by his age." I shoot a look at

James and give him a grin. "Dean isn't as keen on sport and is becoming quite the entrepreneur. He had me discussing the pros and cons of a dishwasher only jut the other night. The biggest con being that he only gets five pounds a week for filling the dishwasher after tea and his friend Nathan gets eight pounds a week for washing up because it takes more effort. He is like James- as sharp as a scalpel when it comes to money."

"I'm sure James would be very proud of him, of them both," my dad reassures her. "He has missed a lot. So has my Dee. Garth, says it about Freya, that Dee has missed her growing up and now her children too."

I am very proud of them and I haven't missed a single thing. I'm with them all the time.

"Yes, they have both missed so much. Lucy talks about him all the time. She has no memory of him being so young when he drowned. The photographs don't do him justice any more. It's so hard to imagine what he would be like now, an old man."

I'm just the same Mum.

"Yes, Freya and Al both say that it's quite difficult only ever knowing Dee through stories because there are no photographs of her. No-one can imagine what she'd be like now, nearly seventy. Twenty-four is worlds apart. She'll just always be twenty-four to me."

I'm exactly as I was, twenty-four and not a day older.

"Are they joining us this year at the villa in Italy with Garth, Al, Freya and her family? Luke and Dean were asking yesterday morning and Lucy said it would be nice to catch up with Freya. Such busy girls they don't get the time now like they used to."

"Yes, everyone is game at my end and all looking forward to it. Garth has called a family meeting to go over it all next weekend. We're all going down to his. He's going to inform us as to which one of us should bring the tea bags, which one of us should bring the coffee and which one of us should bring the candles. You know how he likes to be in control and super organised. It used to drive Dee mad. You should come if you're at a loose end, there is plenty of room and they'd all love to see you. It's been too long."

"Yes, I'd like that," she replies brightly. "It has been a long time. Funny thing, isn't it, time? There was a time when we were always together and now it's just once a year at the villa."

My dad nods. "Time isn't always kind, is it? Everything changes. People get older and busier, technology becomes more advanced but emotion and grief they never change, hurt and pain is absolutely timeless and always so cruel."

They divert from the gravel path and begin to walk over the grass, meandering through the gravestones. Frieda replies, "Time doesn't make things easier either. They are wrong, the people who say this. It's a load of tosh, if you ask me."

"No, it doesn't. And yes, they are wrong. It never heals and it's always there. It's a bit like a scab, I find.

You think it's healed over and then you catch it and it rips off and you're left with the open wound as fresh as the day it first happened." He gave a morose sigh and gazed into the middle distance. "You just learn to live with the hollowness."

"Yes, you're right. You just become numb to the part of you that is missing, which cannot conceivably ever heal," she replies. "It still hurts terribly whenever I visualise James on the last time I saw him laughing and joking with his friends, his t-shirt tucked into the back pocket of his shorts. I still have it in a box under my bed even after all this time. I often get it out and put it up to my face. His scent is gone now, though. It dangled down like a tail on that day. I watched him from my front room window loading all his gear into his little burgundy Astra." She laughs at the memory. "For that last camping trip to the quarry. He didn't have a care in the world, not one. Time is cruel sometimes. On that last day, time was so good at concealing the fact that it was going to run out on him in less than twenty-four hours. I find that so strange. That the last time I ever saw him, my only child, he was in the last twenty-four hours of his life and no-one could have ever known it."

I haven't gone anywhere Mum. Time hasn't run out on me, time is endless for me now.

Dad smiles, "I have similar memories of Dee. We only saw her the weekend before she…" He stops abruptly, unable to finish the sentence, which he never ever finishes. "There were no signs. There was nothing to suggest that she was living her last weekend and that there would be no more Saturdays spent with her.

Even though it's such a long time ago I can still remember every tiny detail. We took her out for lunch and all she wanted was a hot dog." My Dad breaks off and laughs. "She got ketchup and mustard in her hair and she kept laughing and joking looking into the distance with that mysterious vacant look in her eye, tucking her thick hair behind her ear and giggling girlishly at nothing at all, just something that popped into her head, which she never shared. She was always giggling, when she was the Dee that we knew, the real Dee."

I giggle everyday now Dad.

Frieda squeezes my dad's arm. She breathes in the scent of fresh flowers deeply. "I love it here," she says. "She looks at my dad sheepishly, like she has said it without thinking because she has forgotten where they are and what they are doing.

Recognising the remorse flickering in her eyes, my dad smiles at her and pats her arm soothingly. "It's okay. I know what you mean. It's so peaceful and serene."

"Very well maintained," she says. Then she adds, "Those flower beds are stunning." She points at the floral border. "So bright and cheery, in good spirits," she adds, laughing at her own joke.

"Very good," my dad smirks, shaking his head.

"James and his dad were never ones for flowers," Frieda states factually. "But Ciara was, wasn't she?"

My dad nods. "Yes, they both were."

"Once, when we came here without you," Frieda tells my dad. "She told me the story of when she and Dee took floral arranging lessons and they got one over on- well I can't remember what her name was- that awful snob of a woman who lived down the street from you who used to loft it about over everyone. Ciara and Dee took her down a peg or two, and good on them, I say. I wish I could remember her name. This is the trouble with ageing I suppose." She taps the side of her head lightly with the knuckles of one of her hands. "I'm becoming such a scatter-brain. At least it's only the small details that are going."

"Mavis and Erin," my dad says. Then, laughing at the memory, he repeats, "Mavis and Erin. I had forgotten all about those two. What a gruesome twosome. Ciara was full of herself for months after that day. She was the street's heroine, lapping up the glory everywhere she went. She even got a standing ovation once, in the post office I believe."

"Sorry dear," Frieda says, turning to him purposefully, looking awash with vagueness. "I haven't the faintest idea what you are talking about, Mavis and Erin, what do they have to do with anything?"

My dad studies her suspiciously for a few seconds, unaware that we are stood beside him mocking him with laughter.

"He's not actually going to fall for it, is he?" James asks.

"Probably, yes. He always was very gullible," my mum answers.

"She still likes a good stitch up," James's dad chips in. "She used to get me every time. I'm glad she hasn't lost her wit." Then he passes a hand through her short bobbed hair as if stroking it.

"Dad's cleverer than that, though. Surly he will see straight through her, won't he?"

"I don't know love. This is your father we are talking about after all."

Then we all laugh and listen.

Frieda's face begins to crease. "I got you."

My dad throws his head back in good humour and laughs. "Every time, you get me every time. If Ciara and Dee were here right now they would be taking the Michael out of me something chronic for being so gullible."

We are here, and we are taking the Michael out of you.

James's dad slaps my dad on the back. *Never mind, mate, we all fall for it.*

"Do you think they are here?"

"I don't know, Frieda," my dad replies, shaking his head, "I really would like to think so but I just don't know. I can't get my head around the possibility."

"I was the same at first but if they are not still on-going in some way how do you explain us coming together and the whole Simon Thomas encounter?"

Dad shakes his head and shrugs his shoulders. "Well I can't, which is exactly the point. It's unexplainable but at the same time so real. There is no way he could have fabricated what he said, have known that Dee and James were buried so close, which he would have had to know to make it all up. Wouldn't he?"

Frieda nods. "And, then he would have had to somehow manipulate the situation so that we were all there- me, Ciara and Garth- which he didn't, obviously, because he couldn't have manipulated me without me knowing there was some influence."

"Crazy," Dad says. "Absolutely crazy. It's just something we will never know for sure. Nobody ever will until they know, and that means they have to... Well, you know what has to happen."

Frieda nods.

Forty-Nine

After it happened

Garth is scarcely mobile and unmistakably in the final stages of his life. Now we are closer to being reunited than we ever have been before. He shuffles his feet when he moves around his house, hunched over a walking stick, shakily, slowly and painfully making his way from one room to the other. His depreciation is painful for those in the physical to watch and to accept. It would be painful for me if it were possible for me to feel that.

I am sitting in the car beside Freya as she sobs alone in the driver's seat. Her car is parked at an angle because of her haste and panic to get inside. We are in the third parking bay on the left of the hospital's Accident and Emergency entrance. Leant forward onto the steering wheel she cradles her face in her hands and heaves great big heavy sobs, which make her shoulders, shudder. She can't bring herself to be in the cubicle where Garth is being treated for a sprained ankle. She feels like she needs a few minutes to get some air. Andy and their eldest grandson Freddie are still inside with Garth. I am reading her thoughts and she is resolute that this will be the last time anything like this will happen again. There will be no more falls as a result of Garth's stubborn determination to be independent. Whether he likes it or not, he has to move into the extension she and Andy have just built onto the side of their house. Her thoughts are non-negotiable; she is unyielding as she reminds herself of what happened the time before this incident. Garth forgot he'd turned the taps of his bath on. It was only luck that his neighbour had got there before the ceiling came down. If Angela, hadn't popped around with his milk and eggs from the farmers market and noticed the driblets of water forming on the hallway ceiling, Freya tells herself: *it would have been much worse. What if*, she thinks with a shudder, *he had remembered to turn the taps off and got into the bath and then fallen asleep in there? He could have drowned. Or what if he fell asleep with something on the stove? He could burn the house down. Or what if he had another fall? Like today and it didn't happen to be in the hallway by the telephone so that he could easily contact her like he'd been able to do this time. He could be stuck there for hours and die of starvation or internal bleeding.* She shudders again; *it just doesn't bear thinking about. It is definitely too dangerous for him to be at home,* she tells herself one last time.

No matter how resolute Freya is, though, she is forgetting one thing. She is forgetting that her stubborn streak is something she has in common with him. When she puts it to him in point blank terms on her return to his cubicle that he has no choice but to move in with her and Andy, he is just as resolute that he is staying at home with Al. he is adamant that wild horses will not drag him from it, or drag him from his beloved husband. Reassuring her that he will be fine, he reminds her that if he moves out there will be no-one to take care of him. He jokes that her Pa is useless and can hardly even boil an egg, which is exactly why he couldn't possibly leave him. At this point Freya bursts into tears and runs out of the hospital again, shouting at Andy and Freddie to talk some sense into the 'daft old bat'. They both fail to convince him that moving in with them is the right thing to do for everyone concerned. They fail also to persuade him that Al no longer needs him. Even when Andy appeals to his better nature, father-to-father, man-to-man, and asks him to agree for Freya's sake, Garth sticks his heels in and knowing him to be the devoted father that he is Andy realises that if the trump card- asking him to do it for Freya's sake- can't overturn his decision nothing ever will.

If only I was able to talk to Freya perhaps I could put her mind at ease, partially at least but of course she has no idea that now, in this period, I am with Garth every day, watching him, helping him. I am on the days when Al is not helping him, that is.

"The lawn needs mowing," Garth says, placing a wrinkly liver spotted hand on top of Al's smooth, un-ageing hand. "That's a job for a young man so you had better do it. How much younger than me are you now, actually? Seventy-five years younger than me?"

Al smiles back at him, unable to feel Garth's hand. I'm *seventy-seven years younger than you now, actually, Garth. And don't worry about the lawn- it's not on the agenda today.*

"So you're twenty-one, then? I always wanted a toy boy." Garth eyes him very suspiciously, "You have been very cloak and dagger recently and you haven't told me yet why you have come back all of a sudden."

I think you know the answer to that question.

Garth stares at him, realising he has forgotten what his face looked like before the wrinkles and the darkened patches took over it and that he has forgotten how rich and vibrant the colours in his hair were before it went white. His eyes, too, now that he thinks of it. He has forgotten how lustrous they were before they become dull with age.

They, Garth and Al, are sitting in the sun-drenched conservatory with the folding doors to the garden drawn back so that the sound of singing birds and the smell of lavender from the huge pots, which they brought back from Mexico on their last trip abroad in the VW together, wafts gently in. Garth isn't dressed yet and is wearing a light-blue thin cotton robe and matching pyjamas. Al, however, is wearing flawless white linen trousers with a pale pink shirt. There is a certain glow to him that is not yet within Garth. On the inside window ledge of the conservatory, all the way around it, Garth's four-day-old birthday cards stand shoulder to shoulder. I watched Garth open them. Al was also there sitting beside me on the floor cross-legged. Freya stood them up one by one, counting them out as she did; she reached seventy-five, the last one. She stood it up in front of one of his tomato plants. The one that is bursting with bright red plump and juicy-looking tomatoes, which no-one else but Al and me know are so fruitful because of my nurturing green fingers. Above the folding doors, on the red brick exposed wall, hangs a banner made from a torn white sheet with multi-coloured painted letters spelling out, 'Happy ninety-eighth birthday Great-Granddad.'

"Yes, I do know the answer," he says wistfully.

Al smiles. *You are so beautiful; more beautiful than ever.*

Garth laughs, lifting the round red teapot that is sitting on top of the round white wrought-iron table between them. He says nothing whilst he pours a thick treacle-coloured stream of steaming tea through a strainer into two cups. Still in silence, he replaces the teapot on its cork mat and then adds milk to the tea in both cups- just a dribble for Al and two lumps of sugar for him also.

You know I can't drink that, don't you?

Garth lifts his cup to his lips and is blowing into it. "I know. You have been telling me this for two weeks now. Just humour me."

Two weeks, Al says in surprise. *Time means nothing to me now. I have lost all concept of it.*

"I know that too," Garth says. "It's that part I'm looking forward to the most."

Al throws his head back in laughter. *There is much more to look forward to than that, Garth.*

"Oh, I know, but the idea of no time, no pressure of time; it sounds blissful."

Yes, I suppose it is. I don't notice it, to be honest. It's just something that doesn't exist for me any more, a no-need consideration.

"I can't wait."

Well, you don't have to wait much longer.

"How do you know that if you don't have any concept of time?"

Freya is wrong about you, Al laughs. *You still very much have your wits about you. Still the full picnic, you are. Not a sandwich short at all.*

"Is that what she thinks? Cheeky monkey." He is about to ask him what else Freya thinks when he realises what Al has done and then he snappily says, "Don't avoid the question."

Al laughs again. *I do understand time. I know that time exists and I'm aware of sequencing. It's just not a process I live by. I do know when things are imminent. There is warning before an event if I need to be there, like I'm here now.*

"Two weeks' warning strikes me as being quite a lot."

Like I have said before-.

"I know. I know. YOU wouldn't know how long two weeks is and a long time for me is a short time for you. Please don't go over it again."

Okay I won't.

"You are wrong by the way," Garth says.

I'm wrong about what, exactly? Al replies with a puzzled look on his face.

"You are wrong about me being beautiful. I'm not. I look like a bag of potatoes. I'm horrible."

It's your soul I'm looking at and that is as beautiful as the day I married you. You'll see.

Garth smiles. "Will I be young again like you?"

If that is what you choose, he says breezily. Catching himself on and realising this is Garth he is talking to, he adds hastily, *and you will.*

"Are you saying I'm vain?"

Al laughs and says nothing in reply.

"I'll take that as a yes then," Garth says, laughing also.

Freya will be here soon for her once-a-month weekend stay, Al says. *I can't be here when she arrives. You need to make the most of her visit and concentrate just on…* He pauses for a moment. *You and her. I'll be close by, though, and when she has gone I'll come back and stay with you until…* his words trail off.

Perkily, as if he doesn't understand what Al is telling him, Garth says, "How do you know Freya stays here one weekend every month? I haven't told you that."

Al smiles. *All seeing, all knowing. That's me.*

Garth laughs. "Hark the heavenly angel."

Yes, that's me.

"Al," Garth has a vague hint of apprehension in his tone now.

Yes? Al's tone is free from apprehension, detached and free from emotion.

"What is it like? You know, at the end, I mean."

Al smiles reassuringly. *It depends, like everything else in life, on the person and the circumstances. It depends largely on the individual's threshold.*

"That sounds like the nebulous answer of a surgeon, purposefully ambiguous to avoid alarming the patient."

That's a very educated analysis for a simple nurse.

"I used to hang out with this pompous surgeon for a while. His ostentatious carry on was too in-your-face to go unnoticed and not leave a permanent mark."

Touché, Al says. *That means I think you made a good point. Well done.*

"Still a patronising wan-."

Ah-ah, that kind of language isn't acceptable where I'll be taking you. You won't get in if you finish that sentence.

"I know what touché, means," Garth says huffily, thrusting his arms over his chest and turning his gaze towards the folded back door. He watches two white butterflies fluttering around the pots of heather. He notes how striking the white of their wings are against the deep purple heads of the heather plants.

I know, Al says. *You're still as easy as ever to wind up.*

Garth tears his gaze from the butterflies, his antagonism liquefied. "Oh no. You're not going to do this for all eternity, are you?"

Do what?

"Make fun out of me and infuriate me forever."

Yes.

"I'm not coming with you then."

Okay, that's fine.

Al starts fading away.

"No!" he cries, "I didn't mean it. Come back. Please don't go."

Gotcha, Al says hastily adding, *don't worry once we are home you won't care if I wind you up or not. It won't affect you, I promise.*

Garth thrusts his arms across his chest again and turns his gaze back to the white butterflies. "You know, they always remind me of Dee. White butterflies, I mean. I always think that whenever I see one she has sent it or them to visit me and that they fly back to her and give her reports on my progress. I suppose I am wrong. Now I know that she doesn't need butterflies." He turns back to Al. "If you can be here, so could she. If I can communicate with you, I should also be able to communicate with her."

Al recognises the watery look in his eye. *Garth,* his tone is soft. *Are you disappointed that Dee isn't here?*

"Not disappointed as such," he sighs. "I've just spent seventy-four years thinking that she would be the one who came to collect me, that's all. I thought she would never forget me."

I'm here now standing beside the table between them but only Al can see me. Al turns his head and smiles at me. I say nothing and only stay for as long as is necessary. Noticing Al's interruption of thought and his diverted attention and friendly smile to the empty space between them, Garth begins to speak again. "She is here now, isn't she?" Al nods. "How come I can't see her? How come you can and I can't?"

Because that is the way it is for now. You will see her again.

"What does she look like?" Garth says urgently. "Has she changed?"

She looks exactly like your description of her in the poem you read when we visit Ayrl on all of her anniversaries. Al places his hand over Garth's reassuringly. *You will see her again. When it's the right time, you will.*

Garth perks up and his entire face lifts in a huge smile. "I've waited so long. It feels like forever and a day."

And the day is near. Forever has almost been and gone. The day is almost here, he says poignantly like some wise prophet.

Garth's memory jerks inside his head and a hazy recollection seems to stir itself. It is almost like someone sifting for gold amongst rocks in water. The memory brings itself to the surface as he shakes his head like a gold sifter shakes the bowl of its watery contents to bring the gold to the top. "I think," he says, unsure of himself, "I dreamt that she said that to me once." He gasps and claps a hand to his mouth. "It wasn't a dream, was it? She has always been around me, hasn't she?"

Full marks, Al says. *The penny has finally dropped. Garth, Dee is responsible for a lot of things you don't understand: for me being in your life, for Freya being in ours, for this house we found and renovated.*

"I can't believe I doubted her. She has been pulling strings for me from up there." He lifts his eyes to the sky. "And I have spent all these years doubting her."

It's a lot to take in, Al says sitting back on his seat, stretching out his legs and placing his hands behind his head. Garth registers the shards of sunlight passing through his opaque form. *You couldn't have known.*

"Do you think she will forgive me?"

Unquestionably, Al smiles and then adds, *now come on, drink your tea and make yourself decent whilst I get on with the lawn. Freya will be here soon and if she sees you like this, in your pyjamas, speaking to thin air she will have you committed.*

Fifty

After it happened

Garth lifts the receiver of the phone, which sits on top of a small, round, green leather-topped mahogany table beside the dark wood staircase; in his old age, he had become quite old fashioned to the point that his great-grandchildren say that going to his house is like visiting a museum. They had never seen a telephone like the one he owns before. Fluttering on the walls encasing the staircase are shapes from the moonlight streaming through the large square stained-glass window on the midway landing. He brings the receiver up to his ear and in the brief seconds before he speaks, he gazes into Al's eyes. They are exactly how they were at breakfast a couple of mornings ago, the morning of Freya's visit. With the hand that isn't lifting the receiver he blows a kiss at the silver-framed photograph of him and Al on their wedding day. At this moment it's my watch, Al is busy at home preparing, and it isn't going to be long now. I am sat behind him on the stairs. He lowers himself down onto the bottom step beside the telephone table. He is fragile and delicate. His skin is thin and white and almost as opaque as Al and me but you can't see through him- not just yet anyway. He winces and flinches as the brittle bones in his back and legs groan and creak with old age like the old wood of the stairs groans and creaks under his weight.

"Hello," he wheezes into the receiver.

"Hi, Daddy it's me."

"Hello Freya. Did you get home safe?"

"Yes we did, thank you. The drive back was quite bearable, actually. There was hardly any traffic at all. We have been in for about an hour. I was just about to ring you when Alana and Christine dropped round, followed by Freddie, George and Amy. Before we knew it the house was overrun with grandchildren and chocolate cupcakes." She laughs. "No matter how old they get they'll always love my chocolate cupcakes."

Garth smiles. "That's okay, love, I dozed off after you left. You've just woke me up."

"Does that mean you haven't taken your tablets yet?"

"Not yet, but I will. Don't you go worrying about me, Freya. You have enough on your plate."

"Daddy," Freya says pithily. "You are ninety-eight. I worry about you every second of every day. You are the main course on my plate."

Garth is staring at the photograph, straight into Al's eyes, and he smiles. In his head he is having a conversation with Al, mocking Freya. *She is such a silly girl. When will she ever realise that she can't control this? Destiny is much bigger than her. Destiny is so much bigger than us all*. He snaps out of his imaginary conversation with Al and returns to the real conversation he is having with his daughter. "You don't need to worry, dear, I have your pa after all."

Freya bites back the instant hot tears that prick her eyes. "Yes, so you have been saying all weekend. I just don't know why after six months you have suddenly decided he is haunting you."

"I don't think he is haunting me, Freya; I know he is. And anyway it's not haunting, they don't consider themselves to be ghosts."

"Daddy, you told us this morning that for the past two weeks he has been sitting in the rocking chair in the corner of your room. Yesterday when Andy asked what had happened to the picture of your great-grandchildren you said that Pa had knocked it off the dresser and smashed it when he came to have tea with you. And apparently, according to you, he has breakfast with you every morning." She pauses and then in an exasperated tone blurts out, "And as for him mowing the lawn, well, its damn right absurd Daddy, it really is."

"It is all true, dear, and he did mow the lawn. Who else do you think did it?"

"I don't know. I know you haven't- that's damn right impossible. However, it's just as impossible for Pa to have done it too. I don't think you can remember who did it. This is what worries me. I wish you could remember. I'd like to thank them with a bottle of whisky or something."

"I do remember. I keep telling you who it was."

"I know who you keep telling me it was and I know you believe he did, but I keep telling you it can't have been Pa."

"It was him. He's always here now." Then, as if he is describing someone's return from work he chirpily adds," He'll be back later."

"I'm sorry, Daddy, but this is really rather upsetting." Her tone is harsh and firm. "You have to stop this. I won't have it any more. Do you hear me? Pa is not with you, nor has he ever been with you for the last six months and he certainly is not coming back. This nonsense has to stop."

"It's not nonsense, dear."

"Daddy, it really is and if you are still going on like this tomorrow I'm coming back and I'm taking you to the doctors, I really am. No arguments, Daddy. I mean it. I'm putting my foot down now. Please stop this now. I simply won't put up with it any longer." She gives a frustrated sigh.

"I'm sorry, dear, but he has been here. He was here before you came to visit but went away again because he wanted me to focus on you. He said to tell you he is sorry and that we will all be together again. He's come for me."

Freya closes her eyes and dips her head. I leave Garth and go to her, standing behind her. She uses the back of her hands to wipe her watery eyes and then covers the handset with her hand. She turns her face inwards from the dining room where she is sitting to look through the archway into her lounge where Andy is sitting on the sofa with his feet on the coffee table, something he wouldn't do if she was in the room with him.

"Pssssst," she hisses. "Andy."

Andy looks away from the television pushing his glasses up his nose with one finger on the bridge of them. "What?" he says tersely.

"Feet!" She barks sharply. He quickly recoils his feet. Then, shaking the handset at him, she says, "It's Daddy. He is still banging on about seeing Pa all over the place. He thinks he has come for him. I can't handle it, love, I really can't."

Andy lifts himself off the sofa and walks through the lounge into the adjoining dining room. He sits beside her, holding her hand. "He's old, love. He's really very old. He probably has no idea what time of day it is."

"I do know what time it is. It is 9pm," Garth's frail voice seeps through the gaps in Freya's fingers.

We all laugh: Garth, Freya, Andy and me.

I leave Freya now she has Andy, and return to Garth.

"See?" Andy says in a positive tone. "He's not as daft as we think he is," he says, contradicting himself.

Freya smiles weakly. Suddenly she feels better. She lifts the handset off her lap and puts it to her ear. "Daddy?"

"Yes, dear."

"I'm going to let you go now. I think you should take your tablets with some hot milk and get yourself to bed. Can you manage that?"

"Yes, of course I can, dear."

"Me, and Andy will drive out to you in the morning."

"Oh I don't-."

"No arguments, Daddy."

"She means business, Garth. I wouldn't take her on if I was you," Andy says in a raised voice so that it can be heard through by Garth.

"Okay, dear. If you think that's best, you come over tomorrow."

"I am going to," she says rigidly.

"That's fine, but you can't come before Angela brings my eggs and milk around at 10am, okay? Promise me you won't."

"Why on earth not?"

"Because, Freya, I say so. That's why."

"But I don't understand."

"Freya, I am not budging on this." His tone is stern and adamant.

"Oh all right," Freya says exasperatedly. "Fine, we will be around about half eleven, then."

"Good."

"Are you going to take your tablets then now?"

"Yes."

"And, you will take them with hot milk?"

"Yes."

"Then you are going to go to bed?"

"Yes."

"Right then, I'll be off."

"Right you are, dear. I love you. I always will."

"I know you do and we love you too, very much indeed."

"Bye dear, take care and look after Andy."

Freya laughs. "Oh, I always do."

"Yes, you always do. You're a good girl and I'm so very proud of you. I'm so glad I was able to share your life with you. Goodnight, love."

"You sound like you're saying goodbye forever and not just one night. We'll see each other tomorrow," she laughs. "Night-night, Daddy. I hope you have sweet dreams."

"I'm sure I will, dear. I hope all yours come true, darling."

Fifty-One

After it happened

Al, not as his twenty-one-year-old self this time but exactly how he was the day he and Garth met, is with him now and I have returned home to wait. Al is sitting on the edge of the bath watching Garth, who is wearing his blue pyjamas again. He is stood in front of the bathroom sink holding onto his walking stick with one hand to keep him steady, brushing his teeth with his toothbrush in the other hand. He sets his toothbrush down and uses his hand to scoop some of the cold running water to swill out his mouth with.

Al moves in closer, standing right behind him providing the power that Garth needs at this time. Garth looks up and catches his eye in the mirror of the vanity unit and they smile at each other.

"You're back, then?" He rinses his toothbrush, places it in the glass on the side of the sink and then turns off the cold tap. "You took your time. I was beginning to think you were going to never turn up."

Al laughs and shakes his head. *You never did quite trust how I feel about you, did you?*

Garth turns unsteadily. One side of his body weight is concentrated on his walking stick and his other hand is gripping the sink, supporting the other half of his body weight. He has one eye on Al and the other on his reflection in the bathroom mirror.

"That's not true," he says a little coyly.

Yes it is, Al retorts.

"It isn't."

Yes it is.

"It isn't"

Yes it is, Al say's more firmly. *I have the proof.*

"No you don't," Garth says with increasing frustration. "You can't have any proof because it isn't true. It's all in your imagination."

Oh, no it's-. Al stops abruptly and looks down at the walking stick that Garth is shaking through him.

That is pointless, he states with a smug look, the same one that has infuriated Garth on and off for the sixty-five years they shared together. *You know I can't feel anything.*

"I hate you and I've had enough of this," Garth hisses huffily.

He storms off. In his own head he storms off anyway. In reality he shuffles one foot at a time, shaking precariously on his walking stick. He goes out of the bathroom and across the landing where he pauses and grips the banister in exhaustion before eventually reaching his bedroom wheezing and gasping. He finds Al already on the bed laid on his back with his hands behind his head looking up at the ceiling and whistling the tune: *why are we waiting*.

What took you so long? Al asks with very little concern for Garth's wheezing and gasping.

This isn't spiteful. Besides the fact that Al cannot feel emotion, which would cause concern for Garth's decomposing life, he also has the knowledge that new life is imminent. He knows that the end of this cycle is necessary and fertile. Garth doesn't reply; he shuffles over to the bed and draws back the right-hand-side corner of the bedspread and then sits down in the clear section. He rests his walking stick on the bedside cabinet and uses the toe of his feet to remove his slippers at the heel. He picks up his tablets, which Angela has laid out on the top of his bedside cabinet and swallows them one by one, washing them down with a gulp of warm milk. Then he removes his glasses and places them in the top drawer of the cabinet, closing it again with a struggle. Slowly, creaking and groaning and wincing as he does, he lifts one leg at a time up into the bed, easing the bedspread back further and then slowly and painfully draws it back over him. He reaches out for the switch on the wire of the bedside lamp but then thinks better of it and lets his arm go limp and flop down over the side of the bed.

Some things never change. Al's thought penetrates Garth's mind as clearly as they have been doing for the last two weeks.

Garth says nothing in reply.

You always did this.

Still nothing.

You never could keep it up, though. You'll crack sooner or later.

Nothing.

It won't be long now.

Nothing.

Al begins to whistle and waits.

"What did you mean, anyway, about having proof?"

Ha-ha, Al shouts, triumphantly letting out a fist pump and turning his head to regard Garth self-contentedly and with all the cockiness of the young man he has appeared as. *I knew you would crack. I always could read you like a book.*

Garth doesn't reply.

Here we go again.

Garth turns his head towards him and drinks in his young blithe face, which melts him. "I've missed you," he breathes softly and sincerely.

Al hangs his mouth in a coat-hanger grin. *You never could stay angry at me for long.*

"I've been angry with you for the last six months," Garth replies in a half-serious half-joking tone with a hint of a smile both on his mouth and in his eyes. "For six months I've been so angry with you for leaving me here all alone."

Garth, I went into hospital for a hip replacement, caught an infection and died at the age of ninety-nine, he jokes. *You make it sound like I ran off with a younger man and left you high and dry. You've had loads of support and soon you will have me again.*

"You make it sound like you have been gone two minutes. It's been six months. Six months at my age is a long time and you haven't visited before."

I've already explained. I have no concept of time. A long time to you is a short time to me. And, for your information I have visited before, you just haven't been in tune to it.

"You still haven't answered my question," Garth says, changing the subject.

What question?

"What proof have you got that I never quite trusted that you love me?"

Oh, that question.

"Yes, that question."

I was hoping you had forgotten that. You'll find out for yourself soon enough.

"Well I didn't forget and I don't want to wait, so spill it now, please."

It's simple, really. I have read your mind loads of times in the years gone by.

Garth bursts out laughing. "You can't have."

I have.

"You are actually suggesting that over the sixty-five years we were together you were able to read my mind?"

No.

"Good, I'm glad you're admitting that you lied because it's absurd and I wouldn't fall for it."

It's just been, by your measurement, the last six months.

"That might be. Nothing shocks me now. If it is possible that you are here then it is possible that you can read my mind, but that's the last six months since you died, not the sixty-four-and-a-half years before that," Garth says defiantly, folding his arms across his chest and nodding his head resolutely.

But that's just it. Like I've said, time means nothing. I have seen many years in the last, as you keep telling me, six months.

"What, so when you are dead you suddenly become a Michael J Fox time traveller, do you?" he asks, laughing and fully expecting him to reply, in the negative.

Yes, it's exactly like that.

"I knew it," he declares triumphantly. "I knew you were winding me up again."

Garth-. Al tries to interject.

"I just knew that time travel even for a spirit person is not possible."

Garth, but I said-.

"Nope, there is nothing you can say in your defence. I could see straight through you." Garth breaks off and looks at Al, who is gawping back at him with a bewildered expression washed on his face. "No pun intended, as you are actually, at the moment, see through I mean," he laughs. "Just because I'm partial to A Christmas Carol doesn't mean I was going to fall for all that Ghost of Christmas Past malarkey. Time travelling ghosts indeed, yeah, and I'm King Kong. How gullible do you think I actually am?"

I think you're deaf and deluded. That's what I think you are.

"What?" Garth demands. "Why?"

Because, husband dearest, that's exactly what I am saying. Ghosts can time travel. Well, spirit people- we don't refer to ourselves as ghosts. As well you know, I've already explained this to you. It's actually quite offensive. Calling us ghosts is exactly like calling your own mother an old cow, you wouldn't do that, would you? Time travel, however, is exactly what we do. I said yes, not no.

"Don't be silly. Prove it."

All right, I will. Do you remember the first summer we got the VW camper?

"Yes."

It was Freya's first summer holiday from high school.

"Yes, but-."

I'm getting there, Garth. You always were impatient.

"Well get on with it."

I will.

"Good. Go on then."

As I was saying, Al regards Garth with a sharp sideways flash of his eyes, *that summer in the VW, when we both took sabbaticals and drove around Europe for six weeks, can you remember that first night in the Pyrenees in the grounds of that chateaux owned by the hippy couple?*

"You mean vegan valley with side helpings of meditation, tree hugging and yoga?"

Al laughs. *Exactly. Well, do you remember the first day?*

"Yes, just like it was yesterday. You and Freya rode your bikes off the campsite to the local village for bread and milk and came back with two veterans from the Second World War, in their nineties, who ended up having lentil and bean stew with us. They didn't speak a word of English and Freya had to do all the translating for us."

Yes, and whilst we were gone you stripped down to your boxer shorts in the adjoining meadow and spread yourself out on a blanket by the lake to soak up the sun.

"Yes, but how do you know that? I can't remember telling you that."

There was a white horse and she came and laid next to you. You fed her buttercups and told her how happy you were. You said 'I'm the luckiest man alive to have such a beautiful husband and daughter. I feel like I have everything I ever wanted. I feel so lucky. I just hope Al loves me as much as I love him. Sometimes I can't help myself but worry about the fact that he might not. It's like I can't understand why he picked me. He could have anyone. I never tell him this, but sometimes on my way home from places I have been to without him, I get this moment of panic that I'll walk in and find him gone that he'll have come to his senses and realised he can do better.' Then you told her 'Somehow I feel like I know you. I feel like you're my guardian angel or something'. Al takes a moment to look at Garth's bewildered expression and he sniggers at his gaping mouth. *You couldn't stop thinking about her all night and you called her Buttercup in your head. It's why you couldn't sleep. You kept waking me up, and when I asked what was wrong you lied and said that you just weren't tired, but it's not true. You were really tired. You just couldn't get Buttercup and what you had told her out of your mind. They both just went round and round like a stuck merry-go-round. You couldn't switch off and in the morning you slipped away early whilst Freya and I still slept, hoping to see her again, to confide in her again. But she wasn't there. She never was, each time you visited all you ever found was an empty meadow covered in buttercups. You felt like it had been a dream.*

"It's not possible that you know all this. I never told you. I never told anyone. I thought I had imagined the whole thing but it felt so real. She felt so familiar that

I was scared you would think I was ridiculous. And as for what I told her, well, I just would never tell you that. I would never and did never tell anyone that stuff. There is no way you could know it all."

But I do.

"But it's not possible. Not possible at all, unless..."

Unless?

"Well, unless you..."

Unless I was there?

"Yes. But you weren't. Were you?"

Not then, but I have been since. You were right about one thing, though.

"What?"

Buttercup. You were right about her. You do know her. It wasn't a dream, but she isn't a horse either. That was just one of the forms she appeared to you in.

"Dee?"

Yes, Garth. She has always been with you. We both have.

Garth thinks things over for a while and then turns to Al. "Al, Freya will be okay, won't she? And, her family, they'll be okay too, won't they? You know, after tomorrow. They will be okay without me, I mean."

She will. Al smiles gently. *There is still a lot in their future. A lot for both you and I to be part of and we will, just from a different vantage point. In her heart she will know this and find the strength she needs to embrace life. It's all going to be fine. It's all going to be perfect in fact.*

"Good, I can't bear to think of how upset she is going to be tomorrow when Angela breaks the news to her."

Al smiles. *It was a good move, what you did on the phone earlier. I'm impressed. Making Freya promise to come after Angela drops by so that Freya won't make the discovery, it's a genius plan. It's better that it's Angela.*

"Al?"

Yes?

"I'm frightened."

I understand that. I was too, when I first realised what was happening to me, in the hospital. There is no need. You're not going to feel a thing and I'll be right here to show you the way.

"I think it's time now."

Yes, I think so too, Garth. Al reaches out and places his hand over the top of Garth's. *You should close your eyes and go to sleep. I'll be here to take you home when it happens.*

"I love you. Sweet dreams."

Good night, Garth. You sleep tight.

Garth closes his eyes, contentedly smiling, feeling serene and calm. The slight twinges of excitement tug at his insides. It isn't long before ninety-eight years of life surges over him, bringing with it complete exhaustion, which sweeps through him and he falls into a deep undisturbed sleep. He wheezes his last breath without even realising it.

Fifty-Two

When it happens to Garth, told by Garth

Everything is coming into focus. It feels like being under water, like being in the womb and being born. Nothing quite makes sense yet. The only thing I'm certain of is that I left my body behind in my bedroom. I have actually stepped out of my ninety-eight-year-old worn out body and left it behind. My failed, none functioning body, I'm no longer inside it.

I can't quite explain it. I'm finding the whole thing entirely alien, but then Al said I would at first. One minute I'm having a conversation with Al in bed and the next I'm a young man again, standing beside my bed, looking down on my grey, motionless and waxy-looking body. Briefly I wonder where he has got to; he promised he'd be right beside me. Then I see a brilliant white funnel of light and hear the distant sound of his voice. It's as if he is trying to wake me, in the days before Freya, when I was reluctant to get out of bed and he would have to call my name over and over to bring me out of sleep. It feels like this now. I'm suddenly thinking, *ah, there he is.* As my thought of his whereabouts develops stronger in my consciousness, I find myself travelling closer to his voice without physically moving, as if I'm on one of those flat conveyer belts they have at airports to make carting your luggage about easier. In no time at all I find myself here amongst waist-height heather on a staggered descent of a chalky white cliff, looking down at a white lighthouse, which stands on the pebble hem of the chalky cliff only a short distance from crashing waves. There is a brightly-painted beach hut further up the beach and beside that a huge ice construction and then what looks to be a rabbit warren of bubbles. There are two horses galloping about in a gymkhana underneath one of them.

Strangely, I feel at peace and like I belong here. There is a strong familiarity of this place. *Have I been here before? Have I dreamt of this place? This feels like home.*

Garth. Al's voice whistles around me like the wind.

Where did that voice come from? There is nobody here. It sounds like his voice but no-one has spoken. I'm sure they haven't. I'm hearing things.

Garth.

There it is again. It seems to envelope me and penetrates my very mind. Where are you? I think to myself. I know I don't speak it out loud.

Garth, I am here.

How can he answer my question when I only thought it? There is no-one here, I tell myself again. Then I remember the story about Buttercup, the story Al told me about time travel and being able to read thoughts.

Garth, it is me. I am here. You just need to open your mind and let me in.

Open my mind? How ridiculous. I prefer my mind shut thank you very much.

Then you won't see me.

How are you doing this? I'm not speaking, so how can you be responding to me like you are? How can you read my thoughts?

That's how we communicate here. We use telepathy. You know this. You have just answered the question for yourself.

Here? Where is here?

You are home, Garth. This is the place I was telling you about before you closed your eyes. When we were in bed and we were talking about Freya, our daughter. Oh Garth, let me in.

I'll try closing my eyes. I'm doing it. I'm closing my eyes.

Open your imagination. Let go of what you know.

I'm trying. My eyes are screwed up really, really tightly. I'm trying with all my might. I really am, honest.

I know, keep trying.

I can feel him now. His strength is swirling around me. I feel connected to something as if I'm an electrical appliance being plugged in. Something is surging through me. It's not painful or uncomfortable; just ever-present, pulsating and flowing. It's so powerful. *What is happening to me?*

You are changing. You are becoming your higher self.

It is you.

Yes.

We are really communicating in the same way both with our minds and not our voices. I can hear your thoughts and you can hear mine.

Yes.

No, I mean I'm not just thinking things; I'm saying them. In my mind. And I don't just think I can hear you in my mind. I actually can hear you in my mind. It all makes sense.

Yes, Garth. You are ready now. Open your eyes.

My husband is standing right in front of me just like the first day I met him on a busy platform. He has that same look in his eye that he had then. Lustful. I'm just as excited as I was when he severed a piece of his lemon cheesecake with his spoon and fed it to me. We are both just as we were on that day: young, vibrant, carefree and surging with love. *Actually, how many years ago is that? Why can't I remember?*

Because, Garth, we have no concept of time here. Time doesn't exist. It's not important.

Why? Suddenly a stooping seagull catches my attention and I break my gaze from Al and watch it fly over the cliff edge, then I turn back to him. *Hey, stop laughing at me. What's so funny anyway?*

You remind me of me when I first got here. So naïve. Just like a small child learning the ways of the world for the first time. Don't you remember when Freya was like this? Every new piece of information we gave her was followed by 'Why?'

Are you teasing me? You always do this. I haven't missed it.

No. I'm not teasing you.

He moves closer to me and puts his hands up to my face. The front of his body is up against mine. I can actually feel him. I actually feel his body against mine like it used to feel. It feels so good, so safe, and so gentle. I'm tingling all over with the sensation of him. It's like I am the plug and he is the socket, electricity is joining us.

I can feel you.

Yes.

I can actually feel you. I couldn't before back at the house but now I can.

I'm very giddy now. I can detect the high-pitched squeak in my voice just like it used to get whenever I got excited.

I'm not teasing you, Garth. You have a lot to learn. You are new to this.

I'm still thinking about the fact I can actually feel him. I've forgotten about everything else. Then the lighthouse swims back to me. I turn away from him but not so that our energies disconnect. *How do I know that we are energy now? I have no idea.* Something draws my attention to the beach. *That lighthouse.*

Yes. It's our home. The home I built for you.

You built it?

I did, by power of thought.

What? I don't understand what he means.

You will understand. What would you like right now? If you could have anything, what would it be?

Anything?

Yes anything.

I'd like an ice-cream sundae as big as our kitchen sink." I laugh, I'm being very silly but he did ask.

Think it.

Think it?

Yes, think it. Think what it looks like. Think what it tastes like. Think everything about it. Imagine it and bring it to life.

Is this a trick?

He's laughing at me again. I hate it when he does this. Only I actually don't, hate it, I feel nothing but sereneness. *No, it's not a trick. Think it, like I said.*

Okay then, I will, I say defiantly as if I am willing to take on the challenge like it's a duel or something noble.

I close my eyes and I think it. I think a huge glass-frosted bowl the size of our kitchen sink. I think of several large scoops of different flavoured ice cream the size of footballs. I think strawberry cheesecake, white chocolate chip, double chocolate, pistachio, toffee, mint chocolate chip and walnut. Then I think about a mountain of whipped cream on top of it, stabbed with five chocolate flakes the size and thickness of those large pepper grinders the waiters have in Italian pizza restaurants. Then I think about crushed nuts, those tiny colourful sprinkles and lashings of chocolate sauce. Finally I think about a huge glacé cherry the size of a beach ball sitting on top of it.

Open your eyes, Al's voice fills me and I follow his instruction.

There, right in front of us, is what I have just thought about. I have literally dreamt up my favourite dessert, and it's huge.

Can I actually eat it, though?

You can experience it in the same way that you created it by power of thought.

I have to think myself eating it?

You're catching on quick. Yes.

I close my eyes and I think about using a huge spoon and digging it through all the toppings, sauce and cream until I feel it hitting something hard. I think it digging in and scooping out some of the ice-cream. Then I think of the whole lot being fed to me, the spoon levitating itself to me. I taste it. I really taste it. I taste the smoothness of the cream, the textures of the toppings, the velvety chocolate sauce and the coldness of the ice-cream and then its fruity flavour, strawberry cheesecake. It all bursts inside of me. My entire being is as if I am a giant taste bud being tantalised and tingled with flavour. It's divine.

Mmmm, it's yummy. I can really taste it. I look over at my ice-cream sundae and there is a sunken section where I have just delved into it. I'm about to delve in again when someone catches in my mind like a fly in a spider's web.

Dee! I suddenly exclaim.

Al laughs. *It took you long enough.*

But where is she? I thought she'd be here with you to meet me.

She's waiting for you. She wanted me to be the first person to meet you.

Waiting for me?

Yes, she is waiting for you to think her. They all are: your parents, Dee's parents, and my parents, Priya, Polly and Rita, all of them.

Think them? I know what you mean.

I close my eyes and I think. I think about Dee and I think about all of them. I think about how I want to meet them and what I want to happen. Distant chattering and laughter begins to float around me and I feel Al's energy come closer into mine.

Open your eyes, Al says, *and turn around.*

I do as he says. Like an ascending army, they all come. They are just as I thought them, carrying everything I want them to be carrying. Dee and James are at the front. James's arm is thrown over her shoulder and she has an arm around his waist, her hand resting on his hip. James is whispering something into her ear and she is throwing her head back in laughter. She is just how she was the day before she left me. Young and beautiful- a complexion just like snow, not a blemish or pimple on show. Vibrant curls flecked with different shades of autumn bounce around her face as she strides. In their free hands they grip huge bunches of helium balloons all with a different word spelling out 'Welcome home, Garth'. Behind them come my parents. They each look full of life, beautiful fresh faces a normal colour and pasted with huge grins of contentment; nothing like their last days in the hospice. They each carry trays of cakes. Slightly behind them are Priya, Polly and Rita, all hand in hand like paper dolls chatting gaily. On the outside of the trio are Priya and Polly, and each of them carries a plate of finger sandwiches. Priya's hair has grown back and her breasts are full again in a yellow low-cut slip dress. Jo-Jo and her husband are also coming towards me; they are carrying the scones and cream. Then there are Dee's parents and her grandparents, mine too. Members of Al's family, his parents and his brother and three nieces who were killed in a car crash the year after our wedding. There is a little girl no older skipping towards us with a skipping rope. I know instantly it's his sister, who died of leukaemia when he was a teenager. She was his inspiration for going into medicine. Her treatment had stopped working and he had helped his parents pack her things into bags for the charity shop including her beloved blue and cream sewing machine. Instantly I recall Dee's second hand sewing machine. Then I know it had been Al's sisters first: *is everything in life interconnected like a jigsaw?*

They are all coming and all carrying something for my welcome home party. In front of me springs, from nowhere, a huge white circus tent the instant I think it and inside it appear tables and chairs around the circus ring. Inside the ring animals begin to appear just as I think them; my welcome home circus. Then she is stood right in front of me inches from me.

Hello, Dee.

Hello, Garth.

We enter each other's energies. She feels so good, so familiar. It feels as if no time has passed at all since the last time I saw her, not a single second.

Today is the day, isn't it? I say excitedly. *You told me it would come in a dream. Only it wasn't a dream. was it?*

No, Garth, it wasn't a dream. They were never dreams. I was never, not there. And, yes, Garth, the day has come. I told you it would. Forever starts here, if that's what we chose.

Fifty-Three

The day it happened to me. The truth of it, written by me

The others are spread far and wide, visiting the people we have left behind and who are still living in the physical. Garth and Al are with Freya and Andy, sharing with them the christening of their first great-grandchild, Garth and Al's first great, great grandchild. Priya is with her eldest son in his hospice bedroom, waiting for him. Polly and Rita are with her, supporting her and him. James is with Lucy, sharing her youngest grandson's- his great-grandson's- wedding.

I am in solitary contemplation, sitting on a firm mattress of autumn leaves at Aryl's gnarled and knobbly foot. A letter that I had written, before it happened, flutters down, riding the wind like the leaves underneath me had done before I came to sit on them. It is addressed to my mum; I had written many like it in those times before it happened. The flowing ink of my wounded words seeps in to the writing paper. Not all of them were to my mum. At one time or another I wrote one for everyone. I'd hide them. I'd stuff them into my mattress and into the pockets of clothing hanging in my wardrobe or inside my shoes kept under my bed.

I watch the letter descend and land with all the grace and poise of a swooping bird landing on the ground.

I was there, standing in the rain, not getting wet, not jumping and cowering at the thunder and lightning the day Garth handed the cardboard box full of the letters he had found to my mum. This one was sitting on the top. It isn't the oldest or the youngest. My mum put them into the attic and waited, waited until she was strong enough to read them and then, one day, I don't know how long after, she started to read them. She started with this one. Resting my head against her shoulder as she read it, I wished I could stop her. *No Mum, it won't help you now. It will only make everything worse, don't do it. Please, don't.*

Dear Mum,

When you read this you won't be a mum any more. You'll just be a wife. I know how much this will hurt you. I know how much you longed to be a mum as a little girl. I know how much you love being someone's mum, being needed, having a purpose. It hurts me, to think of you without a purpose and I hope that one day you will be able to forgive me for doing this to you; perhaps one day you will understand. I hope that you will. Although I wouldn't blame you if you couldn't find it in your heart to ever forgive me.

I can't be your daughter any more, not because I don't want to; I really do want to be, Mum. I really do. Unfortunately the world, life, has other plans. I don't belong here, Mum. There is no place for me in the world, and it doesn't want me here. I'm different, Mum, so different to everyone else. I wish I could explain. I wish I could tell you why I look at everyone else and I see bright, beautiful appetising fruits and then I look at myself and the mirror shows me something different- a fruit that is rotten to the core, a fruit that doesn't belong in the fruit bowl.

I'm not scared of going and being alone. Wherever it is I'm going to, somewhere else or nowhere at all, like the place under the stairs where I sometimes hide, can feel like somewhere and nowhere. I'm not even scared of going and being forgotten. I know life will move on without me. I know people will change and grow old without me and I know that new people will come into their lives, taking my place. None of this scares me, Mum. Staying here and being forgotten scares me, staying here and being alone scares me. Being old and forgotten in a lonely place, scared of the voices outside and imprisoned inside on a chair under blankets with only the radio for company scares me.

This is why when you read this you will not be a mum anymore.

I'm so sorry, Mum. I love you and I always will. I hope that you will always love me too. Goodbye, Mum.

Love Dee xxx

I finish reading and the letter bursts into flames quickly, turning to ash that disintegrates into the autumn air I have manifested. The letter was written just before the time I experienced limbo, the time I attempted to leave her but didn't succeed. It was never found, though. Not then, not until it actually happened, which had nothing to do with how I explain I feel in this letter. I begin to think about that day, the day Garth and Rita found my lifeless body submerged in cold water my protuberant eyes opened wide, polished and inoperative, giving the effect of being made from glass.

Suddenly, Aryl, the autumn leaves and the open space begin to change. The features wash away as if they are part of a landscape that has been painted only moments earlier by their artists and then carelessly left under grey clouds that burst open with rain. They wash and run and then wash away completely. For a moment there is nothing but a blank canvas. Gradually, new features casually drift in, creating a new scene. I'm back there. The day it happened, visiting the memory of it. I'm back in my attic bedroom where it all started, watching physical me sleep restlessly, as if in combat with sleep itself, the blackout blinds defending me from the bright and cheery mid-afternoon sun.

The strength required to heave myself out of bed is immense when I eventually wake up. I feel like a crane lifting a heavy load and transferring it from one place to another, only I am both the crane and the heavy load. I think about staying put, hiding under the covers like I have been doing for days but something inside me clings to the edges of the dark well I seem to be falling down. Something spurs inside me, urging me to dig my fingers in and use my feet to climb up and out of the top again. From somewhere I find the strength.

Sitting on the edge of the bath, wrapped in a towel, I watch the water gush from the taps. The stereo from my room, plugged into an extension lead that is plugged into the socket just outside the bathroom door, is by my feet. I begin to train myself to think positively with thoughts of pampering myself, relaxing in a hot bath, shaving my legs, scrubbing and lathering myself. Rubbing moisturiser into my skin and drenching myself in expensive perfume and then dressing up in something bright and colourful that my lovely blue and cream sewing machine injected some Dee-dazzle into. A smile manages to birth itself inwardly, travelling up from my stomach. It begins to show outwardly in the twitching corners of my mouth. My morale boosts as I imagine the infectious laughter that lies ahead of us, all of us crammed in one of the booths of Ye Old Victoria.

In my clenched fist are two pink tablets. Sometimes they were my friends and other times they were foes. The doctor had renewed my prescription the day before. Uncurling my fingers to reveal the two tablets sitting in the palm of my hand, they smile up at me promising support, promising rescue. Today they are friend, my fairy godmothers that say to me 'You shall go to the ball.' Swiftly, my hand travels up to my mouth then clasps against it, thrusting the pills into my mouth and sending them tumbling down my throat. Closing my eyes I will them to work, will them to decorate my mood with bright colours, pick up my morale and dust it down, take my vitality and inject it with life. I look at the bottle, the full bottle, which they came from sitting on the tiled ridge at the end of the bath beside a glass of chardonnay and the three-quarters-full bottle it came from.

The bath is almost full now and the small room is full of steam. I can no longer see my reflection in the mirror above the sink. I lean over, reach out and doodle a love heart in the steam on the mirror. Turning my head to check the water levels of the bath, I discover that it is almost full. The foamy bubbles, from the half-bottle of bubble bath I emptied into it before I turned the taps, have risen like snow-covered peaks. After turning the taps off, I stoop down and press 'play' on the stereo. The room is suddenly filled with the sound of feel-good club classics. Lifting the stereo up, I place it on the tiled ridge at the end of the bath beside the pills and the wine. Standing up, I lift up the glass of wine and down it in one go. After refilling the glass and gulping down another mouthful, I tug at the towel and let it fall away from my body to the floor.

I climb into the bath and let my body sink into the hot soapy water. Closing my eyes, I sink underneath it, pinching my nose. I feel the water cleansing me. Already I feel different. I feel like I'm transforming. Rising up again, causing waves to crash against the sides of the bath, I lean forward and reach for my wine, the pills catching my eye. I stare at them for a moment, not noticing the water driblets from my arm pitter-pattering onto the stereo. Talking gulps of the wine, the bottle of pills still holds my gaze. I can hear them whispering to me. I place my wine glass, now almost empty, back and pick up my shaving foam. My legs are up on the tiled ridge, my feet pressed against the stereo. I reach for my razor. Pausing, I hear my bottle of pills whispering to me again. Swapping the razor in my hand for them is something I consider, like they ask. Summoning all my strength I manage to block the whispers out and I feel triumphant.

Beginning at my left calf I glide the razor up my leg, smiling at the smooth track mark left in its wake, shaving foam pushed to the side of it like snow at the sides of a road after a snow plough has ploughed through it. I lean forward again and begin to shave another section. The sting from the nick I take out of my shin shoots up my leg. I kick out against the pain, my foot slamming against the front of the stereo its back smashing hard into the tiled wall. As my foot retracts I feel the stereo pushing forward, squaring up and preparing a counter attack. I realise instantly what is going to happen next. With both hands on the sides of the bath, blood fanning out in the water from the cut on my shin, I thrust upwards, intending to hurl myself out of the bath before the stereo hurls itself in. The stereo is too quick for me. It's too light on its feet. It jumps like a child jumping high into the air at the side of a pool, tucking its legs into its chest and bombing the water. The splashing sound is intermingled with a crackling and then there's a flash. I feel my body surge, my back arching, and my head pulling backwards as if someone is pulling my hair and the front bones in my neck pushing their way through my skin. It's not exactly painful; just all-consuming and overpowering. It's over quickly. I'm stood outside of myself. I'm standing over the bath even before the body I have just vacated slips below the water's surface.

Nobody ever realises the truth and they all assume it is suicide. Realising they are wrong is a lesson that comes soon after returning home. It's a common crime for everyone in the physical at one point or another- judging a book by its cover. It's not their fault; it's simply in the programming of the physical body- making assumptions based on a set of circumstances. This doesn't change until they come home, here to where I am now.

THE END

Made in the USA
Charleston, SC
14 January 2016